FALLING FOR THE ALPHA GODS

MARIA WARREN

Falling for the Alpha Gods

Cover by Mibl Arts

Dedication

THIS BOOK WAS A labor of love and wouldn't have been possible without those that helped support and encourage me throughout.

To my editor Michelle, you always find the strangest errors I make when I'm far too tired to be working. Your support and focus is more than appreciated. Thank you so much for staying with me for this crazy journey.

A special thank you to Tori, she took down multiple plot holes and character issues before it even made it to Michelle. She's an incredible beta-reader and this book would have been a little worse without her.

Andrea, my chubby dragon, you've been a pillar of support from the beginning. When it looked like I was about to be swept into the fires of hatred, you helped rescue me and inspire me to keep going.

Kristen and Raven, you are my Vella Queens, and your support and cheering helped me reach the finish line.

Mai and Heather, you have no idea how much I appreciate your check ins, and constant support.

A special thank you to Robyn, she's been with me since the start, and I truly believe she'll be with me until the end. I'm hoping to announce the release of her book soon so I can help cheer her on

Thank you to all of my friends and fans for loving our Alpha Gods, and I hope you enjoy getting to know them better.

And because I don't want to be sat on, to my beloved sister, who probably won't read this book because the 'good stuff' doesn't come until a later book. She's supported me since the start, and it's still crazy cool that I can talk to her for hours about the worlds I've created. Thank you so much, I love you.

And thank you hubby, for letting me use your name for my asshole, it fits him well.

Warning:

THE SILVERTON WOLVES THEMSELVES have abusive backgrounds, both physical and mental, and it might be something hard to read through. If this is something that will bother you, turn back now.

CONTENTS

MARIA WARREN

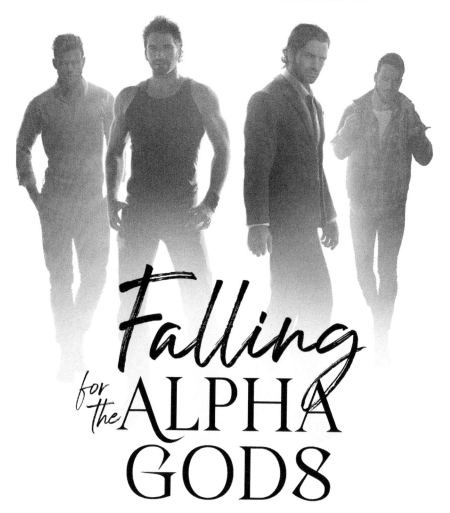

Falling
for the ALPHA
GODS

CHAPTER 1

BROKEN TRUST

I'D FINALLY GOTTEN WHAT I wanted, to be left alone, and all I could do was worry about the two men that I had kicked out. I didn't know what I should do to try to fix the situation and Barb, my wolf, wasn't any help.

Should I run after them and try to stop the impending fight, one that seemed to involve me? Or would it be better just to keep my door closed and wait this strangeness out?

I hated to admit it, hated it more than I hated every other moment I'd spent in this school so far, but I was worried about Julian. Just thinking that almost made me break out in hives. How could I worry about that fucking asshole? After everything he'd done to me, I should be relieved.

But I wasn't.

He was sick, and I wanted to take care of him. I'm not sure if it was some sort of mothering instinct or if maybe I had snapped while serving him, but I couldn't fight it.

I took a step to the door, fingers reaching for the handle.

If I left, I'd have to confront Elijah too. The thought left me chilled. I still couldn't get over the glint in his eye or the pain of having to submit to his Alpha aura.

Stepping backward, I retreated from the door. There was no way I was about to throw myself between feuding Alpha Gods. It wouldn't be worth it. I returned to my room and plopped down on my bed.

My controller waited for me like a shining beacon, tempting me to forget about everything and slip into the World of Clevania. I didn't have to worry about things like this craziness there. Maybe I'd even run into Rusty with my new character and tease him for a bit.

I smiled at the thought before faintly frowning. Wait, if he saw me as a healer, he'd try to make me follow him around everywhere and be his personal healing servant and keep his health topped up.

Sighing, I stared down at my trembling fingers. I had to go after them, no matter how much the thought of facing Elijah made me want to hide under the bed. Why did I want to do this? It was stupid of me, insane. I hated one of them, and the other terrified me, yet here I was, ready to go save the day in some warped way. I got to my feet, prepared to put an end to the fight.

The handle of my front door jiggled. Had one of the men already returned? Or was it one of the other Alpha Gods?

In either case, it was a good thing that no one else had the key to this place. Albedo had promised me, and I trusted him.

A soft click echoed in the front room as the door opened. A soft giggle made me freeze.

Whoever was there, wasn't an Alpha God, and they had a key to my place.

Barb growled, ready to shift, to fight whoever was intruding. But, I couldn't let her do that. Not until I figured out who was invading. Maybe it was Albedo and he had lied about not having a key? I didn't want to hurt anyone I cared about on accident.

My bedroom door swung open and Zelda strolled in, fingers brushing against my painted walls. She held up a key and smiled. "Just like Albedo promised, the key works."

What was she doing here? How did she get here? It shouldn't have been possible. The Alpha Gods dorm building should have only been accessed by the four of them and myself.

Cindy trailed in after her, her lips puckered as if she had licked a lemon. "What is all of this?" she demanded, shuddering at my decorations. "If I didn't know better, I'd think she was fucking Sterling and not your Bedo."

They shut the door behind them, cutting off any chance of escape I had.

"What do you two want?" I questioned, eyes flickering between the two. I backed up, the back of my knees brushing against the bed.

"What we want is for you out of this school, and away from our men," Zelda announced like she was a fucking queen. "You've been toying with the wrong guys, mutt. We're here to put a stop to it, and remind you exactly where you belong." She glanced around my room. "And it's not here."

Cindy grinned. "Due to your missing classes, we've been authorized to move you out of here, and escort you to new living arrangements, more suited to a student of your talents." She smirked and glanced around the room. "Zelda?" she called, as her lips curled and her eyes twinkled.

Zelda glanced over. "What?"

Cindy pointed to my walls. "I think we should redecorate in here."

My stomach dropped. No! I scrambled to get to her but before I could reach her, Cindy took her claws and scratched them through the rabop monster that Albedo must have painstakingly painted.

She laughed.

The bitch laughed!

She turned to me, a finger to her lips. "Oh, that's right. We've got a little house-warming present for you, a little something to help you stay away from our Alpha Gods. In fact, it's waiting for you in your new room."

I couldn't respond. I stared at the wall where Cindy had gouged out all the hard work that Albedo had done.

"Do you choose not to listen to your betters, or are you just not that bright?" Cindy questioned, staring me down. Her claws were still out. She lightly dragged them over another image. "Come on, bitch. Are you really going to make me tear up Zel's walls some more?"

Zelda snorted and made a dismissive gesture. "Cindy, when have I ever cared about this shit? It's childish, take it all down. I'll redecorate with something more befitting of a woman about to be married."

Wait. What? The world spun around me like I had been set on a merry-go-round and someone had turned the speed all the way up. This couldn't be happening. How were they here? "He's not," I whispered softly.

Zelda's smile faded before returning and she held a hand over her mouth, giggling. "Oh, he didn't tell you the news?"

I hadn't seen Albedo since he had left with his father, the Dean. I didn't want to admit it to this bitch though.

She was more than happy to keep going. "I'm marrying Albedo in a month." Zelda thrust her hand at me, showing off a sparkling diamond ring that looked like it could have paid all my brother's medical debt in an instant. "See? He proposed today." She gestured to the room we were in. "And since my soon-to-be husband doesn't need someone like you hanging around him, he gave me this room."

Ice formed in my stomach. What?

She grinned at me. "I have the key, you're not that stupid are you?"

Cindy snickered beside her. "Imagine, being so dense that you can't even see when the heartbreak king is playing you! I bet he told you some lie about how he was going to stay by your side and protect you."

There was no way Albedo had done that to me! Doubt ate away at my assurance. "How did you two even get into this building?" I kept my voice as calm as I could, I wouldn't let them enjoy a second of this.

Zelda laughed and ran her claws through another section of the wall, more of the images that Albedo had spent so much effort perfecting were ruined in a second. "The answer is obvious. I'm getting married to Albedo, and he made sure I could get in."

Cindy burst into laughter, bending over and holding her stomach. "Tell her the best part, Zel!"

I looked from one to the other. The bad feelings wouldn't stop. All the happiness this room had brought me before was being drained away. I refused to believe Albedo was responsible. I had been wrong about him, he wasn't a heartbreak king. There was someone that cared in there.

"What's so funny?"

Cindy peered up at me, wiping tears of laughter from her eyes. "It's just, you're so clueless, mutt. You really bought into the Alpha Gods and this fake protector act. Did you really think they were falling for you after what, three days? Get a grip. This was all a set up."

"The best part," Zelda crowed. "You're locked out of this building the moment I throw your skanky ass out." She celebrated by grabbing my stuffed cabbit, and ripping its head off, letting the fluff float around her. "Get out of my room, bitch."

Cindy's arm darted out and she grabbed me by the wrist. "Come quietly or we're going to make you regret it."

I snapped my hand back. The odd faint scent of vanilla and almonds clung to them. It was almost unbearably sweet, but it made my mouth water. Without thinking about it, I stepped closer.

Cindy chuckled. "How obedient," she mused, opening my door. "Are you done out here yet?"

A sharp scent invaded my senses and my nose wrinkled. It was such a strong odor, almost like a paint thinner.

For the second time that day, my stomach turned to pure ice. Whirling away from the two, I rushed through the hall.

The smell intensified.

The instant I stepped foot into the front room, everything clicked into place. My walls were smeared as if somebody had carefully stripped them down, one by one.

They had taken all of Albedo's hard work and wiped it away.

"The kitchen is done, and so is the restroom, all that's left is the bedroom..."

The world around me came to a complete standstill. A man walked into view from my kitchen. The scent of almonds got stronger the closer he got to me. Our eyes met.

My wolf screamed the one word I never wanted to hear.

"*MATE!*"

Tears pricked my eyes and I fell to my knees. The stranger rushed to my side, peeling his gloves off and pulling me to his chest. Firecrackers exploded at his touch, it was almost painful.

"Surprise," Zelda chuckled into my ear. "We found your mate for you. Mutt, meet Carl."

Carl grinned at me, holding me close and sniffing me. His golden hair was pulled into a high ponytail that tickled my nose.

I scrambled away from him, fighting my wolf's every instinct.

Freckles dusted his nose like a jar of red pepper had been shaken all over it, they were everywhere. "I can't believe it," he whispered. His voice was soft, musical almost. Maybe at another time I would have thought him handsome, but compared to my classically beautiful Elijah, this guy was average at best.

Barb struggled to wrench control away from me. She was desperate to force me to throw myself into his arms, but I resisted.

Carl took my cheeks into his hands, staring into my eyes. "You're my mate, I finally found you."

My control slipped as Zelda and Cindy watched, laughing the entire time. My wolf burst through my mental barrier, and instead of shifting, she took full control of my body, shoving me deep down where I couldn't escape.

"*Sorry, Lee,*" she apologized. "*But he's our mate, I have to do this.*"

She locked me away with only the bitter scent of burned almonds as a lingering reminder of what she planned to do.

It was over, she'd won.

CHAPTER 2

TOUGH CHOICE

STERLING

One moment I was messing around in Clevania, waiting for my Kitty and Lee to get online, and the next I was curled into a tight ball. Pain surged through the bond I had with the other Alpha Gods, it came over me in waves.

"Albedo!" Rust yelped.

Our friend was suffering, and we were sharing the blows. What had happened? I had to get to him!

Rolling off the bed, I hit the ground on my hands and knees and forced myself forward.

We'd all been through a lot together, but this was the first time there was so much pain. It was nothing like the slight discomfort of Julian's earlier agony. That idiot tended to eat things that tried to kill him all the time and he never learned his lesson. That I could ignore. But this was too intense. It reminded me of the kiss that Albedo had shared with Lee before, it had zinged through all of us.

Forcing myself to crawl to my door, I did my best to not focus on the pain. I'd endure it all. My friend needed me, and there was no way I'd let him down.

Unfortunately, I couldn't really tell where he was. It would have been easier if we could use our bonds like homing beacons, but alas we didn't have access to such a cool trick.

Fortunately, I did know someone who could probably find him. Digging through my pocket, I pulled out my phone and thumbed through the contacts until I found her.

Kelly picked up on the third ring.

"Sterling? Why are you calling?" I could just envision her rubbing her temples when she saw my name pop up on the screen. We've never been the happy couple our family had tried to force us to be year after year.

"Albedo," I wheezed. "Something's wrong. I need help," I bit back a scream as my entire body throbbed with the pain.

"Sterling? What's happening?" her irritation was gone. "Please, I'll do what I can, say the word."

That was the problem, any kind of words was hard to do. "Find him," I whispered.

"Got it," sharp taps came from the other end of the line. I could just imagine her hunched over her keyboard with all the screens popping up all over her triple monitor as she poured over them. Her typing came to an end and she chuckled. "Got it. Ready?"

"Please," I grunted.

"Are you sure you looked around for him? It says he's in the Dean's office according to his marker."

What? Why would he be in this amount of pain if he was merely in his father's office? I growled. My elbow shattered in a burst of pain so intense, it was as if a blazing fire had been set off inside my skin. The scream almost ripped from me, but I kept it in by biting down hard until blood trailed down my chin.

I wasn't going to worry my childhood friend.

"Sterling?" Kelly's voice was like a lash. "What the hell is going on? Speak to me! I heard that!"

I couldn't help but laugh through the agony. "It's fine, Kel," I panted. "I'm going to go take care of him." I wasn't sure how I managed to get a whole sentence out before collapsing into another heap.

"There's one other thing," Kelly added, softly. "You remember how you asked me to keep an eye on Alexandra's friend? Her signal from her phone isn't in any of the usual areas she frequents. She's on the other side of the University completely, in the abandoned storage facility."

A chill struck me. What? I'd just left Lee and she had been happily involved in her game. There was no way she had just abandoned that, especially not to end up in the middle of nowhere like that.

No, Albedo was the one that needed me. What did I owe some random woman I barely knew? Kitty could be disappointed, I had to go to Albedo's side. "Hey, Kel," I grunted, knowing she hadn't hung up yet.

What the hell was I doing?

"Yes?" She sighed deeply on the other end. "You're not about to ask me to help anyone, are you? I'm not the savior type, that would be Alexandra. There's no benefit in me helping more than I am."

That's Kelly for you, always obsessed with the bottom dollar. I wasn't sure why she acted like she was broke all the time. "Call Elijah, tell them where to find Albedo," I requested.

What kind of piece of shit was I? Instead of running to his side, I was going to hers, someone that didn't mean anything to me.

"Why does it sound like you're not joining them?" Despite the seriousness of the conversation, Kelly's voice was teasing. "You running off to go help your new friend, Sterling?"

"It's Clevania code, we stick together no matter what. Something's wrong if she's all the way over there," I answered, with a grumble.

The pain had died away becoming a dull throb. I wasn't sure if that was a good or bad thing at this point.

Kelly snorted on the other end of the line. "I'll send you a map of the area as well as the schematics of the buildings, they've been in disuse for a long time so I can't guarantee these will line up. Also, Sterling?"

I paused in the midst of stuffing my pockets with any necessities I might need while I wasn't curled into a ball of suffering. "Yeah?" I cradled the phone between my ear and shoulder, slipping a bone-handled knife into my boot.

"I've known you for a very long time, you need to be more honest with yourself. There's no doubt you love Kitty, but you're about to run off and play the dashing prince. I promise there's more of a reason for it than the simple, she's a Clevania player. Anyone else and you wouldn't have even batted an eye, or you know, you might not have had me watching for them in the first place."

"It's not like that, Kel. I told you."

"Uh-huh." She didn't sound convinced in the slightest. "You know, I don't know what's going on with you and your Kitty, but she might just have a rival with this new piece on the board. Alexandra is on the other line." She sighed and chuckled. "I'm sure she's on another ghost chase for the secret, go have fun being prince, Sterling."

"Bye." I hung up on her and stared at the door. There was still time to do the right thing, go to Albedo, and save him from whatever he was enduring.

Instead, my thoughts only turned in one direction, and this time, it wasn't my precious Kitty.

"*Hey, Sterling?*" My wolf's voice was soft, edged with the earlier pain.

"I know, you think we should go to Albedo, but there's something wrong, Rust. If I don't go, who will? If anything happens to her..." I trailed off. No, I shouldn't think like that. "Besides, the guys can save Albedo."

"*What if there's nothing wrong? What if she's just out seeing a guy?*" Rust suggested, though he didn't sound convinced either.

My brows furrowed. I imagined Lee in the arms of one of the male students and something inside of me hardened. The idea of her with Albedo when he was flirting with her, or even kissing her, hadn't been that bad. Maybe a little when he had forced a kiss on her because of the lust, and the surge of intense emotions distracted the hell out of me. I'd lost a rare card drop to a stupid bot, I'd been so pissed.

"*Even if that's the case, I have to find out for myself. I know Kitty will understand about this.*" Running a hand through my hair, I prayed. I hoped with every fiber in my being that she would. If Kitty ever hated me, I didn't know how I'd be able to function. She was the only one that knew the true me.

If Lee was in danger, as her friend and fellow Clevania player, I needed to get her out of it. Besides, I had failed her the last time I was supposed to protect her. If this was caused by those bitches, I would make them pay.

If they were involved...

I winced and left the dorm, glancing over at Lee's room as I passed by. The door was closed, but a sharp strong scent leaked from beneath the door.

Something really wasn't right.

Praying she'd forgive me for this, I went to the closet, and with Rust's help, we tore the door off its hinges and barged into her dorm.

Albedo's work was ruined. Smears of color dripped off the wall and some areas were even gouged as if a claw had been dragged through.

No more hesitation. I turned, and I raced for the area Kelly had told me about. There was no way I was going to get there fast enough.

Those women were in the business of destroying people and enjoying themselves while they did it. I would not let that happen to Lee no matter what.

This time, I would save her.

CHAPTER 3

FATED MATE

LEE

It took far too long for me to claw my way out of oblivion and regain control of my body. A strange warmth heated my back and I blinked as I got used to being the one in charge again.

The stranger's arms, there was no way I'd ever call him my mate, were tucked around me, holding me against his chest. The almond and vanilla scent hovered over me like a fine mist. The only thing protecting my naked body from his was an extremely thin sheet.

How had I gotten naked? *"Barb! You didn't!"* I screamed at her with everything I had.

"What? He's our mate, Lee, but I would never do that to you. We're a team, I'm not sure why you can't understand this is how things should be. Mates complete us."

He was trying to complete something alright. My Casanova had a handful of my boob, his thumb idly flicking my nipple as he snored in my ear.

It took everything in me not to shift and tear his throat out. *"What happened here, explain,"* I ordered her, peeling his hand off of me.

"Those bitches tossed us both in here and locked us up. I've tried everything I can to get us out of here, but it's like trying to escape from inside a safe. Henry couldn't even manage to make a hole in the wall."

"Henry?" I had the distinct impression she was pointing her muzzle at Carl sleeping beside me. "His wolf," I guessed, and she nodded.

I twisted around and studied him. He looked almost innocent while asleep, despite the lack of boundaries, obviously. His golden bangs scattered across his brows and he gently snored.

This was the mate the Moon Goddess had chosen for me? How could I believe that? It was far too easy of an answer. Besides, there was no way that Zelda and Cindy just happened to find my mate all for the sake of helping me.

They'd destroyed my new home in a matter of minutes. My eyes stung with tears at the memory of how much damage they'd done in the space of minutes. I hadn't even had a chance to sleep in the place!

As soon as I got out of this strange hell, I was going to force Albedo and Julian to handle their women and leave me out of it. It was their trash to take care of, not mine.

Beside me, Carl stirred and groaned. Reacting on instinct, I grabbed the sheet, wrapping it around my body until I was a mummy. I'd left him just enough to cover the important bits. From the looks of his bare shoulders and the way the sheet dipped into his ass crease, the man wasn't wearing anything either.

"Barb! Why is he naked too?"

She shrugged. *"When we couldn't do anything in our human forms, we shifted to see if we could find a solution. Calm down, I promise nothing happened."*

At least the sheet was soft. I just wished it wasn't so thin, and white. Instead of hiding my body, it only served to highlight my curves and tease at what lay beneath. Once I did find a way out of this jail cell, I would make damned sure that neither of those bitches would ever do anything like this again.

His eyes flickered open and the piercing blue threatened to suck me in like a rampaging whirlpool. He reached out, fingertips brushing across my skin as he stared at me. "You're real," he whispered.

The sparks exploded at his touch and I winced, pulling away. No matter how satisfied Barb was with this, I wouldn't be. I knew who I loved, Elijah, there was no doubt in my mind.

But... Hadn't Elijah felt the same way about Alexandra?

"Don't forget you were also soft to Albedo," Barb chipped in, sounding far too smug.

She was right, but I wasn't about to admit it. Carl stared at me as if I had kicked a puppy. First things first, I needed to try and understand this situation. "Carl?" I questioned.

A grin sped across his lips. "Yeah," he answered with a duck of his head. His hair was scattered over his shoulders, equally cursed with countless freckles. "And you're Lee, right?"

I pulled farther away from him, and the sheet crawled over his body, becoming dangerously close to sliding off. "Yes," I replied, staring at the ground.

"Woah!" Carl yanked the sheet back, forcing me to stumble closer. His body heat radiated, even from a few inches away.

"Turn around!" I snapped at him.

He did as ordered, shoulders trembling. "I can't believe I found you, I thought I'd never find my mate or that I didn't have one."

"I'm not your mate, Carl," I corrected. "When you touch me, I don't feel anything."

"*Lee!*" Barb's cry was ignored.

No, I knew what my path was, and no matter what this man turned out to be, it was impossible to think that he was destined to be at my side. It was better to lie because while I did feel something, it was all skin deep. The one thing he hadn't been able to move yet was my heart.

"You... don't feel it?" Carl whispered. His voice was thick and he slumped forward.

"I'm sorry." My first instinct was to comfort him, but touching him would undo the break I was trying to form.

"Did I do something wrong?" Carl questioned, staring at the wall.

I winced. What if Barb was right? What if all of this was some big horrible mistake I was making?

No, it couldn't be.

"It's not you, Carl. It's me. I'm already in love with someone else and nothing is going to change that."

He glanced over his shoulder at me, giving me a warm smile. "You're kind. You didn't have to try to comfort me, and yet here you are. Thank you."

I breathed a sigh of relief. At least he wasn't going to try to fight me over this. Maybe we could figure out a way out of this place together.

"Lee? I'm not ready to give up on you yet. Whenever I touch you, I feel like I've found another piece of myself, that you're the light that banishes the darkness from my soul." Red spread across his face and he jerked his face away. "I mean, just..."

How was I supposed to respond to that? It was cheesy, but there was such sincerity in it that I found myself hesitating. If this kept up, I would be forced to crush him completely.

Barb growled at the thought.

"What do you remember before we were tossed in here?" I scanned the room. It reminded me of a forgotten attic. Piles of junk as tall as me or higher were everywhere, and the windows were at the top of the room, out of reach and barred. Everything was coated in dust and more than a few spiders scuttled around, trying to avoid my inspection. "There has to be a way out of here."

"Not much. We came here and those two locked us in, something about this being your punishment. I'll do my best to get you out of here, I promise." He got to his feet, keeping the sheet covering him, just barely, and frowned. "Hey, what's that weird smell?" He put a hand to his head, wincing. "It's so strong."

"Lee..." Barb's words were slurred. "*Something is wrong, get to a corner of the room! Away from the center, now!*"

I didn't question her, I obeyed. Taking the entire sheet with me, I dashed to the corner, leaving Carl bare in the center.

He stood still in the center of the room, his breathing changed somehow as he took deep breaths. "Mate," he whispered.

"Wait, no," I argued. "We just talked about this!"

He lifted his head. His eyes were clouded and yet focused at the same time. He raised his hand and pointed at me. "Mate," he repeated, getting to his feet. He shuffled toward me, the grin from before gone, replaced with a glazed sneer.

I growled at him, edging my way around the perimeter of the room until I got to the door. I tugged hard on the handle, but there was no give. I pushed against it, desperate to try to break through it, but it was too heavy. Whatever it was created from wasn't going to shatter easily.

The windows were barred, and besides the door, the only space open was a huge skylight in the ceiling. I was trapped, and there was something seriously wrong with him. The strong scent of burnt almonds drifted through the room and I winced. It made my eyes heavy and I was as far away from it as I could get. Carl had been in the center.

Carl stumbled toward me, fingers outstretched. "Mate!"

He lurched forward, acquiring a speed he didn't have a second ago.

I barely managed to evade him. My precious sheet got tangled in my legs and I hit the ground, hard.

No!

I struggled to get up, but the sheet was wrapped too tightly.

A heavy weight shifted onto my back, a heat that brought the sparks back. "We're mates," Carl whispered into my ear, nuzzling my neck. "Mates, mates, mates," he mumbled each word, kissing his way down my neck.

No!

I went still and he laughed above me. Using that spare amount of time I threw my head back with all the force I could muster and headbutted him. Carl yelped and staggered away, enough for me to crawl out of my sheet prison to safety.

The fact I was naked didn't bother me anymore, but being locked in a room with a crazed wolf did. "Help!" I screamed, praying against all hopes that someone out there could hear me.

The thick door buckled in on itself in a display of wood and splinters flying as Sterling's eyes met mine.

My hero had arrived.

CHAPTER 4

TWISTED TIES

ALBEDO

I'd never lost control before. No matter how bad things had gotten, I'd always kept it inside.

The world buzzed around me. Lewis was ranting about something, but I couldn't focus on him.

The bastard had shattered my elbow, but that hadn't been the reason my control had slipped.

No.

He told me what he planned for Lee.

I had to move, get out of this damned cage, go to her, and protect her, but the pain was so severe that the slightest movement was enough to make me curl into a ball. He'd taken pleasure in my screams.

My fists dug into the center of my back, bound there by the heavy ropes he'd used to make sure I learned my place.

At least I still had my eyes. When he'd taken the lighter to my face, I hadn't been sure if they would survive the assault.

The cage meant he'd grounded me for a week, with no food, minimal water, and absolutely no contact with anyone else. He'd come back tonight to unleash more of his frustrations, as he lectured me on what being an Alpha God was supposed to mean for the family.

No, it was what it meant to him. At the moment I couldn't care less about the position.

"I'm sorry..." Lewis's voice finally broke through the haze surrounding me. He whimpered. It was the one time I hadn't shared my pain with him, and it had flooded through to the others. They'd got to experience the real man my father was. The guilt of being unable to protect me ate at my wolf.

"I might have shared the pain with them, but they won't know where to find us. They'll be worried, but that will fade. Besides, I'm sure Dad will come up with some great story for my disappearance like he has in the past. Probably have me visiting another university or something."

Lewis whimpered again. *"What are we going to do? We have to get to our mate, you heard what he's planning!"* he snarled. *"We have to make a decision about our mate, Albedo."*

There was only one choice that made sense. Even if she was my mate, my priority was keeping her safe. *"I'll have to stay far away from her. It should make things easier for her in school until I figure out how to stop his plans. I won't let her be some cog in a corrupted machine."*

Lewis scowled. *"He's not sacrificing my mate, I'll bite his balls off if he tries."*

I winced at the mental image. *"It won't come to that. I'll stop him. Besides, even if I have to marry Zelda for cover, we have time until graduation. There's no need to rush, if we let anyone know about this before we can figure out a way to rescue her, we're risking everything. I don't know if Dad can move the sacrifice date up, but I don't want to test him."*

Lewis was quiet, absorbing my words. His head hung low. *"But, Bedo... what about you? There's no way you can keep enduring this. He only keeps getting worse. I've done what I can to suppress it from the others, but this won't be the last time his control slips."*

This again. How many times have we had this same argument? It was impossible to save myself. Even if I did somehow run away, I'd be hunted down and forced back and what I'd suffer after, would make what I endured now seem like a child toppling over and getting scratched.

The ability to escape this fate was lost the instant I was born into this world. Maybe I could use this curse to save Lee, she didn't deserve any of this. *"I'll endure whatever I have to, Lewis. You're the one that insists she's our mate. If that's true, then this is the least I can do."*

The handle of the room jiggled, and I jerked to attention, ignoring the pain that came from my sudden movements. No one knew of this place, and my father was usually quiet, loving to sneak up on me instead of announcing his arrival. Silence was a virtue, it made you one step closer to the true God, according to him anyway. Deities didn't interest me.

The small door buckled in a show of breaking wood, and a fist appeared in the middle of it. A hand appeared through the new hole and it reached for the lock, ignoring the dangerous spikes of wood they created. I winced as fresh pain seared across my arm, as whoever it was unlocked the door.

Wait.

The door slammed open. Elijah and Julian barreled in, followed by Alexandra of all people. What was going on? I looked beyond them, searching for her. I wanted to see my kitten, but at the same time, I didn't want her anywhere near me.

Lewis wilted upon realizing she wasn't with the group.

My two best friends stood frozen, eyes locked on me. I could imagine what they were witnessing for the first time. My dirtiest secret was finally exposed for them to see. Every part of me that would be on show, normally looked fine, besides the shattered elbow of course, though that's why he had left me here.

"What the fuck is going on?" Julian snapped. He tugged at his hair, staring hard at me. His eyes traced the paths of the scars that had been left for my father's pleasure, the ones I'd always kept hidden.

"You can barely fit in there." Elijah knelt beside me, yanking the lock completely off the bars and crushing it in his hand. "Who did this?" he snarled, his eyes completely golden.

"Is that..." Alexandra put a hand to her lips. "Albedo..."

Ah, she must have noticed my special bucket left in the corner for me to take care of my business. I couldn't blame her for her reaction.

"Bedo, what the fuck is going on?" Julian trembled, barely able to keep it together. His rage flowed through our bond.

Elijah tossed the door open and squeezed himself into my prison.

I winced. There was no way he wasn't being assaulted by the stench all around me.

"*Albedo, we need to tell them what's going on,*" Lewis lectured.

I ignored him as Alexandra peered into the cage at me, her eyes brimming with tears. "I'm so sorry. I never imagined this was going on... I overheard you earlier, but I would never have guessed..." She gestured at my condition. "This."

Elijah's claws sliced through the leather laces that bit into my arms. It's not that I had been helpless to be able to do the same thing myself, but I'd learned early on that rebelling against my father only brought pain. I'd barely been able to save Fireball the last time I had defied him. He'd broken all my fingers for that little stunt, keeping eye contact the entire time as he snapped each and told me how much I deserved this for my defiance.

That had been the start of many 'vacations' I would take, where it would be me in solitary until I healed, while everyone else assumed I was traveling the world with a dozen different women. It had been before we were linked as Alpha Gods, so it had given me time to learn how to hide my pain behind a wall.

But my father wasn't stupid, he made sure I was trained on how to force my wolf to keep all the pain to himself and not let it leak to any bonds. Something that should have been impossible, but the threats we were given about Fireball were all we needed to do everything in our power to protect her.

I hissed as the blood returned to my damaged limbs. Didn't they understand how much harder this was going to make everything? "What are you doing here?" I wheezed, taking time to stress each word through the pain that throbbed through me like a heartbeat.

"Dumbass," Julian shook his head, staring down at me. "Once we felt your pain, we weren't about to let you face whatever caused it alone. We are more than friends, you know that. Albedo, be fucking clear. What's going on here? Who dared to touch you?"

Alexandra interrupted him, sweeping in close to me and her fingers trailed across my scars. I winced and shied away from her light touch. "It's true, isn't it? Your dad wants to sacrifice Lee to give the Alpha Gods power?"

How pissed would Dad be if he knew how close she'd managed to get to the truth of this rotten university? The question was, should I break and tell them what was really going on, or should I keep the secret so I could save Lee myself?

My bones cracked, as they slowly shifted back into place, my ribs realigning and my arm settling back into place. My arm tingled, but we had time until my father would return.

Time for me to reveal the full story.

"The Alpha Gods are always paired with a scholarship student, and though I'm not sure how the worthiness is decided, our scholarship student is Lee."

"The hell it is," Elijah interrupted. "Nothing is happening to her. Enough already has."

"Bedo, I'm not going to ask again. You're going to tell me what the hell is going on in this room and who dared to do this."

"Don't worry, I've got this," Lewis assured me before he took all control away and he shoved me into the backseat of our mind. A golden haze took over my vision as he remained in charge. "Hey, all of this was done by Bedo's fucking old man. When he finds out you guys stopped his little punishment ritual for Bedo getting Lee into the dorm, he's gonna be pissed. I wouldn't be surprised if he tries to carve into him next time. This isn't the first time Bedo has been punished like this, and it won't be the last. If you guys care

anything about your safety, get the hell out of here. You're only going to make everything worse."

"You really think we're leaving you, asshole?" Julian scoffed. "In your dreams. Albedo, stop hiding behind your wolf and get your ass out here. I'm going to take care of all this, then I'm going back to Lee's."

What? When had those two gotten so close?

Elijah helped me to my feet and when I swayed, he picked me up in a princess carry. I'd make him pay for that later, but I was too exhausted to fight back.

I wanted to ask what was up with Julian and Lee, it ate at me like a disease. Why the hell was he wanting to go to her place after everything he'd done to her?

"Hey," Lewis growled, twisting in Elijah's arms and making eye contact with Julian. "Stay the hell away from Lee, she's our mate."

Lewis was going to be a dead dog when I got control back.

CHAPTER 5

THE HERO

STERLING

Crazed glazed eyes flickered up to me, barely acknowledging my presence before they focused on the victim squirming beneath him. I had no idea who this asshole was, but Lee had called for help. There was no way I was going to abandon her.

"Mate," he groaned licking her neck. Lee struggled beneath him, bashing the back of her head against his nose, but he didn't even register the blood flowing down his face.

A flash of bright light filled the scene, and I blinked the stars from my eyes. I turned to see Zelda and Cindy side by side with their phones in their hands. I should have known it was something to do with those jealous bitches.

"Get the hell off her," I demanded of the stranger, with a growl.

"Maybe we should have waited a few seconds longer for him to actually mark her," Zelda mused. She strode past me as if I wouldn't move, putting her foot on the top of Lee's head, and pushing her against the cold floor. "Stay the fuck out of my way, and away from the rest of the Alpha Gods. They're way beyond you."

"Zelda," I snarled her name. Rust screamed in my head for us to draw blood. We normally ignored the bitches following the others around, but this was too much.

Cindy glanced over her shoulder at me. "I suppose you can chase that failure. He should have never been made an Alpha God, he's practically worthless."

The insults didn't bother me, her heel digging into Lee's skull did. "Move your fucking foot or I'm cutting it off," I warned her.

Zelda glanced up and away from Lee. "What is all of this to you anyway? All we did was help this mutt find her mate and get them together." She clicked her tongue. "You're not sniffing around this pitiful creature too are you?"

Cindy tucked her phone into her bright pink purse. "Come on, we don't have to be enemies here. Turn around and forget this little lesson we're teaching her. I'm sure there's some sort of silly event going on in your game."

"Do you really think I'd just turn and walk away from this?" I rushed forward and Zelda backed off. Thankfully the man, whoever he was, hadn't managed to mark her. Though from the amount of drool and red marks on her skin, it hadn't been from lack of trying.

I grabbed him by a handful of his hair and bodily threw him back to a corner in the room. His head rebounded off the wall and he went limp. Lee continued to cling to the floor, her hands on her neck. Slowly, she opened her eyes and peered up at me.

"Sterling?"

A burst of warmth exploded inside my chest. "I'm here, scholarship," I bent down, wincing at the state she was in. This wasn't the Lee I was used to, the one that would battle Julian on the daily. She was vulnerable.

And naked.

I needed to do something about that.

Cindy kicked the man on the ground, still completely dead to the world. "Pathetic," she glanced over her shoulder at Zelda. "We did all that work of finding his mate for him, and he couldn't even finish the job. Pathetic wolf, he'll never be an Alpha God that's for damn sure."

"Give me your jacket," I demanded of Zelda. Mine was covered in splinters from bursting through the door, I didn't want her hurt.

Zelda adjusted her long black leather jacket, pulling it tighter around herself, and her lip curled in a sneer. "You think I'm giving anything to her? You've played those stupid games so long you've rotted your brain. Sterling, get out of here."

"Give it to me willingly, or I'm ripping it off you, bitch. Albedo can put up with your shit all he wants, but you're not pulling that with me. *Take It Off.*" Rust threw his aura behind the last words.

Cindy couldn't handle my command, and with a whimper, she craned her neck in submission.

"No fucking way," Zelda snapped, holding it closer.

"Cindy, you do it. Take it off her." I snapped my fingers, keeping an eye on the passive Lee. The longer she stared into space like a deer in headlights, the tighter my chest grew and the hotter my urge to beat these women.

Cindy jerked her head in a nod and stumbled forward, grabbing the jacket off Zelda and yanking it free.

"Fuck you, Cindy," Zelda yelped, but she didn't try to fight the other woman.

Cindy turned toward me with the coat in hand and I nodded toward Lee, who watched us the entire time. "Put it on her," I demanded.

Cindy shook and her fingers clenched the black leather. "You're kidding me," she scoffed.

"*Do it,*" Rust commanded, and Cindy wobbled toward Lee.

"Here," Cindy tossed the coat over her shaking form.

"Do you really want to do this?" Zelda challenged. "You're breaking up a fated mate pair. The Goddess Morgan is going to curse you for the rest of your life."

Lee showed life. She jerked and wrapped the coat around her. "Not my mate," she whimpered.

I wanted the normal Lee back, and I would make both these bitches pay for doing this to her. "Phones," I held my hand out. "Right now."

Zelda's jaw dropped. "No fucking way."

"I'm not here to play games with the two of you. Hand me your phones, or I'll make you," I promised.

The women glanced at each other. Cindy tossed her hair behind her shoulder before yanking out her phone and throwing it at my chest. "I expect you to buy me a new one you asshole."

Zelda threw hers on the ground and stepped on it until it splintered. "There, that's good enough, right Alpha God?" she mocked.

For an answer, I strode over to her phone and crushed it myself. "If you two ever pull anything like this again, I won't rest until your engagements are dissolved and you're tossed out of this university. She's not my mate, but you can be damned sure I'm going to protect her from you," I promised before going to Lee's side.

The roaches scrambled out of the room, leaving me alone with Lee and the still-unconscious man. A strange burnt smell lingered in the air, it made my stomach clench. Lee glanced up at me, before staring at the ground and pulling the coat tighter around her.

"Did... you see?" she whispered, her words were husky, as if she was going to break on me at any moment.

I glanced away from her, pulled her into my arms, and picked her up.

I'd seen everything.

How was I going to explain this entire disaster to Kitty? She would be relieved I'd saved her, I was positive, but it didn't help the guilt that gnawed at me. I had never been this close to another woman before.

Lee leaned against my chest, she tucked her head beneath my chin, and gradually her trembling stopped.

If I had been a moment later, she would have been marked. I'd make it my personal mission to find out who that shit stain was and set Julian loose on his ass. No fucking way was that random wolf her mate. The bitches were playing some sort of dangerous con.

Lee sighed, and the tenseness in her melted as she relaxed in my arms. Her scent was everywhere, and I bit my lip, resisting the urge to groan. I needed to get her home and fast, far away from me.

I'd never smelt anything that was so intoxicating before.

She tempted me in a way that not a single damn thing ever had. I'd sworn myself to Kitty years ago, but that promise was in danger the longer I spent around Lee.

No, I'd never cheat on my Kitty, and I'd do whatever I had to in order to keep that vow.

CHAPTER 6

BROTHERHOOD

JULIAN

Albedo glared from the safety of Elijah's arms as we strode out of the university. They might not know where we were going, but I did.

Fuck. How was I going to explain the place to them? Was there a way I could possibly go about it without being teased or mocked?

Whatever. It didn't matter. All that mattered was getting Bedo somewhere safe, somewhere that no one else knew about. Once he was secure, I'd venture out and bring Lee back as well. I couldn't leave her in that school if something like this could happen to one of my best friends.

I let my mind wander as I stared off into the distance. His wolf had been serious. He really had chosen Lee as his mate, but what would she think about it? Would a chosen mate work for her or was a fated mate the only way to go?

Then there was that whole bombshell with Alexandra. As if I didn't have enough shit on my plate, here she came with a scooping heap of it. I had to find out the truth about what happened to the past Alpha Gods and the scholarship students. Some sort of sacrifice? I wouldn't let that happen.

Albedo wheezed and grunted, doubling over, holding a hand to his side. All too soon he waved our concern off, forcing a smile to his lips. "Sorry, brushed a sensitive spot. I didn't mean to worry anyone. Besides, this all looks worse than it is. I should get going and head back, It's a mistake to take me out."

What the hell was wrong with this guy? Here he was with the shit beaten out of him, and he was talking about heading back into that hell? I was going to tear his dad to ribbons the next chance I got. No one messed with my pack.

Albedo's face was pale, his eyes sunken, and if I listened hard enough I could make out his pained wheezes. He'd be fine my ass. "Bedo, what the hell is taking you so damned long to heal? My grandma could heal a broken hip by now."

He coughed and looked away from us. "Guys, I know you're trying to help. I get that. All of this will heal, but you're making everything ten times worse if you don't let me go back there. He's going to snap when he finds out I escaped."

Elijah glanced at him, a brow raised. "Oh? Okay then, let me set you down on your feet and if you can walk back in a straight line without stopping, we'll let you go back."

His chin dropped to his chest. Everyone knew he wasn't capable of something that small right now. Fucking Bedo and Lewis. Why did they have to hide that?

"Hey, Albedo?" Elijah ventured. He stared at the other man as if trying to peer into his brain. "I have a question. What exactly did Lewis mean when he said Lee's your mate?" There was a tenseness I wasn't used to in my brother, an almost challenge to his tone.

Albedo laughed, hiding a wince from us. "Oh, come on. I didn't say I had a mate. That was just Lewis. When have I ever said I wanted to be tied down with a mate? Can you imagine me chained up like that?" He scoffed. "No fun in that kinda lifestyle. No thanks, I'll just enjoy the women I can get with no strings attached for now.

I imagined him with those women that always fawned over him, crammed on either side, while Lee looked on from the sidelines with that damned sad-eyed puppy look of hers. Fuck it. I hated myself, but I wasn't going to let that kind of fate happen.

"Good, you won't mind when I take her then."

Elijah and Albedo both stared at me blankly. Elijah blinked rapidly like he was some sort of computer trying to decipher a code, and Albedo's eyes flashed. Lewis was dangerously close to taking control again.

What the hell was wrong with me? Had to be those shitty eggs. They were making me act in ways I never would have before. Those devils had tasted oh-so-good sliding down, but were making me suffer for every delicious bite. It had to be them responsible for this lapse in judgment I was having. "You heard me. She's my doggie, remember?"

Beside the two men, Alexandra fumed at me. Her fists were clenched and she trembled. For the first time in my life, her wolf glared out at me. I didn't blame her. I still couldn't really admit why I wanted to treat Lee like I did. One minute I was forcing her to eat off the floor, and the next I sent her to go and get pampered; like that would make up for being an ass.

It had been mere days. How had someone managed to get under my skin in such a short amount of time? She hadn't been the first to piss me off like she had. But maybe the first to challenge me, and to dare treat me like I was just an asshole.

The Lee that had been taking care of me tonight overlaid the one I'd forced into the ears and tail with that collar. Something about the image was hot to me, and what made it all the more bizarre, I knew for a fact if Cindy or Zelda wore the same get-up, I'd be disgusted with them.

What the hell was wrong with me? What had that ... I sighed. I couldn't even think of her as a mutt right now. What witchcraft did that woman possess?

"Julian, I've never been so disappointed in you. To think that you still want to treat Lee the way you do. She's not some toy for you to fight over, she's not a possession for you to use however you want."

With the way her fingers twitched, I was pretty damn sure she wanted to throw something at me. Thank the Goddess her hands were empty.

I smirked at my fortune. "Yeah, you're right. She's not a toy, she's my pet."

Deadpan, Alexandra reached down and unbuckled her sandals. She slid her foot out of them and bent down, picking them up. She grabbed one in her hand, and threw it in the air. I tipped my head back to watch the golden footwear sail into the air somersaulting high into the sky until I lost track of it.

Had she snapped? What the hell was wrong with her?

Taking the other shoe, Alexandra marched over to me and slapped me in the face, my head jerking to the side. I held a hand to my stinging cheek, when a moment later something slammed into my head and her other shoe plopped to the ground.

"I don't say this often to you, Julian, because I know you have a heart in there somewhere. But tonight? I've had enough. Fuck you."

Elijah jerked like she'd slapped him. I guess I couldn't blame him. Alexandra wasn't this type of girl, ever. She'd never lost her composure in front of us.

"And I don't know where you're leading us, but I'm not following you anymore. I'll take Albedo to my house. At least it's safe there. I don't know why I even for a moment, trusted you had a plan."

Damn it. Why couldn't I have just kept my mouth shut? "I do have a plan... We're not just taking a walk to get out here. We're going..." I glanced at Elijah again, but he was too busy staring at Alexandra. "To my place," I mumbled.

"Your place?" Elijah's attention snapped to me. "Wait, you've been at the dorm. You don't have a place. I would have known."

I ran a hand through my hair. Goddess damned, I hated this whole situation. "Listen, before we went to Silverton, before I abandoned the whole heir thing that dad expected, I got myself a place out here on my own that no one else knows about. Well, mom does, because she had to sign the paperwork, but other than that, it doesn't exist. No one in Silverton knows about it."

"You've had it all this time? Why not just get rid of it back then?" Elijah stared at me. "You hid something like this from me?"

I sighed. I knew he'd react like this. "Come on, do you really have to give me that hurt look, bro? I needed a place for myself. Besides, I couldn't give it up after I got it."

Slipping my hand in my pocket, I retrieved the secured keycard and waved it over the security checkpoint we'd come to. The gate beeped and rolled back.

"After you," I offered with a bow, and gestured towards the skyscraper. "Grab the elevator, I live close to the top floor."

Alexandra marched past me, her shoes ignored as she jammed on the button to call the elevator.

Once the doors opened, I slid in and pushed my floor number, waiting for the others to board. Why did it have to be this embarrassing? I'd kept this a secret from everyone else for so long it had become a part of me.

The elevator made it to the 65th floor and I marched out into the sole room on the level.

"Wow, this place is pretty nice," Albedo chuckled. "Got your own bachelor pad, huh? Bet you're getting a lot of tail like that. I wonder what Cindy will think."

Tail? I resisted the urge to groan. Did he know? Is that why he was using something so outdated? "Shut up," I grumbled. I pulled out my key and slid it into the lock, opening the steel door.

Whatever. They could make fun of me all they wanted. It didn't matter. At least Albedo would be safe, and once I went and got Lee out of that hell, she would be too.

CHAPTER 7

SECRET PETS

THE MOMENT THE DOOR opened, there was the chirping of several dozen robotic greetings.

Elijah stared at me, then at my open door and back. "What the hell is that?"

"Just bring Albedo in here. I promise he'll be safe. He can just pass out on my bed, I don't care."

A robotic cat rolled over to my foot and bumped into it repeatedly, meowing my name. Damn it.

Alexandra bent down and pet the robotic dog at her feet. "What is all this, Julian?"

They were the closest things I could get to real pets. If I'd gotten one of those they might have died while I was stuck in the university, or forced to do my parents' bidding. Besides, real animals didn't seem to care for me much.

The cat reared up on her hind legs and scratched at my shin. "Master Ju-li-an, come please," she pleaded.

Albedo doubled over again, laughing his ass off. Well, at least he was feeling better. Elijah continued to stare at my cramped quarters.

"Seriously, Julian, what is this? How could you just keep something like this a secret the whole time?"

I shrugged and headed over to the kitchen, opening the fridge. "I needed a place away from everyone and everything. This was it." I grabbed some beers and set them on the counter. They hadn't expired, but they were not what i normally would have stocked. I'd kept all shopping for this place as far away from my normal life as possible.

"Here have a drink," I offered.

It was getting dark out, and the longer I delayed, the more danger Lee could be in. My stomach still felt like I was trying to surf while eating a greasy triple-stacked burger.

My phone buzzed in my pocket and I turned away from my robotic pets to fish it out. Was Lee reaching out to me? Had she somehow missed me?

Damn it. What the hell? Why was I acting like I was some lovesick puppy? She was my pet, not the other way around. Rolling my eyes, I flipped the phone over to check the caller ID, but instead of seeing Lee's name, I saw that Cindy was sending me a series of messages, though I couldn't make them out from the thumbnails.

I opened the first one and froze. It's possible I even forgot how to breathe.

It was a picture of Lee lying on the ground in some kind of dusty dirty building, certainly not a place I'd ever been before, she was naked with only a sheet covering her body, but the thing was so thin I could see through it. Some man I didn't know was behind her, his face buried behind her hair and an arm wrapped around her body, pulling her against him.

What the fuck?

Lee?

My stomach roiled again, reminding me that the demon eggs hadn't finished their adventure through my body. Who had sent this? I stared at Cindy's name, trying to understand.

She had accompanied this photo with a single line, but instead of it making me hate Lee, which I'm sure was her intention, it only cemented my hatred for the woman I was meant to marry, unwillingly, but I'd still have done my duty to carry on the bloodline.

Not anymore.

See what the little school slut gets up to when you back is turned, love? Make the right choice, free our school of her filth.

The phone fell from my fingers onto the floor. Trixie rolled over it, scratching at my legs, demanding my attention again. Crouching down, I picked up the robotic pet and idly played with the leather collar around its throat.

Elijah set Albedo down on the couch, before returning to the kitchen. I didn't know what was going on in that photo, or any of the others. Elijah bent down to grab my discarded phone, the others questioning me, but I stared past them. She'd been after Elijah hadn't she? Everyone always wanted Elijah. He was the twin they loved.

I was the afterthought.

"Julian?" Alexandra grabbed me by the arms, too short to reach my shoulders, and shook me. "Julian!"

My fists curled. The image was burned into my brain, seared into a brand I couldn't escape from.

Fuck.

Who the hell was he? Why was he with my doggie?

Elijah's eyes flickered over the pictures. Unlike me, he was apparently able to stomach more than one. His lips pressed together, Baron peered out from behind his cold gaze.

Grunting, he rubbed his elbow and set the phone down. "Don't be so easily led, Julian. Think hard about who sent that to you."

Alexandra snatched the phone from Elijah's hands. She stared at the images, going pale as she did so. "You know she didn't do this willingly, right?" she focused her question on Elijah. "Those bitches did this to her!"

Albedo reached for the phone. "Let me see. Everyone else has had a chance."

"Don't," I corrected Alexandra.

She ignored me and handed my phone over to the other man. His fist clenched around the device and he squeezed. My phone had no chance, he crushed it in seconds. "I'm going to kill them," he growled.

I set Trixie down with a scratch behind her ears. "Where is Lee now?" I questioned the group. It's not like I expected them to have an answer, but I didn't want to think about the implications of those photos.

"Hey," Albedo called softly. "There's something else I didn't tell you guys..." He tossed my shattered phone to the side and stared over at us. His eyes were glazed. "I'm being forced to marry Zelda next month. The wedding was moved up because of all the time I was spending with the kitten."

Alexandra tilted her head to the side, eyes narrowing. "What's that?" she questioned.

I fell silent, focusing, and I heard it too. The buzz of someone else getting a phone call. "Elijah, sounds like you."

Elijah jerked, shaking his head, and grabbed his phone from his pocket. "It's Sterling," he announced before taking the call and putting it on speakerphone.

"This isn't the best fucking time, Sterling. And where the hell are you? We needed you and you couldn't peel your ass off your game long enough to care about us? I thought you liked Albedo."

Sterling's voice was raspy and cracked. "I... had to get Lee." He groaned on the other end. "Hey, someone needs to come get her. I can't do this..."

What the fuck was wrong with him this time? Still, at least I knew he had Lee. She wasn't with that scumbag, whoever he was.

A soon-to-be dead scumbag when I got my way.

Sterling whimpered. "Please guys, I don't..." he swallowed. "I can't cheat on Kitty," he whispered.

Cheat on his precious digital girlfriend? My fist clenched at my side. What the hell was going on with the others? When had this happened? In a matter of days, she'd swayed the hearts of men I'd known for a lifetime.

Why? What was so special about my doggie that she was capable of doing this?

"Sterling, I'm sending you an address. Bring her here. She'll be safe, and you need to fill us in on what the hell is going on. I was sent a picture, and I need to track down this guy in it."

Sterling let out a shuddering sigh. "Fine. But as for that Carl guy, I've never seen him before. I'll drop her off, then I'll go hunt those bitches down. I warned them what would happen if they leaked that shit. We both know they won't keep it just to you."

There was little doubt about that. I wouldn't be surprised if by the time we returned to school that the entire facility had pictures of the woman that belonged to me.

I wouldn't let it happen for long, I'd crush every electronic device if I had to.

Lee was mine.

CHAPTER 8

THE DEAN'S CONTROL

LEE

Sterling returned to my side from his phone call. He'd taken me back to my room. I reached out to open the door and froze. My body was chilled, "please," I whispered to him, my voice thick. That man had nearly marked me, and taken me as his own. No matter what kind of assholey stuff Julian had been up to since I got here, it was nothing compared to that.

If Sterling hadn't shown up, what would have happened to me?

Sterling hadn't met my eyes since he'd saved me. Did the man blame me for what had almost happened? Trembling, I pulled the coat around me, trying to find some semblance of warmth in it.

My entire future had nearly been snuffed out.

I hadn't put too much thought into mates before Silverton. I'd been content to throw myself into my studies and try to find a solution to save King. But after entering these hallowed halls, my outlook was rapidly changing.

If that man had marked me, the possibility of finding my mate would be dashed forever. Part of me still believed without a doubt that Elijah was the one.

"*That's not true,*" Barb protested, huffing softly at me. There wasn't a sting to her words, but an almost awe to them. "*Carl is our... mate.*"

"*You don't sound too sure yourself,*" I pointed out.

She answered me with a wave of silence.

"What's wrong?" He wrapped an arm around my trembling shoulders. "Scholarship?"

My fingers trembled on the handle. "Zelda and Cindy had the key... they said Albedo gave it to them."

It's not that I believed them, there had to be some other explanation. Albedo hadn't set me up for that experience, there was no way. And yet, the nagging worry refused to fade.

"That's not possible. She shouldn't have even been able to get into this building," Sterling corrected me. He took the key from my fingers and opened the door himself, letting the door creak open. "Behind me," he instructed, slipping through.

It took only a matter of steps, for the happiness this place had brought me before, to be dashed away in seconds. Everything Albedo had painstakingly painted for me was gone. Great black smudges and splashes of red paint were the only things left. I'd gotten a taste of it when the bitches had snatched me, but coming back to see just how much damage was done was devastating.

My knees gave out and if it hadn't been for Sterling's support, I would have crashed to the floor. "No," I whispered.

Sterling shook his head at the scene. His grip tightened and his free hand rubbed soothing circles on my back. I looked up at him and met his comforting eyes. "You're not staying here, scholarship. We'll go back to my place, I'll let the others know. You'll be safe there. I promise."

Breathing a sigh of relief, I leaned against him. A part of me wanted to break down and sob. This school had put me through a lot, but having something so dear torn away hurt far more than I had ever imagined. I couldn't bare to stay in this place for another moment, so his words were a welcome balm. "Thank you."

He sighed, glancing away from me and at the floor. "Don't worry about it. You can take my bed, I've got a couch in my room, I'll sleep there."

Why did he sound like he'd gone toe-to-toe with some fierce enemy and lost? There was no answer in his tone, but more like a deep sense of resignation.

"Don't worry," Sterling forced a smile, his brows furrowing as he finally met my eyes. "I wish you were someone else, scholarship. It would make all this easier if you were."

He turned and left me, striding out of the apartment and grabbing the hallway wall.

I went to his side, placing a hand on his back.

"Excuse me," hissed a nasal voice behind us.

"Ms. Suga, will you care to explain to me what you're doing in a restricted area? This place is for Alpha Gods only."

Sterling took a stance between us. "She's already been approved to be here. Albedo told me he got permission from you."

The Dean's eyes narrowed on me. "Ah yes, that. It was a mistake, and it's been handled." His lip twitched. "Albedo is paying for that currently."

What did he mean by that? "Where is he?" I interrupted.

He gave me a sly smile. "Do you want me to take you to him? Leave this place, and I'll take you straight to him."

Sterling kept his hand on my harm. "She's got permission from the Alpha Gods, Dean. Last I checked, we were the ones that ran this school, not you. Why are you interfering?"

Instead of recoiling, the Dean's smirk only grew. Why weren't the special Alpha God powers they always bragged about working? "Sterling, you have this sole opportunity to return to your room while I handle the scholarship student. Since you are indeed an Alpha God I'll be willing to overlook this minor offense. As for Ms. Suga here, I can not afford to be so lenient. I'll be taking her to another room, more befitting her station."

Sterling shook his head. "No, I'm telling you to leave, or I'll have your job. I don't care if you're Albedo's father. Lee is under my protection. You won't lay a finger on her."

"Under the protection of an Alpha God?" the Dean clarified.

"That's right. So leave," Sterling insisted.

"Then all I have to do is strip you of that," the Dean mused.

None of this made sense. Why would a school that bent over backward to take care of the Alpha Gods before, suddenly turn their backs on them?

Even Sterling seemed impacted by his words. He had frozen in place. "You... can't do that."

The Dean smiled. "That might have been true before, but considering how this year has been shaping up, the Master of this university has given me certain rights I don't normally get to use. I've wanted to strip your power away for a long time, Sterling. You never did deserve to be an Alpha God. Last chance, step away from the girl, and go back to your room."

The Dean reached for my wrist with his bony fingers, but Sterling intercepted it, grabbing him instead, and squeezing. "Hands off," he growled. His beast peered out, and Sterling's eyes turned completely gold.

Barb was still quiet, no matter how much I urged her to help, there was a passiveness that was unusual to her. "It's okay, Sterling." There was no point in me getting him in trouble. If this little act would protect his place in this school, I wanted to do it. He had saved me not too long ago.

"Where are you planning to take her, Dean?" Sterling pressed.

"None of your business," the Dean snapped back with a growl. His eyes had turned golden too, his connection with his wolf was strong and his claws slid free from his fingertips. He twisted out of Sterling's grip and grabbed me, slicing my arm in the process. "As of now, you're no longer an Alpha God, Sterling. All rights and privileges you did possess are gone. If you insist on fighting me on this, I can make the punishment worse."

"If you don't fucking drop her now, I'm going to claw your face off," snarled a low hiss of a voice behind us.

I craned my neck to see Albedo limp forward, supported by the rest of the Alpha Gods. He looked awful, but there was a monster inside him threatening to come out and it wasn't aimed at me. It was aimed at his father.

"I'll do what you always do, I'll give you a count to three." He, chuckled, his laugh echoing in the small space. "Drop her and run. One," he didn't waste time and started his count.

CHAPTER 9

THE FOUNDER

LEWIS

My attention was held captive by the vicious red streaks that marred my mate's flesh. No one else existed at the moment but her, and the bastard that had dared to touch what was mine.

What Albedo wanted or didn't want, didn't matter any longer. I was confident he was still on my side, and that he too would want to rescue Lee, but I wasn't chancing it by giving him a second of control. Not until this matter was handled.

I would stop the crazed man. "Get your filthy hands off her," I snarled.

The other Gods glanced over at me, their wolves peered out, uncertain if they should join my crusade. I didn't need them. I was enough. She was my mate, and I'd protect her with my life.

My vision was a red haze as I focused on the precious blood that dripped to the ground. I stepped forward, growling. My body was prepared to shift at a moment's notice, and I would.

I needed to pay this bastard back, for not only what he had done to my precious, but what he had done to Albedo, for years. This asshole would pay. I'd die before I let him drag Lee off to the punishment cage, or to his secret chamber.

The Dean didn't look phased at all. He had to know that I was the one in control, yet his smug smile never so much as flickered. "Are you sure you want to insist on this? You'll be the reason Sterling is not only kicked out of the Alpha Gods, but also banned from the entire Silverton University."

I laughed, my lips curling into a sneer. Humans always had the wrong priorities. "All I care about is my mate, and getting revenge for your son." I stepped closer, my bones cracking, preparing for a shift.

I would rip him apart.

He tightened his hold on Lee's wrist before tossing her to the ground. She shook, curling in on herself, a pose I was far too conscious of, thanks to Albedo. A strange coat was wrapped around her body, but from what I could tell, not much was beneath it. Strange scents clung to her that were far from natural, and she was pale as a sheet of paper.

What had happened? This wasn't the woman who had faced down Julian without fear in order to save her friend. The fire that had burned in her, had been all but put out.

Sterling stared down at her, his hand was outreached, but he wouldn't take the next step to pick her up and comfort her. I'd claw his eyes out later.

"Lewis," Albedo's father greeted with a nod of his head. "After everything you've done to Albedo, now you want to get his position taken away? I'd rather be fed to rabid domestic dogs than to ever let him mate with a filthy mongrel."

Elijah rushed to her side, kneeling beside her while Julian took a protective stance above her.

I barely held back the urge to launch myself at Elijah as she melted against him. Hadn't he already rejected her? No, that wasn't important. This bastard couldn't be allowed to harm her again. "Get her out of here," I snapped at the brothers.

Elijah gently helped Lee to her feet with a hand on her back. Julian wrapped an arm around her shoulders, lending her his support.

Elijah had pissed me off, but Julian being soft to her made me want to rip him apart. How could Bedo let these men sniff around our mate all the time? Didn't he understand that she belonged with us?

"Albedo," the Dean hissed at me, and inside, Albedo tensed. The asshole was trying to force me away.

"We've got a matter to settle, Marcus," I sneered at the Dean. I loved the way his eyes narrowed on me as I was disrespectful to him.

"Such impudence!" The Dean was shaking, his wolf glared out at me. "I'll make sure that Albedo is stripped of his powers and banned from this university as well. It doesn't matter to me that he shares my blood, I can always birth another child. This time, I'll make sure that he won't be a failure."

Did he think I was falling for his bluff? I laughed in his face. "A power-chaser like you will never abandon your ambitions so easily. You wanted Albedo to be an Alpha God from the moment he was born, just so you could use the power it would grant him. All of the power, and none of the responsibility."

"So what if I did, Lewis? Have you forgotten? Albedo is my son. As his father, I have the right to do whatever I want with him, just like I did with his mother. All that matters in this world is power, and if he doesn't have the drive to take his talents and put them to use, I'll do it for him. Even if I take it from him right now, all I have to do is control the one I give the power to until my next son is of age."

There was no way he could be telling the truth. Ever since Albedo had been declared a possible Alpha God of Silverton, this bastard had gone overboard with his punishments, and tried to control everything Albedo did, attempting to shape him into a Marcus clone.

Almost everything. Albedo had always flirted and sweet-talked any woman he could to fill his days, and to irritate the hell out of his father. He'd have to figure out another way to bug him, we'd found our mate, there would be an end to that nonsense.

"Please, Lewis, I don't know what you expect to accomplish. You're his ignorant wolf, muscle, and not much of anything else. If I had known how worthless you'd both turn out to be, I would have killed you the instant you were born and tried again with a worthier mate. Your control won't last forever. The instant you retreat, I'm going to make Albedo suffer for all of this. I might just blind him."

My fangs almost broke through as my urge to shift became an obsession. "You will never touch Albedo, or anyone else again," I promised. "I'll keep him locked away forever." I jerked my head towards Lee and the brothers as they hobbled down the hall. "And you will never touch my mate either."

"Mate?" Marcus scoffed. "Juvenile fantasies. For Alpha Gods, there is not a need for those. Albedo will marry Zelda in a month's time, and nothing either of you do will stop that. Even if he's worthless, at least his bloodline might be useful for something. Ms. Suga is nothing but a necessary pawn to bring out the true power of the Alpha Gods."

Julian gently pushed Lee into Elijah's arms and strode back down the hall. Oni was ready to take him over. "She's not going to be anyone's sacrifice." Sterling had gotten to his feet, Rust peering out. Even he was ready to throw what power he had into play if need be.

Marcus's lips twisted into a smirk and he shook his head. "Really, Julian? You're willing to give up your position as well? With all of the antics you've gotten away with, I thought you'd be the last one to want to chance that. All of those cases involving you and the bullying you did will be unsealed. Remember how you drove that student to insanity in grade school? Her family would be the first in line to take you and your family down."

I wasn't the fondest of Julian, he tended to be a dick, and I didn't like the way he stared at my mate, but that didn't mean I was going to stand here and let one of my pack be treated this way. "That's it," I snarled, I launched myself at the Dean, shifting as I did.

"That's it?" he mocked me. "Pathetic wolf." Marcus shifted and his robes shredded, unable to hold his wolf's form. Despite him being old in human years, his wolf was anything but weak and would be a challenge.

Marcus's beast was more crazed than the man, and crueler as well. Neither I nor Albedo had ever been able to win a challenge against him, or even his acknowledgment. Not that I ever needed it.

His gaze turned to my mate and he snarled, leaping into the air and at her.

His physique as a wolf was at its peak, and his speed was blazing. I wouldn't be able to dart in front of him, and the others wouldn't be able to react in time to stop his assault. Snapping at his tail, I grabbed it with my teeth, and yanked back with all my strength, tossing him to the ground.

He was down for only a second before he struck at me with his claws, slicing into my cheek when I didn't dodge in time. He didn't give me the time to adjust. He was like a whirlwind as he bit and clawed at me, trying to force me to submit.

I tried to dodge to the side and away from the punishing force this old man could muster.

He sensed a weakness and sprung at my ear, likely to teach me a lesson. It was the perfect opportunity. Like a snake, I struck, ducking beneath his attack and sinking my teeth into his throat, I bit down with all the force I could. His coat was too dense for my fangs to sink through, but it didn't stop me from trying.

Lee would be safe with the brothers. Someone had to stop this monster. I couldn't help but recall all the times Albedo had to rely on my power to heal, or worse, when he used it to stop himself from healing because his father was a sick fuck that wanted him to take the pain, and wear his injuries as a punishment.

I pushed beyond the strength I possessed, summoning up everything I had. I clenched my jaws, until the tips of my canines slowly punctured his flesh, his blood welling on my tongue.

"Enough!" barked a smooth voice from behind us.

Wait, who else could get into this sacred hall? Had the seals on it been completely broken? But I could still feel their power sizzling in the air.

Something grabbed me by the scruff of my neck, and I was yanked off the old wolf, and thrown into the wall.

I got to my feet and shook the ringing bells away. What the hell? There'd been no one behind me. What had happened?

I stared down the hall opposite the way that the others cradled Lee. A figure strode down the passage, his long white hair billowing behind him, as a black Silverton robe donned his slim frame. A black mask settled over the top half of his face, though the golden-eyed gaze of his wolf could not be hidden through the black mesh eyes.

Who was this?

"He's the one that founded Silverton," Albedo offered, his voice barely above a whisper.

The man brushed off his robes, and the black magic that leaked from him faded away. "Obviously, I made mistakes when I chose the Alpha Gods this time. How dare you attack the Dean of this university."

I was still trying to figure out what this man had used. Magic wasn't foreign, but it was incredibly rare, and those that wielded black magic, even more so.

Maybe I should try to correct this founder and let him know exactly what was going on, but what would be the point? When Albedo had first been abused, he had tried to tell others. Other adults, from relatives to teachers, and no one believed him. How could they ever think the Dean could be so cruel to his own son? It wouldn't be different for me.

"Sir," Lee had found her voice again, but it was shaky at best. "He-he was just trying to save me. Please, don't punish him, or any of them. This is on the Dean, he snapped, he was-"

"Enough," snarled the man. He gestured towards Lee, and black wisps of magic exploded from him and wrapped around her, pinning her against the wall, and tying Julian and Elijah to the floor.

"Touch my mate, and I'll fucking end you," I promised. Death wouldn't be good enough, I needed to make this bastard suffer, both of them.

The founder's eyes barely flickered. "The Dean has stripped both you, and the one known as Sterling, of your rank, but I'm here to take your power. In all of my years of serving this academy, I have never seen an Alpha God deprived of their position. You two are the first."

I shook my head with a laugh, circling him. That strange magic of his hovered around him like a shield.

"Careful," Sterling cautioned. "I don't know what that is... I've never seen anything like it."

And whatever it was, had my mate captured. "I don't give a damn if you expel me. All I care about is her, and nothing will keep me from saving her."

The stranger shrugged. "Expelled," he agreed, flicking his finger at me. Instead of the black tendrils, a gust of wind hit me in the chest and knocked me over. I landed on the ground and grunted.

He was going to take Lee from me. He stepped closer to her, grabbing her by the wrist to rip her off the wall.

There was no time to explain.

Please, Morgan, let my mate forgive me.

I scrambled to my feet and ran full speed at them. I grabbed her wrist with my teeth, biting down, letting the magic of my mark crawl across her skin.

She shrieked when she understood what was happening. I didn't blame her. She smacked me with her fists and tried to wrench herself free.

The black magic that had coiled around her crept away. She stared at her bloody wrist, and the mark I'd left behind, and I faced the man that had just tried to take her away.

No matter what, my mate was mine and nothing would rip us apart.

CHAPTER 10

WORTH OF A GOD

LEE

I couldn't tear my eyes away from the mark that would forever tie me to Albedo. It didn't surprise me that his mark would be as cocky as he could be. The black wolf winked at me from my marked flesh, I could almost see the swagger in the tilt of his head and the raising of his brows.

Like a giant blanket, the bond wrapped around me, muffling me in its warmth as it tied us together, connecting me to him and his wolf.

Barb was pissed, it radiated out of her like a cloud of rage, but instead of coming to the surface and arguing about it, she sunk deep into the darkness and left me behind.

That wasn't all. Though it was faint, and I couldn't make out what any of the other Alpha Gods were feeling, but I could feel their bond to Albedo.

Julian's head jerked to the side as he craned his neck to stare at the situation from his position, tied to the ground.

Lewis didn't so much as flinch from his position. He had maneuvered himself between me and my attacker. He didn't even glance at Julian, just his ears flicked to indicate he had heard him at all.

Sterling gently pulled me away from the chaos. I let him, too stunned by what had just happened. I had a mate. Now, I was tied to Albedo in a way that I could never escape without suffering.

The mysterious masked founder smirked. The energy around him flared, and though it was muffled since it wasn't a direct tie to the others, a wave of pain flooded through the Alpha Gods.

Sterling crumpled at my side. His long fingers tangled in his hair, tugging hard at his roots as he soundlessly screamed. He panted for breath, wheezing as his entire body shuddered. He forced his head up and stared at the smirking man. "What did you do?" he snarled.

Lewis was next. He fell to the ground, growling and snapping as he tried to keep him away from us the entire time, even as he whimpered in pain. His pain echoed through me and I fell beside Sterling, crying as the agony crept through.

What was going on?

"This is what you deserve," the Dean sneered at us from behind the founder. He shifted back, and picked up the remains of his clothes.

Death wasn't good enough for that man. He needed to suffer.

My rage must have unlocked something within the mate bond. Scenes I'd never witnessed before flashed through my head. One image burned into my mind, making me sick to my stomach.

Albedo was leaning against the bars of a cage with his arms tied behind his back. There were bruises all over his body and his arm was twisted at an unnatural angle. Scars were seared into his flesh and there was something dead in his eyes.

"What?" I whispered, trying to make sense of it.

Lewis panted. "Don't look," he pleaded. "Please."

Sterling's pain flickered through me like a live wire, destroying the hold I had on the image before. It vanished in the space of a heartbeat, and only Albedo's pain haunted me through our bond, forcing me to the ground with its intensity.

Whatever was happening between the Gods was only getting worse. Elijah and Julian's magic prison had vanished, and Elijah was curled into a ball, gasping in agony.

"What the fuck did you do?" Julian snarled, a hand held to his head. He pointed at the masked man, and his eyes had turned pure gold. "Stay the hell away from my pack," he threatened.

The man adjusted his mask and I noticed a white stenciled dog carved beneath his right eye. "I don't make it a habit of replacing the Alpha Gods, I've never had to. But here's a little-known secret. All of the Alpha Gods are wholly replaceable, because while you do hold power, you are not true Alpha Gods yet."

Julian's face darkened. "Not true Alpha Gods? That's not right."

"I'm the one that decides who has reached that state, and no Alpha God has ever reached that state. Usually, their worth is decided during the last test, but I already have decided two of you are completely rotten. I've cut the ties and abilities from them. There is no way I will let them remain here to fester and corrupt the rest of this sacred ground."

How could they do this to them? "They've done everything you wanted," I protested, getting to my knees. "They've sacrificed so much."

"That doesn't matter to me. The two I've cut off, I suggest you leave this school now, or you will run the risk of being forever separated from your wolves. I have no sympathy for trash."

Elijah and Julian jerked, staring at Lewis and Sterling in turn, twin puzzled expressions on their faces.

I got to my feet with Sterling beside me. He too was staring at the other Gods with an air of confusion hovering over him. Disbelief flashed over all their faces. I wasn't sure what had just happened, but all four had been touched by it.

"Why are you doing this to them?" I snapped at the Dean and the founder. I'd seen something else for just a moment, another face behind Albedo's when he had been tortured, a face twisted in a satisfied smirk as his son suffered. The Dean's face.

I wanted to rip him apart with my bare hands. Pointing at the founder, I stepped forward. "You talk about not letting anything rotten into the Alpha Gods, and yet you run a university where you let a father abuse his own son?"

The Dean scoffed. "You're mistaken, Ms. Suga, I have no son."

My eyes flickered to Lewis, but he didn't flinch at the words, there was a wave of pain swelling over him.

Sterling grunted, hanging onto the wall. His eyes met mine. "Sorry, scholarship," he mumbled before racing down the hall and away from us.

"I'll go after him," Lewis grunted. He shifted back into his human form and hobbled after his friend. They leaned against each other for support, escaping the Alpha God's hall.

I wanted to run after them, but the founder stood directly in my way.

"You're the one that the school took pity on. We took the suggestion from a classmate of yours, or rather, their family, and helped you with your little family problem, correct?"

I shivered. Was this a threat?

Julian and Elijah scrambled to their feet and stood in front of me like twin walls, protecting me. "You're not touching her," Julian snapped. He glanced over his shoulder, meeting my eyes, and a fierceness burned in him. "She's mine."

Elijah sighed, burying his head in his palm. "Sometimes, it truly is an embarrassment to be around you, Julian," he muttered. He shook himself out of it and scanned the founder. "If you are who you claim to be, introduce yourself. What do you want with Lee?"

"I'm the founder of this university, what else do you need to know?" He inclined his head, glancing my way. "Though, I could make an exception for the one to be sacrificed." He reached for his face, removing the mask and revealing his features.

Strange. Wasn't this the founder of this place? Why did he look like he was our age, or even younger? His face was smooth and there was a youthful sparkle to the twist of his lips.

Something wasn't right. "How old are you?" I blurted.

Elijah winced.

"How old?" he repeated. His silvery eyes twinkled. "I come from a line that was there the very day this world was born, all those memories are retained within me. When you speak with me, you speak to someone that's always been here. I am ageless, I will live on past you until I achieve my bloodline's ambition." He reached for me, the black tendrils of magic gathering around him again. His eyes glowed gold, replacing the silver.

Julian snarled, and thrust Elijah backward so he was beside me. "She's not being sacrificed to anyone, she has a name and it's Lee."

I glanced down at my feet as I considered taking my shoe off and beating him over the head with it. Out of all the times to insist on my name, it was now? What a fricking hypocrite.

Elijah gave the other man a look, like he couldn't believe the words that came out of his mouth, and taking his palm, he slapped it upside the back of Julian's head. "We do not need your commentary. Let me handle this."

I was to be sacrificed, huh? It made sense in a twisted way. Why else would a school such as this have an opportunity for someone from my position, to mingle with the elite in its hallowed hall? "Mr. Mask, if I'm being sacrificed, I have one question for you."

He smiled at me, and turned to glare at the Dean. "You can leave now, I will handle this. Get out of my sight."

The Dean's cheeks puffed out and he huffed, but he waddled down the hallway that the others had left down, cradling his clothes to his chest. Hopefully, Albedo wouldn't have to face him.

The founder slipped his mask into his robe. "I will allow you, and these current Gods, to call me by name. Unless they are monumentally stupid, I expect they will be there for the final test." He bowed. "My name is Inu."

"Well, Mr. Inu," I countered. He inclined his head, and I took the invitation to continue. "After you've killed me off with this little test of yours, what happens to those I've left behind? My family will not be able to afford any of this once I'm gone."

Julian and Elijah stared at me like I'd grown another head. Julian grabbed me by the shoulders and shook me. "What the hell? I didn't give you permission for all that, doggie!"

"I won't let you hold her family to ransom like that," Elijah intervened, pushing Julian away. "If it's money she needs, our family has more than enough of it. You will not kill her off." His words had a bite to them that took me by surprise.

Inu ignored the two, his eyes were only focused on me. "They'll be taken care of, until the day they all naturally die. Your brother will receive the best medical care for the rest of his life. His disease is rare, but our resources stretch farther than you'd think. I've got doctors and medical staff on standby exclusively for his care, including those that could cure him."

Cure? There was a cure to that awful disease? My little brother could get his life back? I swallowed. It was a heavy price, but I was willing to pay it. I ignored Julian and Elijah's protests. This wasn't their life, it was mine. My dreams never did matter as much as other people's, this was just an extension of that. "Whatever you need, I'll do as long as you uphold your end of the deal, and take care of my family, no matter what happens."

Maybe there would be a way to survive this little test of his, I couldn't give up all hope, not yet. Besides, who knew what would happen to Albedo if I was killed? He was my mate now and he'd been through enough pain, I didn't want to add to that.

But if I had to give up to protect my family, it was an easy decision.

I'd give anything for them, even if it meant my life.

CHAPTER 11

BROKEN ENGAGEMENT

JULIAN

My ears had to be playing tricks on me. I grabbed Lee by her marked wrist and dragged her backward, away from Inu. She dared to glare at me the entire time looking like a ruffled kitten. "Stop it, doggie," I scolded, glaring right back at her. "There's no way in hell we're going to just let you do whatever this guy says. You don't even have proof that he's telling the truth! What if you die in this twisted scheme of his, and your family still ends up broken? Would that be worth it?"

"But!"

"No!" I snapped. I wanted to shake her again until her teeth rattled, but Elijah had been pissed enough at me the first time. "I'll take care of her family, me and Elijah got this. No matter what you're promising, you can't compete with us. We've got you covered, Lee, don't listen to this man. You don't have to risk your life."

Inu clicked his tongue. "You have the money to continue their care, but you won't have access to the doctors that will cure her brother's condition. You see, my team knows how to handle tardoxia." He turned his eyes to me. "Think about your decision, Ms. Suga. They can keep your brother comfortable until he dies, I, however, can make sure he's cured and has a normal life. This offer will not last forever."

"She's not interested," I snarled.

Inu chuckled. "As for you two? Beware the enemies you set up for your futures. It's not exactly smart to make an enemy of me. She will become the sacrifice sooner than you think, and nothing you do will change that." He smiled at the two. "And boys, your little plan only works as long as your father still claims you. He's my next stop." He slipped his mask back on and strode down the hall, leaving us behind.

Lee cocked her head to the side at his words, frowning, and then pivoting to stare at us. "Your father?" she questioned. "He said boys."

"Ours," I replied with a shrug. I hated having to do this. "Listen, Lee, Believe in me, got it?" I ordered.

Elijah rolled his eyes at me. "Why would she ever do that when you insist on treating her like an object? I can count the number of times you have used her name on one hand." Elijah's eyes flashed. "Why couldn't you have just let her live her school life in peace, you asshole?"

Huh. That was weird. Elijah only got upset over Alexandra, but he sounded as angry and pissed as I was. The man practically radiated fury as he strode forward. "Lee," he hissed.

Her head jerked to the side as if he slapped her, and she stared at him, her eyes wide and hopeful. "Elijah?" she whispered.

Why did he bring such a weakness in her tone, even now? He'd been nothing but an asshole. Why was she showing this cowardly side to him? He'd crushed her, hadn't he?"

He softened as he smiled at her. The asshole, didn't he understand this would make things worse?

"Julian and I don't agree on a lot of things. But this? He's right. No matter what we have to do or the strings we have to pull. We will help you, we'll keep you and your family safe."

She stared up at him, I didn't exist.

Damn it. I snatched her wrist and traced a finger over the winking wolf. "This means you belong to us, even more than you did before. Lee, I'm not letting Albedo be the only one who claims you." I pulled her wrist to my lips, prepared to leave a claim beside Albedo's.

Elijah punched me in the gut, hard enough I was forced to double over and wheeze in pain. What the hell?

"She's already had one mark forced on her, she doesn't need another, and certainly not from you. What gives you the right to even pull that shit? We need to get out of here and regroup."

Lee yanked her hand free from my grip, and hugged it to her body, glaring at me. What was her problem? Didn't she understand I was offering her protection? So what if it hadn't been my first intention? All that mattered was that it was my current one. With my power, I could protect her and her family.

"I just want answers," Lee replied. "Elijah, where should we go?"

"Damn it!" Growling, I reached for her again. Why did she have to piss me off all the time? No matter how much I tried to shove her out of my mind, she always came back. "Lee!"

Elijah moved her to the side, blocking me from her, and pulled her to him instead. "Julian! Get a hold of yourself. You're acting like a toddler!"

Lee stared up at Elijah before slowly taking a step back and pushing him away from her. He winced and she gave him a small, hesitant smile.

The sight made me grin. Looked like the idiot was in the doghouse as well. I wasn't the only one suffering her wrath.

As if she sensed my thoughts, Lee stared at me like I was the one who had threatened her family. "Julian, why can't you get it through your thick head that I don't want anything to do with an asshole bully like you? All you've done is bring misery to my life." She turned and stomped off with Elijah trailing after her.

Instead of following them, I froze. I couldn't tear my eyes away as they walked down the hall, not even turning back to check on me. Oni wanted to chase her down, pin her to the wall, and force our mark on her, just as Albedo had done.

My hands clenched at my sides. No matter what, nothing I did would change her opinion of me. She wasn't even giving me a chance.

But a chance for what? I stared at the ground, trying to sort it out. What was I trying to do to her? Why couldn't I escape from the shadow she cast over my life? Anyone else I would have burned down to the ground for getting in my way.

I didn't want to hurt her. Damn it, I wanted her to like me. What the hell? I hadn't been that big of an asshole since she met me, had I? I'd gone out of my way to get her a spa treatment, and even new clothes. And, I'd let her stay in our dorm when Cindy was being an uber bitch.

Elijah and Lee vanished into our dorm. I doubted they would be there too long, it wasn't safe with everyone having access to our fucking realm of safety. I needed to go for a run or I was going to tear my hair out.

By the time I got out of the building, the others were already long gone. Probably for the best. If I saw Albedo I was going to punch him in the fucking throat for what his wolf had gone and done without permission. And yet I was the asshole? He'd forced a mating bond on her!

"Julian," cooed a voice nearby. Goddess fucking damn it, why did I have to deal with her of all people? "Julian," Cindy interrupted my thoughts again, fluttering her hand in front of my face before she grabbed my chin and jerked my gaze down to meet hers. How had I ever considered marrying this bitch?

"What do you want, Cindy?" I snapped, tearing my face away from her talons.

She pouted up at me, tapping her toe. "Did you get the picture I sent you? I was so shocked when I saw it, but I knew you had to see the truth."

The fire in me that had sparked to life when I witnessed that cursed image flared hot and heavy again. "What about it?" I snarled. I imagined myself strangling the man, pushing a foot on his neck, and forcing him to eat the slop I'd tried to force on Lee.

Hesitation flickered through me. Maybe that was one of the reasons she hated me. But I'd been the one that ended up eating the fucking shit. Why did she have to be mad? I'd treated her with kid gloves considering what she'd done. The mutt only got what she deserved, right?

I frowned. The rage faded away. Lee wasn't a mutt, not in the same sense I had treated her like it before. No, I wanted to be around her, wanted her to smile at me, and maybe even one day, for me.

"Julian," Cindy simpered, butting her way into my thoughts.

"I saw the damn picture. What, do you want a fucking medal? Or wait, no you want a head pat, right? Since you're so jealous of my bitch, is that how you want to be treated?" I regretted the words almost the instant I said them. Lee wasn't a bitch.

I took my frustration out on Cindy, aggressively patting her head until she shrieked and stumbled backward. "Julian!" she complained.

The stupid woman didn't know how to say anything else. "I don't care about whatever it is you're trying to say, Cindy."

She adjusted her hair and pouted at me. "That's not the right way to treat the woman you're going to marry. You're supposed to be my prince charming."

Cocking my head, I turned on her, thrusting my hands into my pockets as I towered over her. She hated this stance. "Your prince charming?" I laughed in her face, and her fake smile vanished. "All I'm ever going to be for you is a devil trying to wreck your life. The wedding is off, I'm not marrying a selfish bitch like you."

Cindy's eyes widened so much I thought they would pop out, and her mouth worked like a fish. "You-you can't do that! Your father-"

I snorted. "You think I give a damn what that man wants?" I shook my head. "Listen, Cindy, I don't care what anyone else wants from me anymore. Not you, not my old man, and no one in this damned university. I've finally understood what I really want, and nothing is getting in my way." I stepped around her.

She grabbed for my arm, but I shook her off. "Julian!" she shrieked, screaming my name as loud as she could, as if it would change my mind.

"Sorry, there's only one woman I'm willing to fight for right now, and you're not her. Nothing you do will ever change my mind, I don't care how many pictures you send or what positions she's in. But I promise, if you ever pull that shit again, I'll string you up to the top of the Silverton steeple and leave you there for a week, but first I'll roll your ass in honey, and sprinkle birdseed all over you. That way you learn to stay out of my fucking way."

Cindy trembled. "Fine," she growled at me. "We'll see what your father says. I won't forget this, Julian. I'll make you pay, you and that little bitch of yours."

I turned to head back into the building and paused, turning on my heel to glance her way. "There is one thing you can do for me, Cindy."

She brightened, like I hadn't just threatened to torture her. "Yes, Julian?"

"How did you get in? Only Alpha Gods are supposed to be in there."

She waved my question away. "That's all you're asking about? It's obvious, isn't it? The Dean turned that little system off and gave us keys to the dorm. If that bitch was allowed in, why did you guys deserve any exclusive rights?"

"Give me the keys, Cindy. Yours and Zelda's."

"Why would I do that? I have every right to go wherever the hell I want. You can't stop me."

Getting into a fight wouldn't solve anything. I would figure out a solution for this mess, even if I had to cram everyone into my apartment. No matter what, I would keep her safe, even if she kept hating me.

If I had a heart-to-heart with her, there was a chance we could start over, before it was too late and she hated me forever.

CHAPTER 12

STOLEN RANK

ELIJAH

Lee stayed stuck to my side as we entered the room. We couldn't afford to stay long, this entire building was compromised. My head swam with all the information dumped on us. Julian had nearly pushed me over the edge, and I would have lost my cool. It wouldn't have helped if both of us were fired up and pissed off. Someone had to be sane enough to keep him under reign.

"Thank you," Lee whispered. Her voice was shaky, still probably considering that bastard's offer.

Then again, I'd been a bastard to her as well when I'd snapped. I ran a hand through my hair. "Lee."

She looked up at me, though she couldn't meet my eyes for too long.

"About earlier, I'm sorry. I know I've said this before, but it's important that you know I mean it. What just happened in there? Julian was right, neither of us are going to let you throw your life away."

Hope shimmered in her eyes, and I cursed myself. That hadn't been my intention. Didn't she understand I could never be what she wanted? The bond I had with Alexandra could never be broken. I loved her unlike any other.

The pain in my head that had crawled through my scalp like the tip of a knife had been bearable up till now. My skin crawled, and the intensity magnified as if something was prying my mind apart. I doubled over, and only Lee slipping a hand around my waist stopped me from crashing to the ground. "Elijah!"

I tried to answer but the pain was too intense. Clenching my eyes shut, I tried to regain some semblance of control, but all I could do was scream as claws plunged into my brain and shredded it. The ties that I'd had with the others had been dormant, but now they were being ripped away from me. I couldn't even sense Albedo and Sterling anymore.

From outside the room Julian howled, I assumed he was facing the same situation. "Bastards!" he snarled.

Lee pushed the door open and stared at the man crumpled on the ground. "What's going on with you two?" she questioned, staring from one to the other. She pushed a hand to her head, whimpering. "Why does it hurt?"

The pain must have been ping-ponging back to her through the bond through Albedo. I could feel her like a specter, hovering at the fringes of my mind, but she was fading fast, just like the connection I had with the other Alpha Gods.

"Damn it," Julian grumbled before grunting and getting to his hands and knees. "What the hell is going on?"

"Our pack bond," I admitted. I had never given two thoughts about the ability to feel my other Gods like they were extensions of myself, but now that it was being torn away, I was lost. Two of our members were gone, like they'd been erased. And since Albedo had been the one that marked Lee, her faint presence was stolen away as well.

"It hurts," she whimpered, curling in on herself.

Julian had gotten to his feet and grabbed her from me, cradling her against his body and massaging her head like he was trying to towel dry it.

She stared up at him before bursting into laughter, and ducked away from his touch. "What are you doing?" She patted her hair, trying to get it into some semblance of order.

Julian glanced away, unable to keep her gaze. If I didn't know better, I would bet my brother was blushing, but that was impossible.

"Whatever," Julian huffed. "I can think again, it must be over," he grunted, wincing as the barrage continued.

I had to find a way to undo this. Our bond was one of the things keeping Julian sane, without it, who knew how far he could fall? Or what he would end up doing to Lee.

Julian massaged her head again, and this time she didn't pull away as he gentled his touch. I didn't know there was anything gentle in him left. "What do you mean our pack bonds? How can they take those?"

"Everyone's gone," Lee whispered. "Everyone but Albedo."

Julian's eyes flashed at the way she said his name. Now that she was Albedo's mate, even the way she spoke of him had changed.

Had the founder, that Inu person, had he always had so much power? If so, why hadn't we met him even once? It had to have been him, the pain hadn't started until he had attacked us. The Dean was another matter. One I would personally handle.

How had we as a group been so blind to Albedo's suffering? He'd put up with that torment for years, and none of us had caught on. How had he managed to hide it? Wasn't privacy something that didn't exist for us? Or used to not exist. The only one I couldn't hide things from now was Julian, lucky me.

"Can you still sense Albedo?" I questioned her. I ignored Julian's death glare, the man could probably register that as a trademark. It was still weird to see him actually jealous, even if he didn't realize it yet. I had seen his obsessive side in the past, but this was nothing like that.

Lee winced, and pulled away so she was by herself. Her thumb rubbed against the mark on her wrist. "I need to undo it," she whispered.

My stomach dropped. She wanted to undo a mate bond? Why would she ever want that? With Albedo at her side she would be better protected, besides, I didn't want to think about what it would do to the man if she rejected him.

"Fuck," Julian growled, pulling at his ear cuff as he tugged at his ear lobes. "Damn it, Lee. You can't do that to Albedo. I wish you didn't have that damned thing either, but if you reject him, you're going to break him. Please, don't do it."

I was a dirty bastard for the manipulation I was about to use, but it was necessary. Taking her hands in mine, I squeezed them to get her attention. Her head jerked up as she stared at me and a delicate blush spread across her cheeks at my touch. The same hope I'd noted earlier flashed across her face, stronger than ever. I'd at least stopped her being afraid of me, but I was still an asshole for this. I had to play the role of her prince charming she seemed to think I was. "He's been through enough. Let's just think about it before you make a decision that will tear you both apart for the rest of your lives."

She turned pale as my speech wore on. By the end, she only mustered a small nod and bit her lip. "What should I do now? My room was destroyed, and I don't feel safe going back to my original one. I won't hurt Albedo by rejecting him, but I wouldn't feel right just moving in with him either."

"You're moving in with me," Julian announced. "My place is small, but I can protect you if you stay there. I'll even hire Albedo to come and decorate the whole place again like your apartment was. I just hope you like robot pets, I have a few."

"With you?" Lee questioned, looking past Julian and focused on me. I didn't need to be connected to her to know how hopeful she would be about my answer. How was I going to let her down again after feeding her all this false hope?

"Yes, I don't like it, but it's a smart move. Julian's apartment will be secure."

"Julian's apartment?" she echoed, her eyes widened. "Wait, I thought you meant your house or something. There's no way I'm staying with him. Why can't I just stay on my own? I can go back to live with my family."

"No," Julian interrupted. She shot him a glare, but he held a hand up in defense. "Listen, at my place Elijah and I can keep you safe without a doubt. You won't be touched by Cindy, Zelda, the Dean or that Inu guy, you'll be completely protected. However, I can't do that and protect your entire family. I swear, I'm not going to mess with you anymore, at least not on purpose. I just want to help you, get it?"

"Julian is right, as much as I hate to admit it," I grumbled with a sigh. "You can't stay on campus, not when there are no safe spots left. Julian is an idiot, an asshole, and he's stubborn as hell, not to mention he doesn't really seem reliable-"

"Elijah, I'm going to kick your fucking ass!" Julian snarled.

I ignored him. "Despite that, whenever something really important happens, he's always someone you can count on. If he's saying he'll keep you safe? He means it. He'd probably die before he let anything happen to you. Also, as long as they're still trying to get something from you, if they think they can get it without force your family should be safe."

Julian grumbled as he crossed his arms. "Thanks."

I chuckled at him. He really had fallen for this woman, it was too bad for him that she was still completely into me. Even if Albedo hadn't marked her, it's unlikely she'd give Julian a date, ever.

My vision flashed red and Baron screamed obscenities a moment before a raging fire was set off in my brain. I collapsed to the ground at the same time as Julian did as our minds were ripped apart.

CHAPTER 13

NEW GODS

JULIAN

Heavy bombs exploded behind my eyes, and I tried to claw the pain away but it only made things worse. My head throbbed with every moment and every time I so much as breathed too much, the pain was almost unbearable. Each second only brought more intolerable pain. I howled, desperate for relief.

"Are you okay?" Lee's voice drifted to me, but she wasn't at my side. No, she was still simpering over Elijah. I grit my teeth. Not only was I in agony, but she hadn't even thought about checking on me. Did she really hate me that much?

My head continued to pound and the ability to focus on the ball of rage in my gut was taken away. It was even worse than when Sterling and Albedo's bonds were ripped away. Not my entire brain was melting and falling apart in protest.

"What's going on?" Elijah panted, grunting with every word.

Heh, at least he wasn't the smooth and suave person he normally was right now. It was the only solace I had as black stars blinked in front of me, threatening to blind me.

Then it was gone.

"What the fuck?" I snapped. It was like invaders had been forced inside my brain.

"What?" Lee questioned. This time she actually asked me.

I couldn't answer her as a snarl tore through me. It wasn't at her, but the minds pushing against mine. "Who the hell are they?" I demanded. I forced my eyes open and glared at my brother like he could give me my answers.

Elijah's head was cocked to the side before he buried his head into his hands. Lee was at his side in an instant, running her hands through his hair as she attempted to massage his head. Much gentler than I had done before.

I ran a hand through mine, imagining what it would be like if it was her touch instead of mine.

"You know who," Elijah spat. Even my brother was growling. "You're smart enough to figure this out."

I pulled my hands away from my head and focused. The pain was fading, but I could still feel the echos of it with the two new minds in our network. Bonds that didn't belong to Sterling or Albedo.

"Are you telling me they really replaced them already?" I hissed. Those fucking assholes. Whenever I became this true Alpha God or whatever, I would use all the power I had to expel the Dean and Inu.

"They did," Elijah agreed with a deep sigh. Lee helped him get back to his feet, and after doing so she turned to me. She hesitated before coming to my side and staring down at me.

"Here," she thrust her hand out. "I'll help you up."

Was she going to pull her hand away the instant I touched her? I stared at her, unsure if she was going to play a prank on me. But she kept it out there, stubbornly staring away from me.

I curled my hand around hers and struggled to my feet with the offered hand. "Thank you, Lee."

She glanced over. "You're welcome." An instant later she let go of my hand and pulled away, retreating to Elijah's side.

"Come on, let's get back," Elijah announced.

I sighed. It wasn't that I was against his decision, protecting her was important. But I wish I could have time alone with her like I had earlier. Those demon eggs had done something for me I'd never expected, and if it hadn't been for Elijah, who knew how things would have turned out?

"Do you need anything?" Elijah asked her, glancing through our place.

"No, let's just get out of here. I don't want to be here any longer."

I grunted and grabbed the door. Why was I the third wheel for these two? He was madly in love with Alexandra, who was still at my place. All he was going to do was hurt Lee again.

Footsteps down the hall caught my attention and I craned my neck to see who was coming to fuck with us now.

I froze.

The man I hated more than Elijah was strolling through the hall like he deserved to be there, and he wasn't alone. Fucking Rue was behind him.

What the hell?

"Where do you think you're going?" the stranger that had been in the picture with Lee questioned me.

Behind me, Lee stopped. She grabbed the back of my shirt, hiding her face. Elijah took a position beside her, slipping into a protective stance. Lee trembled behind me.

"Lee?" the man questioned. A strange longing ping-ponged through my brain, and it didn't belong to me. I positioned myself in the doorframe so the man couldn't see her.

"What the fuck are you doing here?" I demanded of the prick.

He ignored me, glancing past and catching sight of her. "Lee, come here," he encouraged, opening his arms. "You don't have to be afraid, we're mates, remember? I know that something strange happened last time we were together, but I'm fine now, I won't hurt you."

Lee whimpered, a terrified little yip escaping her.

Oni snarled. The man took a step backward, his neck cocked for a moment in submission before he shook his head and straightened up. "Stop that, you can't do that to me anymore."

Anymore? I didn't know exactly who the pissant was. "Who do you think you are? You know I'm an Alpha God, and if you and that runt don't leave now I'll break the two of you, right?"

He shrugged at me. "I'm an Alpha God too, and she's my mate," he pointed at Lee. "Come on, Lee. Stop playing. We need to go to our room. The Dean gave us our own so we would have some privacy."

"Hey!" Reuben objected. "Hold on, I never said I was going to let you do that, Carl! Lee's staying with me." He thumped his chest as he growled at the other man. He paused, and glanced her way. "I mean as long as she wants to."

They had to be shitting me. "The two of you, Alpha God material? Hell no. You barely qualify to breathe the same air I do, let alone are free to roam this school. That dumbass Dean made a mistake."

"Oh, the Dean isn't the one that initiated us," Reuben interrupted. "It was this strange guy in a half-mask on his face. He said he was the founder of the school. Which is quite the feat because I've studied the history of Silverton, as you know, and it's been around for ages. He must be extremely old."

From behind me, Lee snorted. Despite it being for someone else, I was glad to experience an emotion besides fear from her. I didn't know what to do when she was acting that way, it just wasn't Lee.

"Rue," she giggled. "You really are a Silverton fanboy."

Rue grinned our way. "You don't have to hide, Lee. It's okay."

Slowly, she eased out from around me. I tensed, prepared to shove her back if these asshats tried anything. She pointed at Carl. "I'm not your mate," she said, her voice ringing clearly. "I never was. There's no way."

"Come on, I know you felt the bond..." he trailed off, his brows wrinkling. "Wait." He nodded to the mark on her wrist. "What is that?"

I smirked and leaned against the door frame. "Oh, that? She's been marked. Too bad for you wannabe, Alpha God, she's already taken."

He shook his head, backing up to the wall. "That can't be right. No, you have to reject him. Why in the world would you become mates with that asshole, Lee?" He waved a hand at me. "I know what we felt. Your wolf felt it. There's no denying that we're supposed to be."

"She agrees with me," Lee replied softly. "We are not rejecting our mate. You're nothing to me, Carl."

He grunted like she had hit him, and his eyes flashed gold.

Ever since I'd seen that picture, I had wanted to punch this man's face. Lee hadn't been in that position willingly, I knew that beyond all doubt, and Oni growled in perfect agreement.

"Besides," I added. I dropped my hand from the doorframe to around her shoulders. She stiffened at the touch, but didn't shove me away. "Lee is mine. She doesn't need you, or you either," I nodded at Reuben.

Elijah glared at me from over her head. I'd get an earful later, but I didn't care.

"Lee," Reuben interrupted yet again. This guy never could take a hint. "There's something you should know. Before we were turned to Alpha Gods, the Dean was talking with your family."

"What?" Lee pushed me away, striding forward. "Tell me everything."

Carl smirked at me, but he didn't try anything beyond trying to piss me off. If he had taken one step, I'd have punched his teeth out.

Reuben glanced at us before turning his focus back on Lee, and he scratched his neck. "It's just, they told them you were going to be mated and wed to one of the Alpha Gods." He glared at Carl. "He didn't say it was going to be him exactly. They thought it was me." he said if it didn't happen, he would have to relook at the funds the school is diverting to take care of your family, especially when you can't be bothered to attend most of your classes."

"No," Lee whispered.

That was it. Maybe Rue hadn't meant to bring back this frightened version, but I'd had enough. "She doesn't need anyone else to take care of her family, I've got it handled, and she doesn't need to be blackmailed. Not that it matters, she's already a mate to an Alpha God."

Carl scoffed. "You mean the guy I replaced? Besides, even if he forced it on her, she's still supposed to be mine. I can still feel the bond now."

I laughed. "Oh, you can huh?"

Carl frowned, uncertainty flashed across his face. He sensed a trap. Too bad for him, he'd already fallen into it. "Of course, I can. She's my mate. All I have to do is brush against her and it's like I'm touching a fire."

My smirk only grew. "I fucking knew you weren't her mate."

He stared at me, his brows knit as he tried really hard to understand my point. Idiot. "You're not making any sense. Now get out of the way."

"Alpha Gods can't feel their mates. It's one of the drawbacks when we get all that power. If you were really her mate, it would be cut off right now."

He whirled on me. "You're the one that said she was your mate! How do you explain that?"

Elijah sighed and shook his head, but for his part, he didn't interfere. I appreciated that.

"Easy, I decided she's mine, and that's it. I'm not letting a little upstart like you take her. You'll never be a true Alpha God."

"Julian," Lee protested at my side.

"Don't worry," Reuben interrupted. "I won't let Carl do anything to Lee. I'm an Alpha God now too, I can protect her."

I resisted the urge to slap myself, really fucking hard. This kid was on something. "She doesn't need you, either of you. She's got me and the original Alpha Gods."

"Lee," Reuben protested. "You're not going to let him talk for you, are you? You're my best friend. I know you don't hate me."

"Rue, thank you. Really. I appreciate everything you've done for me and what you're trying to do. However, I will be safe with Elijah."

I scowled. Really? She couldn't just throw my name in there with his, even with something like this? "And?" I pressured.

"And Julian," she agreed with a long sigh.

"You're not going to be safe for long," Carl protested. "He sounded serious about making you break contact with all of the old Alpha Gods. Besides, Lee, I don't care what he says, you're my mate, the reason I still feel it is because I found out before I became an Alpha God. Barb knows it, Henry knows it, you should know it too. We can't defy the Moon Goddess, Morgan."

Reuben frowned, stepping between Carl and us. "Hey, I know we're both on the same level, but you have to accept that Lee doesn't acknowledge you. Accept your rejection and move on..."

He huffed. "It's not like she wants you either, Reuben."

Their anger at each other flared in my brain, and I grit my teeth. Was I really going to be subjected to this all the time? I'd rather undergo the excruciating pain again

Reuben frowned, shaking his head. "Lee doesn't acknowledge you, that's all I have to know. Just accept your rejection and move on."

Carl growled at us, his eyes turning a deep golden as his wolf threatened to take over. "Mine," he snarled. "Come, mate."

Lee's eyes flashed in response and her wolf came to the surface. Lee's expression became sharp and she growled back. "I've got a mate," she answered, showing her wrist. "Give up, it'll never happen."

Carl grunted and shook his head. "You're confused. You'll change your mind. I know you'll remember what you should do. What we're supposed to be, I know you'll accept it eventually."

"Get out of here," Elijah snarled at the two of them.

Both were startled. What the hell? Why hadn't they responded that way to me? Assholes.

"No..." Carl shook his head. "I'm not going to let her go. She's mine, and I won't let you stand in my way. Even if I have to play dirty to do it." He glanced away and reached into his pocket, pulling out a collar, similar to what I had her wear, but arced with electricity.

What the fuck? Did he really think he was going to get away with this? I cracked my knuckles and Oni moved forward, prepared for battle. "Elijah, get her to my place. I'll be there later." There was no way in hell I was going to let this asshole win.

CHAPTER 14

FALLOUT

ALBEDO

"Where are they?" I asked for the millionth time, we'd had to endure the raging pain seeking to tear our brains apart. Whatever it had been, had ripped everyone but Lee away from me. Only our bond remained. "I need to get back to her." There was far too much wrong, and me not being with my mate was the biggest thing.

Sterling put a hand in the middle of my chest, gently pushing me back. It was hard to even look the man in the eye.

Lewis had been out of control, he hadn't given a single thought to the consequences of his actions when he'd marked Sterling's kitty.

"*Mine,*" Lewis reminded me with a huff.

I didn't want to argue with him. I'd betrayed one of my best friends in the absolute worst way possible. He wasn't going to forgive me for this when he found out. I didn't blame him, I would never forgive me either, even if it was my idiot wolf's fault.

"We need to stay here. You know we can't go back until whatever happened is fixed."

"My mate is back there!" I hissed. My fist clenched. Those words were so foreign to me. Sure, I'd planned to marry Zelda and be the good son my father had expected, but I never would have referenced her as my mate. I snorted. "At least I don't have to worry about marrying Zelda anymore."

Sterling's phone buzzed interrupting us, and with a great sigh, he fished it out of his pocket. "Man, sometimes I really don't get how we're friends. Your humor is out there."

He glanced at the screen, his brows furrowing. "Huh." He answered it. "Kelly? What's up? You rarely call."

He walked away from me so I couldn't hear their conversation. I figured she was scolding him for losing his position, because his shoulders slumped as the conversation went on.

One of Julian's strange little pets rubbed against my shin, and I picked it up. Why did he have so many robotic pets anyway? It was more than a little strange. I scratched behind its ear as I stared out the window and back toward the university. All I wanted was to run back in and pull Lee out. With every second that passed, fear and dread filled my being. That founder couldn't be trusted.

The door creaked open behind me. I whirled, ready to grab Lee and take her to the side to talk. However, it was just Alexandra. She had a handful of bags in her hands, and gave us a thin smile. Damn it. I thought I'd get a chance to talk to my kitten and explain things. I had to apologize for Lewis, and talk about what she really wanted. If she didn't want me, it was going to fucking hurt. But, if that happened, I would push her toward Sterling. Those two deserved to find each other.

Until Lewis decided to ruin everything.

Alexandra set her bundle down carefully and smiled at one of the robotic pets that waddled over to greet her. "I'm glad you two are okay. I've been keeping watch on this place, but I went out to get Lee some things she'll need. I want her to be comfortable when she returns."

"Did you hear what happened?" I asked. If she knew what Lewis had done, she wouldn't be smiling at me so gently.

"No, but considering that it sounded like your place wasn't safe anymore, I assumed that everyone would end up here. Or at least Lee would." She frowned. "I just hope Julian can be nice to her."

"Sterling and I..." I sighed. There was no way I wanted to admit this. "We're no longer Alpha Gods."

"What?" Her eyes widened as she stared between the two of us. "What happened? Are the others okay? Where's Lee? Why are you guys here alone without them? How?" With every question, her grace and poise faded.

"The founder stripped us of our positions, the others were okay when we left them, but we were forced to leave, it was too painful to be on campus grounds. Julian and Elijah will bring Lee here."

Instead of making her feel better, it appeared my words only made Alexandra more upset. "How could you leave her like that?" Alexandra snapped. "Lee isn't used to any of this!" She frowned, eyeing me closely. "Why aren't you looking in my eyes, Bedo?"

Damn. I thought I was doing a good job masking it all. "I..."

Sterling came back in, his call with Kelly was finished. He scowled at the two of us. Something had pissed Sterling off? That was new. He nodded to me. "Pretty sure he's trying to tell you that his wolf went and marked Lee."

Alexandra slowly turned on me. "What?" she whispered.

"I lost control.... Lewis just did it out of nowhere."

Her eyes twitched and she whirled on me. "What the hell were you thinking, Albedo? She's Elijah's mate!" She put her hands on her hips and glared. "I've never seen you serious about anyone, you're not capable of it."

I winced. Her words were true, but they still hurt. Besides, things were different with the kitten. I'd always chosen to not get serious with anyone. It was easier to hide my true self that way. The only one that had ever seen my scars, besides Lewis, was my dear Fireball. "I'm serious about her," I replied softly.

"I don't understand this. Sterling, are you really okay with this? He stole Elijah's mate! Our best friend, and supposed to be yours too. How could you do it, Albedo? It's been obvious to me from the first day they were supposed to be together." She took a deep breath and shook her head. "I'm sorry, but I'm going to suggest that she reject the bond."

Lewis tensed. He was prepared to go to war. No, I couldn't hurt Alexandra. She'd been our friend since we were kids. "Alexandra, I'm not playing with her. This isn't some trick." This felt so awkward to say, and Lewis refused to interfere, he was letting me confess all this. Damn, how could this be true? "I genuinely care about her."

"Okay, you care about her. That's not the same as love. That's what she will gain with Elijah, and it will last their entire lives. He only thinks he's in love with me, but I'll make him see the truth."

I stalked away and to a small chair where I plopped down. A robot cat jumped in my lap and rubbed against my chest before kneading its sharp claws into my leg. Why did Julian have so many of these things?

Did I love Lee? It was a huge step from caring, she was right. The answer had already been decided the moment Lewis marked her. The instant he'd connected us, everything else had changed. It was why I felt so guilty, I didn't want to give her up.

"I love her," I agreed softly.

I didn't want to. Doing so put her in danger of my family. I knew what my father was capable of, and yet, I couldn't hold back. Nothing would stop this feeling from seeping out of my heart. Lewis would never let me turn away, and I didn't want to.

"I'm sorry, Alexandra. I know you had everything set up for Elijah, but I'm not going to reject her, and I'll make sure she doesn't reject me unless it's her will."

"Very well, I'll guide her to the right choice. I can't take you seriously, Albedo. I've heard you tell other women you loved them before. You've broken a lot of hearts, even if that wasn't your intention. I won't let you add Lee to your list."

"Wait," Sterling ordered us. I jerked and focused on him. This was my chance. I needed to tell him the complete truth about Lee. It would be like yanking off a bandaid. It would hurt, but it was easier than slowly peeling it away and letting the pain simmer.

Just confess, and get it all out of my system. He would hate me for keeping it a secret as long as I had, and he'd really hate me for marking her. However, if I did it now, there was a chance to avoid hatred between us.

"That was Kelly on the phone. There have been some developments at the university over all this already." Sterling interrupted.

My lips twitched. "Oh, she didn't just call to bitch at you for losing your spot?" It was fun to give him hell, and who knew how many more opportunities I would have for it?

Sterling didn't even crack a smile. "No, this is serious. After we were expelled, they replaced us."

"Wh-what?" I stared at him. I had considered us being punished, I never would have imagined it was for good.

"Two new Alpha Gods, and if I look at the picture she grabbed, one is that bastard that I saved scholarship from," he grunted. "Bedo, you have to keep that mate bond and protect her. I've got a bad feeling about all this. I know what we went through to get those spots."

He didn't notice my wince, and Alexandra was too busy staring at him, speechless about her words.

This was the moment. I needed to tell him. If I failed, I would be worthless, no, worse than worthless. "It's funny you bring her up," I mumbled.

Sterling turned on me. His eyes narrowed. "Why?" he pressured. He hadn't taken a step toward me, but his aura threatened to bend me over in submission.

"Sterling, I found something important out this week. It's about your kitty, and I think you should know."

His lip curled and his eyes turned gold. Rust threatened to take control. "What about his kitty?" he growled.

"I-"

Alexandra's phone buzzing interrupted me. She glanced at the screen before she brightened. "It's Elijah!" She held her phone up to us before answering it. She nodded, listening intently. "Got it." She turned back to us, and her smile was bright but something was strange in her eyes.

"What's wrong?" I questioned.

"That was Elijah, he's got Lee, and he's heading this way. He wants us to have a strategy meeting." She paused, glancing away. "Julian isn't with them. He stayed behind, and he's fighting one of the new Alpha Gods."

CHAPTER 15

LEE'S GUARDIAN

JULIAN

"Why won't you give up?" I snarled. I kept my eyes on the collar he held tightly in his grip. Lee had gotten away for now, but there was no guarantee he wouldn't try to go after her if I didn't stop him.

Carl smirked at me. "Why won't you give up? You keep claiming she's yours, but I have yet to see her wear a mark from you. You're nothing but the school bully, and I know you've been bullying my mate. I've watched what you've done to her."

I scowled. This was the last thing I wanted to hear. "Can it, stalker psycho."

"I'm the psycho? You're the one who made her wear a collar, tried to get her to eat dog food, made her eat off the floor." He ticked off each point on his hand, eyes focused on me. They flashed golden. "And let's not forget the rumors of what you've done to those around you before. I won't let you break her."

Me, break her? I wanted to strangle this fleshbag. "Maybe your little promotion has made you forget your real place in our society. You are nothing to me, and nothing to her. Just because we have the same title, doesn't mean you have the same power as me. You can't threaten me, and if you try again I'll rip your fucking throat out." I grinned at him. "You've heard the rumors, I'm sure. I'm an Alpha God, I can get away with murder."

"You guys okay?" I was grateful my connection with Elijah hadn't been cut. I would have been riddled with worry if I couldn't mind link with him. He was the only one I could trust Lee with right now.

"We're fine, we're almost to the apartment. Julian, be careful. Those two weren't promoted for just any random purpose, they had to have a reason to do it. Get back in one piece, I won't be able to handle this situation without you."

I was snapped out of the mind link as a fist smashed into my cheek, forcing me to take a step back from the force. Carl chuckled at me, bouncing back and forth on his toes and punching the air. "This concerns my mate, I don't care what powers you have, or what rumors surround you. What kind of man would I be if I didn't stand up for the one I'm fated to be with? Back off, Julian, she's worth more than you are."

The tongue on this one. A taste of power and he acted like this? I wasn't an Alpha God just because of my family line, I had to prove myself through countless tests. There was no way this pea would ever be worthy of Lee, even if he was somehow her mate. Which, I knew was impossible. She didn't need a mate, she was mine.

"Did you forget she's got a mate already? You're too late, wannabe."

Carl flashed the collar in his hand. "Did you forget? I told you, I'll have to make her. It will work out in the end. She'll just need this long enough to reject that bond. I know she felt it, just like I did. Besides, he's not a real Alpha God, he has no right to anything with her. If I want her, they'll give her to me."

"She's not some object you can own," I snapped.

The look he gave me almost made me slap myself. Whatever, I wasn't about to take the words back. He shouldn't be treating her like an object. "She doesn't want you. If you want to keep your spot as a fake, you need to give up on her."

"Why are you so obsessed with controlling her? She's not your mate. I don't know what she did that has made you so set on torturing her, but I won't let it continue. You're the one treating her like a toy, Julian. Besides, you've got a wife-to-be, remember poor Cindy?"

The name made me snarl. That bitch reared her ugly head again. "I wish I could forget her. She's lucky I don't make her the target of this school. When I'm done she'll be left with nothing, I'll even make her family cut her out of their life, lower than a mutt for everything she's done."

"You really are a heartless prick, Julian. Not that I expected anything more. You can attempt to play prince charming for Lee all you want, but we both know your true colors. Then again, I've known about those for a long time. That student you drove to insanity because you turned a mob on them. You do know once you're in college that kind of bullying is more powerful, you'll get people killed. If you ever lose that mantle of Alpha God, you can be held to blame for every disgusting thing you've done."

I crossed my arms. "Are you really going to stand there and lecture me while you're holding a collar meant to do more than humiliate? That's going to do more than tickle, you sick fuck."

Reuben stared between the two of us. His eyes were focused on the collar, but the coward wasn't saying a word. "And you, some best friend you turned out to be. Are you going to let this guy do whatever he wants to her? If you were really there for her, you'd want her to be happy, no matter what. Oh wait, I get it. You're just waiting for him to hurt her enough that you can step in and be the faithful white knight, huh?"

Reuben winced while Carl laughed. "That's not it," Rue defended. "It's hard for me to believe she's better off with you and the other Alpha Gods after I've seen what you've done to her. What you continue to do to her." He whirled on Carl and shoved the man from behind, sending him stumbling forward. "However, that doesn't mean I'm going to let you do whatever you wish either. Lee deserves to be happy, she's been through enough!"

Carl turned on him, laughing in his face. "What, you're scared of that prick, and you call yourself an Alpha God? I'm going to put this arrogant fucker on his back, and show him that no one will get between me and my destiny."

I'd had enough of both of them. Neither deserved Lee. Carl did his stupid bouncing again, and the second he shifted his weight to his weaker leg, I pounced. I rushed at him, striking him in the gut with my shoulder. He grabbed me around the middle, stopping my momentum from throwing him over my back and stomping his head in. Throwing a sharp series of punches aimed at beneath his ribs, I refused to hold back. Every blow was a testament to my rage that this creature was trying to hurt Lee.

Instead of letting go and defending himself, Carl squeezed me tighter. The tips of his claws slid out and cut into my back deeply. Hot blood gushed down my skin, but I focused only on him. "You're staying the fuck away from Lee," I snarled into his ear with every blow I delivered. There was a satisfying crack with the last one, and he grunted, his hold weakening.

I had no bloody idea what I was going to do about Albedo and our relationship, but when I finally got back to Lee, my mind was made up. I was claiming her. No one else deserved to touch her or to receive those soft little smiles of hers. They would all belong to me.

Reuben kept from getting involved, watching from his safe place, the chaos we caused. Blood trickled from Carl's lips. "Carl, stop this, we need to get out of here and get to classes. We have an introduction to do, and if you keep it up, you won't be in any shape to do it."

Running away? Why wasn't I surprised? This Reuben guy never deserved her either. He was like a gnat hanging around, trying to find the right time to swoop in and take advantage. A true friend would have stopped me from the start, before things escalated, not bend to my will in a sick urge to placate me.

"Oh, he's not going to be in any shape for anything but to step down from his new position," I growled. I slammed my fist into him again, into the spot that I had heard crack before, and he coughed up a puddle of blood. It dripped onto my shoes, and he growled like a wild animal before he leaned down and bit into my shoulder, and his caws curved, peeling my skin away.

"Enough!" Reuben roared. He grabbed Carl by the back of his long ponytail and yanked him off of me with one vicious tug. He ducked as Carl whirled on him and attacked.

I had to admit, that part was impressive. I didn't think the little runt knew any fighting skills. Still not worthy of Lee, but maybe not a complete failure of a wolf.

"Carl, we're leaving. I didn't work my ass off to become an Alpha God for you to risk our position on the first day!"

I snorted through the tinge of pain. "Work your ass off, huh?" I sneered.

Reuben turned to glare at me. "I'm not on your side, Julian, I never will be. I used to look up to the Alpha Gods, yes, you were brutal, but this school ran efficiently and everyone knew their place. I'll never forgive you for what you've been doing to Lee. She's not a pet for you to break, I'll never let anyone crush her. She's my best friend, and even if I have to throw my life away to save her, I will. I didn't get her into this place for an animal like you to try to dominate her."

Blood flowed down my chest. When Carl had been pulled away, he'd taken a chunk of my flesh with him, bitten right through me. I held a hand to the wound to suppress any more blood loss. My eyes turned a golden haze. Oni wanted to slaughter the man, and decorate the dorm with his entrails. I did want to stay and fight, but I needed to get back to Elijah and Lee. It was only a matter of time before my mother discovered her, and that wasn't a conversation I was looking forward to.

Besides, she was in my apartment, and we'd be spending the night in the same space. Not even a hole in my shoulder could take that aura of pleasure away. I stumbled forward. "This isn't over, I'll see both of you again. When I do? We're finishing this. You'll both learn your place, and leave Lee to me."

Oni surged through the new bond we had, and both their wolves shrunk back from his ferocity. They weren't expecting to deal with a demon wolf, and Oni had never backed down to another.

Carl spat out the chunk of flesh he'd gouged from me. "You're in way worse shape than I am, Alpha," he snarled. "But yeah, come at me again, I'll kick your ass harder. I'll tear one of those eyes out of your sockets and carve your nose off. No one will ever want to look at you again."

I turned away from the two of them as they limped down the hall. I needed to make it back to Lee's side and get to the bottom of all of this. We'd find out what the Alpha Gods really were, and why the university thought they could sacrifice my woman. And the one who was giving me answers, was my best friend Bedo if he wanted to or not.

CHAPTER 16

REVELATIONS

STERLING

Sitting on the edge of one of the chairs, my knee jostled up and down as I stared at the wall. Alexandra had excused herself to clean up the place, since cleaning was not Julian's forte.

Why was it taking everyone so long to return? What had just happened worried me. Albedo was stretched out in a chair beside me, one of the mechanical cats curled up on his stomach, and he stroked it while staring up at the ceiling.

Lewis had marked Lee, claiming her as his own. It was still hard to believe scholarship had a mate, and why did it bother me? I had Kitty. But it did bother me, in a way I couldn't describe. It wasn't like I wanted her, but she needed to be taken care of by the right person. I wasn't so sure if Bedo really was it.

"Hey," I questioned, glancing over at him.

Albedo's head jerked over, his eyes unfocused. "Yeah? What's up?"

"How do you feel about all this? Lewis just marked scholarship, and it didn't look like you had a say in it." I glanced away. "Plus, I don't think Jules is going to be happy. He's going to be pissed, dude." It wasn't a lie, Julian had some sort of possessive thing going on when it concerned her, though I wasn't sure what his intentions were.

At first, I had assumed he was going to find a new way to torture her, but then he'd done things I'd never seen him do. He'd pampered her and cared for her, yet at the same time, he'd kept up with the stupid collar and leash act.

Then again, maybe the dude was just kinky that way.

Albedo scoffed. "Yeah," he agreed. "That's putting it lightly. He ran a hand through his hair, pressing his head back against the chair.

Elijah sure was taking his sweet-ass time. I regretted starting this conversation, why was it my business what the others did with her? She was a friend, that's all. She was nothing like my Kitty. I would be loyal to her until the day I died, no matter what.

"I couldn't stop him," Albedo admitted. "I don't know what came over him, why he went to that extreme." He put a hand to his lips. "She's gonna hate me for forcing that on her." His voice was choked as he spoke.

I doubted that completely. "Dude, she liked you already. She wouldn't have kept hanging out with you after that kiss if she didn't. And yeah, maybe she'll be upset you didn't get her permission for the mark, but that wasn't you, that was Lewis. He's the one who has to deal with the consequences."

He answered me with a snort. "Her liking me, and her being bonded to me are two different things, man. He tied her to us in a way that will tear us both apart if she rejects me. Lewis might have been the one that put the mark on her skin, but I wasn't able to stop him. If she wants to reject me, I'll accept it. She deserves to make her own decisions."

I nodded along. "Hey, do you love her?" I don't know why I even asked such a stupid question. I hated myself for even being curious. This was it, I needed to message my Kitty. Talking to her would help get my mind off everything. Besides, she was probably worried sick by now, I was never offline for this long.

"Love?" Albedo echoed my words, and his brows furrowed. He stared down at the cat on his stomach happily kneading away with its metallic claws. He stroked it, staring at its shiny body as if it held the answers he sought. "I haven't thought about anything like that, but I know without a doubt that Lewis does. He's decided she's our mate."

Mate.

The word was enough to suck the breath from my body. There was only one person in the world who could fill that position for me. Decision made, I fished in my pocket for my phone and opened it. I wasted no time in loading up the game.

Kitty was the one I loved, the one I'd always love, and the only one I ever could. True, scholarship's vulnerability, and the way the others softened around her had weakened me. Maybe it was even through our bond that their feelings had leaked through and corrupted me.

I was a bastard for even thinking about someone else, if even for a second. Mogan herself had interceded on my behalf through Lewis. With Lee marked and bonded, it would be impossible for me to fall under her spell.

As long as she didn't reject Albedo.

No! Even then, I was loyal, and would always be. Kitty was the only one who knew the true me, and she liked me for it.

The music from my game filled the room and Albedo went back to stroking the cat, his eyes fixated on the door. How was he going to handle that conversation when she came in?

I opened up my mailbox after the damn thing finally loaded all the way. What? It was like someone had punched me in the gut. Not a single message waited from my Kitty.

Maybe things had been crazy for her too, but the lack of worry still hurt. I bit my lip. Should I message her instead?

My attention was stolen as the door jiggled and Elijah entered the room, an arm was wrapped around scholarship, leading her in. "Julian will be here soon. He stayed behind to fight." He guided her to a seat on the other side of the room. "Take a seat," he encouraged.

She nodded, plopping down and turning away from us. She refused to look Albedo's way and he stared, but didn't go to her side. She held her middle and stared at the floor. The smirking wolf on her wrist caught her attention and she bit her lip, clenching her eyes shut.

I scowled, and Rust growled.

Sighing, she dug her phone out and idly turned it on.

Whatever. It wasn't my place, I'd made my decision.

I turned my attention back to my phone and tapped on the keys. What should I say to Kitty about everything? I couldn't tell her the truth, or rather, I shouldn't tell her. The last thing I needed was her actually worrying about me. It sounded like she had enough to deal with in that school of hers.

Kitty,

I'm sorry I haven't been on much. There's been some more stuff happening at the college, but don't worry. This won't change anything for us getting to finally meet. It's just a bit chaotic right now.

I found a healer, she just started fairly recently, but she's played the game on an actual good class. I promise she's not worthless or anything. If you want her to join us, let me know.

Rusty.

I pushed the send button, and at the exact same time, Kitty's avatar popped up. Seeing her digital profile pic made my insides warm and I smiled down at it. How could I have even once thought about straying from her? No, she was all I needed. I grinned, and waited her reply.

Thankfully, I didn't have to wait long. Within minutes I had a message of my own.

Rusty,

Sorry, things have been really... weird for me around here. Um, don't hate me, but I don't think we should meet anymore. I'm sorry, I'll try to explain later. Tell your healer I'm sorry, but I have to deal with a lot of things before I can play too much again.

Barbed Kitty

The smile faded from my lips. All I could do was stare at the words on the screen, each was like a dagger. Don't hate her? I could never! Was she serious? Was she quitting? And most importantly, was it all my fault?

Kitty!

I'm not sure what's going on, but I could never hate you. Did I push you too hard about wanting to meet? Please, tell me, I'm sorry. We don't have to do it right away at all, I can wait for however long you need. Please, you can even forget about everything I said. The last thing I want to do is put any pressure on you. And if you leave... Never mind, just I'm always here for you, no matter what you decide.

I hit send and across from me, Lee's phone beeped as she received a message on Clevania. I hoped she had better luck with her conversation than I was having. She was typing furiously, her eyes dark, and she bit her lip so hard I thought she would bite through it.

Rusty,

No, it's not you at all, I promise. But, things have changed for me in ways I can't even begin to explain. Besides, once you saw me, you would hate me and wouldn't even want to be my friend. I've got something to confess, but I know when you hear the truth it's going to crush you and I can't do that.

Let me go and try to think of how to break this to you. I don't want to quit either, our time here means the world to me. You mean the world to me, Rusty.

Please, for both of our sakes, do what I ask, let this go.

Barbed Kitty

How could she be serious? Nothing she said could ever hurt me. But did that mean someone had hurt her? That damned school of hers had to be responsible. I'd get her transferred out, and here with me where she was safe. Hell, she could even be scholarship's friend.

I froze. Wait, I wasn't an Alpha God anymore, I didn't have any of the powers I needed for favors that big. I would have to tuck my tail between my legs and beg Julian or Elijah for their help, and I wasn't sure either really would. It did nothing for them, and both treated my relationship with Kitty like some fantasy thing.

No, whatever it took. I would rescue her. Even if she was never mine, it didn't matter. As long as she was safe and happy, I would be content in life. It's all I needed.

I thought about my words, typing carefully.

Kitty,

If this is about you being bullied, I can pull strings to get you into my school. We've got our share of assholes here too, but I can and will always protect you. No matter what, you've got my promise on that. Whatever you're worried about, forget it. I'll never be mad at you, and even if you don't want to be with me, it's okay to just say it. I've got your back, no matter what you decide, and always will.

Rusty

I hit the send key again, and once more at the same time, I heard a familiar ding from scholarship's phone. I frowned. Huh? That was oddly specific, we were having conversations with people at the same time?

Lee typed out another message, shorter this time and she huffed as she did, her eyes were filled with unshed tears and a spear stabbed my heart. I wanted to tear apart whoever was hurting her, rip them limb from limb.

But before I could think more about it, a new message flashed across my screen.

Rusty...

I was marked.

There was a big fight and the one defending me, he marked me. I'm someone else's now. I can't ever be yours, we probably shouldn't even talk anymore.

Barbed Kitty

My hands trembled and my eyes teared up.

No way.

How could she expect me to accept all of that? Someone had claimed her? Without her permission? I growled low in my throat. I needed to strangle the bastard.

Lee's head jerked up, her teary eyes met my own. "Is something wrong?" she all but whispered.

"Just game stuff," I replied before typing out one last message. I would probably regret this, but I was going to lay it all out. She had to understand that my feelings would never change.

Kitty,

I'm never leaving your side, I don't care that you're marked. Join my school, stay with me, I'll protect you forever. I love you.

Rusty

I glanced back at Lee, unable to watch myself press the send button. This could end my relationship with Kitty forever, or improve it.

And just like it was magically connected, scholarship's phone beeped again, announcing she had another Clevania message at the same moment.

My stomach dropped.

No Fucking Way.

I opened the inbox one final time, and typed a single word.

Lee?

CHAPTER 17

HIS KITTY

Lee's phoned dinged at the exact same time, but she didn't open her messages. Instead, her head jerked up as the door opened and Julian limped through. A hand was pressed to his bloody shoulder.

Thankfully, Oni had already thrown his healing powers at the task, but from the amount of damage done to his clothes, his fight hadn't been an easy win.

Lee's phone fell to the floor, abandoned, and she rushed to Julian's side. She slipped a hand behind his back, helping Elijah support his weight.

Rust growled. *If this was our Kitty, if scholarship was the woman we'd loved all these years... Nothing would be able to hold us back. It didn't matter that Albedo had marked her, it solved everything.*

It explained it all. Why scholarship had been able to slip under my guard and worm her way close. Why the thought of her had intruded when I just wanted to be with my Kitty. All because she was my Kitty. The more I thought about it, the more sense it made.

"Julian!" Lee's cry filled the air and she helped him to her chair. She paused, checking him over for any more wounds. She hissed at the state of his back, her fingers gently brushing against it

I shuddered as the foreign sense of jealousy filled my soul.

"What happened?" she questioned the both of them.

Julian plopped down in the seat and leaned against Lee, his forehead pressed against her chest. "That asshole Carl. Don't worry about any of this, it's nothing. I left him some parting kisses too, he won't be bothering you anytime soon."

She glared at him. "Asshole! Don't joke about your health like that! Why stay behind if you're going to limp back here looking like you're ready to die on us?"

Albedo growled from his chair. He set the mechanical pet on the ground and moved between the two. He put an arm around her stomach and gently pulled her away. "Save your anger, we need to check how bad the wound is."

I didn't mind. His moving her had put her beside me again. "*Lee.*" It was time to get to the bottom of this.

However, she ignored me, her eyes were only focused on Julian.

I hated it.

"I need answers about all this," she insisted. "Albedo, what's going on? I want to know the truth about the Alpha Gods and this whole sacrifice shtick. If you guys were truly so important, how did you get replaced like that?" She snapped her fingers for emphasis.

I leaned closer to her, almost directly over her. "Barbed Kitty," I whispered.

Her whole body shuddered and her head jerked to the side, her wide eyes met mine. For a moment, her brows furrowed and she stared. It took her a minute to understand that I had called her user name.

"What?" she whispered. She bent down, and retrieved her phone. With her eyes locked on me, she scrolled to Clevania again and opened her messages.

She whispered the word I'd sent her and her mouth fell open.

"Rusty?" her voice quivered.

My heart soared. I'd been right. Everything would be fine now, I understood what she was going through, and I could be by her side, protecting her through it all.

Albedo's eyes flickered gold. Lewis was doing his best to interfere with us. But it was too late for him to stop any of this. Not after I'd waited for so long.

"Kitty, I've finally found you." I reached out to touch her cheek but Julian groaned and she turned her back on me.

I wanted to strangle him for ruining our moment. Didn't he understand what this meant to me?

"It's about time you guys got back. Julian, I swear you must have never washed down your bathroom. I'm ashamed of how big of a mess it was. Instead of robot pets, maybe you should get yourself a robot maid..." Alexandra trailed off, her long braid swaying to the side as she frowned at me.

"Now what's going on?" she pointed at me. "Sterling, I've never seen you with that expression, ever. And Julian, what the hell happened to you? Elijah, aren't you supposed to be taking care of your brother?"

Elijah winced at the rebuke. "I'm not sure about them," he gestured my way and took a seat, steepling his long fingers and studying us. "But all that matters right now is we sit down and share all the information we have. Alexandra was obviously correct, maybe not accurate about what's happening, but something unusual is happening in Silverton. And Albedo, I think you need to share what you know since it's clear you're aware of more than us."

As one, we turned our focus on Albedo. Lewis backed away, leaving Bedo to stand on his own about the matter.

I bit back a growl. The frustration was setting in. Everything that was about to be discussed was important, but it also was driving home a fact I didn't want to consider. Despite my bluster, I couldn't protect Lee on my own, not with my rights and powers stripped away. I couldn't even step foot on the campus property without extreme pain.

I was useless.

"You better have a good fucking reason why you never shared any of this," I snarled at him. It's not like I didn't understand. I'd gotten a good view of what his worthless father had put him through. Likely he'd been threatened with worse if he ever revealed the real truth.

But this involved Kitty, I'd break every bond I had if it meant keeping her protected. No one else was more important to me.

Albedo glanced at Lee, then back to us. He ran a hand through his hair, twisting the end of a spike around his finger and sighed. "Not even I know all of the details. Just my father has been involved in it for generations. Every time the Alpha Gods are selected and are tested to see if they'll ascend, there's a ritual that involves a scholarship student." He took a breath. "I'm not sure what happens to any of them, but none of them have ever returned. My father called them all failures, but I would be different."

"Why scholarship students?" Lee insisted. "Why let us in if they just plan to do that to us? It's sick."

"It can't be anyone that the majority would miss. People who are desperate are the prey picked over and over again. Lee, your situation was perfect when dad heard about it. He knows how to cure Tardoxia, so it was easy to use that against you."

Something curdled in my stomach. "Wait," I held up a hand to interrupt his explanations.

"What the fuck?" Julian snarled, talking over me. "Are you telling me that they could have already helped Lee's family? He could be cured?"

Her little brother. How could I have forgotten about him? My fists clenched. "I agree. If he knows how to cure it, why hasn't he?"

"Because her job wasn't done yet. I confronted him on all of this. I told him I wouldn't let Lee be sacrificed for some dumb ritual." He glanced away. "He was a little less than pleased about the idea. He thought he could break me if he threw me into the punishment cage with a little beating first. That I would give up and agree to lead her to her fate."

I wanted to burn the entire university to the ground. What sick fucks. She'd been so desperate to save him, she'd thrown herself through countless programs to improve herself to even get a chance to come here. All to save him. And for what? To be used in their sick experiments? For her life to be taken in return for his?

"Even with my situation, how did I ultimately get picked? I wasn't the only one in a bad position. There's more to that too, isn't there?" she questioned.

Albedo looked away from her. "Your friend, Reuben. His family made a plea deal. They sacrificed to get you to be the one chosen to attend so you could be with their son. Once the review board saw the rest of the situation, you were an instant acceptance. They knew even if you found out the truth, what your answer would be, what your moral character was"

She'd never let those she loved die. She would always be the type to throw herself on a live grenade if it protected one person.

"What do we do about this?" I growled. I was shaking. All Rust wanted to do was rampage. How dare these bastards use her.

"Nothing," Alexandra noted from her spot.

I whirled on her, ready to rip her braid off her head and force her to eat it. "What do you mean, nothing?"

"I'm going to get to the bottom of this while we still have time. It's not graduation yet, the semester has barely begun. They don't know that Albedo will have given us all this information. Besides," she gestured to me and Albedo. "You two have been expelled. You can't do anything. Lee, you should stay with me on campus."

Lee nodded like that made sense.

The hell it did! "No, there's no way she's stepping foot back in there again. She can move in with me. I lived off the remains of my family's estate, but it would be enough for the two of us. Now that I'd found my Kitty, I wasn't about to let her waltz back into a lion's den.

"No," Elijah turned down my suggestions. "The safest place for her is this apartment. No one knows about it, it's been a safely guarded secret. She should continue to attend classes with us, and we'll all investigate the situation. We don't know that all of the previous scholarship students and Alpha Gods were killed. Maybe they've been imprisoned and we can find a way to rescue them. With their power, we could overcome everything. Besides, we're not here to just stop this one instance."

Lee and Alexandra nodded as if they shared a brain. "That's right," Alexandra agreed. "Whatever this whole ritual is, we're going to find a way to end it for good. Once we're done, Silverton will be the fair university it always should have been, and it will herald a new generation of those that will improve the world."

Lee's eyes shone. "That's right. I don't care who that Inu guy is, we won't let anyone else be hurt. No matter what it takes, we're stopping them."

It was her words that bothered me. There was no way in hell I could let scholarship do whatever it took to end this. If it came down to it, I would stop her, in order to save her.

CHAPTER 18

SAFEHOUSE

ELIJAH

Tensions were high, and Julian was still bleeding all over the floor. Oni might be healing him, but he was still weak. I'd never seen my brother this pale before. "Julian, bed," I ordered. His little mechanical companions flocked around his legs, rubbing against him trying to bring some comfort.

Slowly, he lifted his head and stopped staring at Lee. He glowered at me. "Some sympathy," he scoffed.

Sighing, I resisted the urge to slap the back of his head. At times he could be so mature, an older brother I could be proud of; and then there were times when he acted like a spoiled toddler. I shook myself, it was time to don the older brother guise. I couldn't let him know how exhausted I was. There was a role I had to fulfill.

I rolled up my sleeves to be more comfortable if I had to heft his weight. "Julian, you're useless to us as you are right now. You're going to get into bed and allow yourself to be properly cared for so you're worth a damn. If you don't get your sorry ass up, I'm going to pick you up and throw you in bed myself. Would you prefer that?"

Julian grunted and leaned over, resting his head on Lee's shoulder. She tensed beneath his weight and glanced up at me with a wince. She still hadn't given up on me, even after being claimed by Albedo. I hated hurting her, but I knew who I had always been always meant for. No matter how many times Alexandra rejected me, she was the only one I could ever love. It didn't matter that Baron was softening to this woman, he could be as stupid as my brother at times.

Julian grunted. "I'm staying here. If I move, this is only going to tear open again."

"I think he's right, Elijah," Lee agreed. She didn't seem convinced.

"No," I corrected her. "He needs to rest in his bed. Even if it tears open, he'll be better off there than sitting in a chair. Unless he gets solid sleep, he can't go back to Silverton with us."

This entire situation had spiraled out of my control. I'd expected to have a difficult time with Julian, that was standard when it came to us. I'd never planned for all the complications of the university and the secrets of the Alpha Gods. Nor had I ever imagined that Albedo's wolf would take Lee as his mate, or the reveal that Sterling had just discovered. This single woman had wormed her way into our group, becoming an integral part of it.

As close as Alexandra.

I couldn't push this aside. Baron refused to let me. I would get to the bottom of this, and help Lee in any way I could, as long as that didn't involve her getting closer to me.

"Kitty, we need to talk," Sterling went to her side, trying to get her attention away from Julian.

Couldn't they go elsewhere for this? We had more important things to handle than this love affair of theirs. It was only a matter of time before the Dean of the school contacted my parents, and I'd have to deal with my father. Once he discovered more about Lee, there would be too many questions I would be expected to handle as the perfect son.

Would she really be safe in this tiny apartment? True, the school was not right for her. Even if she was with Alexandra, the danger was too great. That Carl character had fought hard against Julian. "It's getting late," I gestured to the darkness outside the window. "Everyone that doesn't live in this apartment, besides Lee, needs to go home. We all need rest."

"Whatever, but Kitty is coming with me," Sterling insisted. "She'll be safe."

Albedo frowned. "Sorry, but my mate is staying with me, Sterling." He got up from his seated position, and put a hand on Lee's shoulder, trying to draw her to himself.

I groaned. Why did this have to be such a big issue? We needed to work together, not fight over Lee like some mongrels fighting over a juicy bone. "Lee is safe in this apartment. Out of the four of us, I only trust myself and Julian being capable of protecting her. We're the only true Alpha Gods since you've both been stripped of your powers. This is about her security, not your perceived rights."

Albedo scowled. "That doesn't matter. She's my mate, I can't leave her. I have to take care of her."

It didn't surprise me that Sterling wasn't too far behind. "That's my Kitty. If you think I'm leaving her here, you haven't been paying attention."

Alexandra rubbed her forehead, scowling at the lot of them. Finally, I would get back up on this issue, she always spoke sense, well almost always. Her rejecting me wasn't part of that. "Everyone needs to stop this. What's happening here is more serious than who she should be with. Lee, I was wrong, you wouldn't be safe enough at my place. Here is best."

They opened their mouths to object, but I held a hand up for their silence. I wasn't going to be diverted by any of them. "There will be no discussion, I've made up my mind." I pointed to Albedo and Sterling. "Both of you have been stripped of your powers. You wouldn't stand a chance against me for sure, but you couldn't even defend yourself against Julian in that state." I had no doubt they'd lose and suffer, and I had no desire to hurt my friends. Even before their powers were taken, they were no match for Julian and I.

Lee stared around the space. "Is it really safe to stay here?" she whispered. "I don't want to put anyone else in danger, and I have a feeling they won't stop until they get what they want from me." She glanced at Julian as she spoke, debating what he might do to her, no doubt.

"Lee, you're staying here tonight. I give you my word Julian will not try anything with you. If he even breathes on you the wrong way, I will personally carry out his castration by pulling his special little piercings out with pliers."

Julian paled, grabbing at his crotch with a wince. He groaned louder than he had when we'd got to the apartment. Had he been faking the severity of his injuries for sympathy? I'd deal with his shenanigans later.

"Thank you, if you say it's safe, I believe you." A trace of a blush tinted her cheeks, and Baron wagged his tail, pleased with her response. How many times would I have to crush the both of them? There had to be a way to make her understand without breaking her. I didn't want to be cruel, I'd already been that to her. I could never forgive myself for the fear that I'd put into her eyes.

At least it had finally faded, if only to be replaced once more with that warm hero worship.

Sterling sighed hard. "Fine, if she agrees, there's nothing I'll do to stop it. Elijah, Julian, I'm trusting you to protect her with your lives. No matter who stands in your way, protect her. She's my Kitty."

Lee stared at the ground, her fingers gliding over Lewis's new mate mark. Would she reject Albedo after all this? Would he be able to withstand it? I'd failed him like I had many others. I'd never suspected his father of being such a monster, despite having dinner with my father countless times.

My phone buzzed, the ringtone ringing loudly. Julian's head jerked my way. "Answer it," he insisted.

Why did he want me to do this here? "I'll do it outside. He'll have questions that you won't want to hear."

I adjusted my sleeves again, as if I was preparing for battle. Even if my father couldn't see me face to face, it wouldn't be an easy battle. If I wasn't careful, all my promises would evaporate into smoke. The others were counting on me. No, that was too simple of a thought. It was up to me to keep my father away from the truth, and protect everyone else.

Baron tried to tell me something else, but I ignored him. Lee's fate was just one of many I needed to protect. She had no special place in my heart. I would answer his questions, and protect them all.

"Answer it," Julian pressed again. "I want to hear what dear old dad has to say this time. We deserve to hear it."

I groaned. He wouldn't stop. "I'm not going to do that to the rest."

"Elijah, please answer it," Lee agreed.

Sighing, I gave in. I answered the phone. "Yes, father?"

"Elijah," his voice was a low growl. He'd been drinking again. "We need to talk, boy. You need to come home."

I glanced at the door, but the glare the group gave me was clear. They wanted to hear this conversation, but Julian was a fool. I knew what my father's favorite subject was, especially when he was drunk. My brother was going to regret this.

"We'll talk on the phone. I'll come see you after we're finished."

That was if I could trust him again. There was a chance I was about to be as much of an outcast as Julian was forced to be.

CHAPTER 19

SETTLING IN

LEE

Elijah and Julian's father was nothing like his sons. His loud deep voice was impossible to ignore through the phone.

"Elijah, I've just gotten off a phone call with the Dean, and he tells me that worthless child of mine is about to get you expelled? You are aware that I will never allow that disgrace to take you down with him, correct? He'll be disowned completely before that happens, and you will break all contact. You're going to return home and stay away from that negative influence. Unlike you, he's worthless to me."

Ouch. I winced, glancing at Julian. He didn't look upset, in fact, he looked like he expected it. There was no hurt in his eyes, just a stoic resignation. What the hell? Why was he willing to accept his father talking like that about him?

"Father, you shouldn't treat Julian like that. He might not have lived up to your expectations yet, but he's far from worthless. He's still an Alpha God, and we all respect him."

He scoffed on the other end of the line. "You all respect him? There are only two of you true Gods left. I heard what happened to those other black sheep as well. I don't get why the Dean didn't throw Julian out with them at the same time. Once he loses that position, he'll end up a loser like those friends of his. He'll have no place in this family."

"Father," Elijah growled under his breath.

"And it would be wise for you to mind yourself too, Elijah. Do not think that just because you've been the model child all these years that I won't tear your inheritance away from you as well. You too were hanging out with those disappointments. Sterling and Albedo, was it? Pathetic creatures. The first to ever have their status as Alpha Gods stripped away. I suppose I should be grateful that Julian wasn't the first to be kicked out. Morgan knows he's the type to ultimately humiliate me in that type of situation."

What kind of father did these two have? I growled deep in my throat at his callousness. No wonder Julian was such a prick! I reached for the phone, but Alexandra put a hand over mine, shaking her head and putting a finger to her lips for silence.

I hated having to obey, but clenched my first and reluctantly obeyed. I'd accept this for now, but if I ever got a face-to-face with this guy, he was getting an earful.

"I have a question."

He sighed loudly. "What is it now, Elijah? You should already know my views on this situation."

"There's a secret involving the Alpha Gods that involves the sacrifice of a student with each class. While you were not chosen to be an Alpha God, you still went to this school. Was there anything similar to that when you attended?"

The sigh this time was longer and deeper. "You're asking me about something that happened so long ago I can barely remember it? I stayed out of the Alpha Gods' way, I let them do whatever they wanted, to whoever they wanted. When it was time for graduation, they vanished without a trace, no doubt to be taken to where they can do the most good."

Elijah scowled at the phone. A look I'm sure he wouldn't reveal in person to his father. Funny, it was pretty similar to one of Julian's death glares. Maybe they really were brothers. "What happened to the scholarship student they were paired with, father?"

"Elijah, whatever happened was none of my business. You should only be focusing on keeping your position, and graduating as an Alpha God. I don't need any further embarrassments in my life. Also, I'm depending on you to keep a muzzle on that mongrel of a brother of yours. Come home, get rest, don't let that moron's idiocy rub off on you."

The call ended and Elijah's shoulders slumped. "I should go," he mumbled, reaching down and grabbing his phone. He avoided Julian's eyes and left us behind.

My heart stung from his coldness. How could he be so warm in one moment, and like a block of ice the next?

"Asshole," Julian remarked, turning away and studying the wall.

Alexandra gracefully rose to her feet and clapped her hands. "It's been a long night for all of us, and this room is extremely cramped. Sterling, Albedo, since you two can't enter the university, I need you to put all your time into researching it. We need to find out as much as we can about it, and those who attended. Between the two of you, we should be able to find a lead to start our investigation."

"Of course," Sterling agreed.

Rusty... I would need to find time to talk to him soon. How could my precious friend be one of the very Alpha Gods I'd been saddled with? A person I cared about more than any other, before all this chaos rained down on me.

But now, I was a branded woman, I didn't even have the right to glance his way. All because of Lewis. Why had Albedo's wolf decided to claim me?

"What do you want me to do?" Julian questioned, still staring at his wall.

"You?" Alexandra blinked. "You're willing to get involved, Julian?"

He glanced over at her, his eyes flashing gold. "I will protect her. That's why we brought her here."

She sighed. "Because we have no choice right now, but don't think for an instant I'm approving of you being anywhere near her. You don't deserve her either, she's supposed to be Elijah's mate. It's obvious to everyone but him."

He snorted. "Elijah's mate? You know as well as we do that the only one he'll ever try to protect is you, and that's it."

She waved away his words. "Despite that, I do know you're very adept in battle, Julian. Lee is one of the few friends I possess, and I know that as long as you're committed to protecting her, she'll be safe with you."

Maybe I was being slow, but with the way they were discussing everything, it was starting to sound like they planned to leave me with Julian for the night in this apartment. Would the others really let that happen?

Alexandra walked over and hugged me tightly. "I promise you're going to be safe. I'll put my number in your phone, if he even looks at you cross-eyed, call me. The others won't put up with it."

"Wait, why do we have to leave?" Sterling scowled. "I'm not leaving her with Julian."

"Agreed," Albedo huffed.

Alexandra scowled at them. "This place is tiny, and the fewer people here, the easier it will be to keep it hidden from the Dean until we figure out an attack plan. I've got some ideas, but I need a chance to sit down and structure them out. Julian, if you dare try anything, I won't hold Sterling or Albedo back."

Alexandra gave me a hug and I hugged her back just as tightly. "I'll see you tomorrow, right?" I all but whispered.

She gave me one of her dazzling smiles and my heart warmed. "You can bet on it. Come on, Sterling, Albedo," she commanded.

Albedo came to me first. He wrapped his arms around me, mashing me against his chest in a tight hug. His heart beat against mine and everywhere our skin touched, sparks danced through my body. There was a sense of all was right with the world I'd never experienced before.

Was this what a mate bond could do?

"We're still going to talk about all of this," he assured me, nodding at my marking. "I owe you an explanation and an apology, and I will deliver it. Stay safe, okay, Kitten?" he requested with a brush of his lips against my forehead.

Before I could answer, he jammed his hands in his pockets and followed Alexandra, leaving me alone with Julian and Sterling.

Sterling scowled at Albedo's back before he grabbed my hands in his and stared into my eyes. "Kitty, there's so much I want to say to you, so much that we need to talk about. You know I don't care who you're mated to, you could be with the entire school and it wouldn't cause me to love you any less. All I need in life is to be able to love you."

Fire blazed through my cheeks, and I stared at the ground. This wasn't like the non-direct and aloof Sterling I'd gotten so accustomed to. This one was passionate, and staring into his eyes made my blood sing. "Sterling," I whispered.

He gave me a half smile. "It's okay, we'll talk tomorrow. You need to get rest, and I'll keep watch on this building from outside. Don't worry, no one is ever going to hurt you again, Kitty. I promise." He hugged me tightly, brushing his lips over my cheek before gently pushing me away and heading for the door. "I've gotta go have a talk with my supposed best friend. Jules, I'm counting on you."

The door closed behind them, and Julian grunted as the back of his head hit the wall. "I should have accepted Elijah's help to get my ass in bed," he groaned.

I bit my lip. I wasn't as strong as the others, but maybe I could help this idiot into bed. He wasn't going to be any use to me unless he healed up anyway. "Here," I offered, leaning down and slipping an arm around his shoulders. "Let me help you."

He didn't answer, but he allowed me to awkwardly guide him to the small bedroom, where he collapsed on the bed. The bed was big enough for two, but I wasn't about to curl up next to one of my worst enemies.

I'd sleep on a chair, it would be fine.

Julian glanced up and patted the spot next to him. "You should rest too. Look, I'll turn the other way, I won't bleed on you. But tomorrow is going to be hell. We all need to be ready."

I hated to agree with him, but I obeyed and slipped beneath the covers. It was hard to ignore his body heat, but I flopped around so I was facing away from him and stared at the wall, as the little mechanical pets made sleeping nests around us.

Was I really going to survive the night?

CHAPTER 20

SOFTENING

JULIAN

All I could do was focus on her breathing and the heat of her body so close to mine. I should be more concerned about the ball of fire that throbbed from my shoulder where that bastard had gnawed on me like some sort of chew toy.

Should I try talking to her? I'd been surprised when she agreed to lie down beside me. "Are you still hurting?"

Her soft voice caught me by surprise. I glanced over and met her eyes. She was staring at my shoulder where I clutched it with my hand. "Of course I am," I snapped.

Damn it. Why was I treating her like this? How could talking to her be so difficult? She glanced away from me.

"Sorry," I mumbled.

She pulled her hand back, clenching her fingers into a fist. I hadn't even noticed her reaching out to me in the first place. "It must still really hurt. You hid it from the others, and you never apologize. Move your hands. Let me see."

My shirt was a bloody mess. Did she expect me to take it off? The thought made me shudder. No, she didn't need to see. At least it had healed a lot since the bastard had taken a bite out of me. "It's a mess," I protested.

She ignored me, grabbing the hem of my shirt and tugging it up. "It needs to come off, and don't get any perverted thoughts. You're an idiot by just lying here in your own blood and not tending to your wounds. Werewolf or not, you can still get sick, dummy."

Her cheeks were red as she undressed me, or at least tried to. My weight was stopping her from getting too far. I chuckled at her. "What, want to see the whole package? I can take the pants off too," I offered with an eyebrow wag.

She let go and glared at me. "Idiot," she grumbled. "Sit up, you can at least do that right?"

One thought crossed my mind, I could just lie here and let her put her arms around me to pull me up. I could feel her heat as she wrapped her arms around me as she tried to help me sit up. But no, I didn't want to lie to her about something so small.

I pushed against the bed until I was sitting up. I grunted as her fingers brushed against the wound, a fresh sheen of bright red bled through the fabric. I'd messed the scab up again.

Lee slipped her arms around me helping me the rest of the way up, and lean some of my weight on her. "Goddess, I'm so sorry," she gasped. "I didn't mean to hurt you."

Her scent wrapped around me like a blanket. I inhaled, enjoying the rare moment. We weren't this close often. Oni was practically purring, something no self-respecting wolf should ever be caught doing. "You're fine, it only stung for a second." I helped ease the sticky fabric away from my body and ducked beneath it as I peeled the shirt off. I resisted the urge to just fling it in a corner, but I didn't need to give her more reasons to not like me.

She grabbed the shirt from me and tossed it in a corner. I gave her a look and her lips twitched. "What? We'll take care of it later. Right now I'm worried about this." She prodded the wound and I grunted as the throbbing continued.

How much had that asshole chomped out of me in the first place?

She got up from the bed and left me to my thoughts. My pets followed after her, scampering at her feet and making it hard for her to move around. The water ran in the bathroom, and I sighed.

What was I doing? Yes, I could keep her safe, but this situation was nothing like I expected it to be. My pack was all falling for her, besides Elijah. Not that he'd ever show any interest in anyone other than his precious Alexandra.

That worked out for me. It was bad enough that Sterling and Albedo both had an interest in her. One was bonded to her, and the other had been Sterling's love for years. Competing wasn't going to be easy.

I almost groaned. It was hard to admit, and I still didn't want to, but I wanted this woman to pay just as much attention to me as she did the others.

She returned with a wet cloth in hand and climbed onto the bed. She grabbed the uninjured part of my shoulder and pulled me closer. "Here, we need to clean it out. You don't have any medicine, but we can at least use some simple water."

I yelped the instant she prodded the spot. Fuck! I was going to tie Carl to the steeple and carve his nose off. The fucking bastard hadn't held back. There was a thin layer of new muscle that had healed just over the bone but it hurt like fucking hell.

"At least you're healing," she mused, settling back on her heels. "He bit an entire chunk out of you." Her fingers trailed around the ragged red edges of my wounds. She didn't even glance at the rest of my body and what I had to offer.

Was I just someone to be pitied? I scowled, but she didn't notice that either.

"Julian?" she prodded, she bit her lip as she glanced my way.

I forced myself to give her a noncommittal grunt. "Yeah?"

"You got hurt like this protecting me. You stayed behind and fought him, but why? I'm nothing to you."

She was nothing? I snorted, and her brows furrowed. "You haven't got it through your thick skull yet, doggie?" Damn it, I'd meant to stop doing that. Though she had zero issues with the others calling her pet names. Why was it okay for her to be compared to those instead?

Lee scowled. "Why'd I even bother?" she grumbled, turning away.

"Sorry," I apologized again. She never reacted like any other person I'd dealt with before. "I didn't mean to call you that again. You don't like it, right? But, I'm going to keep you safe. You're mine, Lee."

She laughed in my face. "You're such a fucking asshole, Julian. On one hand, you verify I'm tired of that insulting nickname, and then you try to claim that I'm just an object for you to control. I'm never going to belong to you." She pointed to one of my pets. "I'm not another robot for you to control, you ass."

"You're more than that," I agreed with a snap. None of this was going the way I wanted.

"Whatever, Julian. Go shower. You're going to leave the bed a bloody mess if you stay here. You won't let me do what I can to clean it."

I couldn't help it. My lips twitched. "You're going to help me take a shower, right? You can't possibly expect me to be able to do a good job cleaning this when I can barely move my arm, right?"

I waited for her to slap me, or throw a pillow at my head. Instead, Lee shook her head with a deep sigh. "Fine, but nothing other than the shirt is coming off. I'll take care of your wound, because you got it for my sake, but that's it. Got it?"

I couldn't stop the grin racing across my lips. My heart soared and I nodded. That hadn't been the reaction I had expected, but I'd take it. "Understood," I agreed.

Once more, Lee offered her support and together we limped to the shower. I plopped down on the toilet while she fiddled with the water. "Is there anything we can put in here that you can sit on? It's going to be hard if I'm trying to hold you up and help you get cleaned up at the same time."

"Maybe we can put a chair in there. You want me to grab one?" I winced at the thought. Carrying anything was going to hurt.

She shook her head, rolling her eyes. "You do know I'm trying to avoid you from getting hurt, right? Dummy. Stay put. I'm not as helpless as you treat me." She stomped off, leaving me alone in the bathroom.

I leaned over the edge of the tub and ducked my head beneath the spray of still-cold water she had set up, and let it beat some sense into me. This was too much fun. Every response I got from her only made me want another. If I wasn't careful, I was going to be addicted to her.

What would it take to convince this woman that all she needed was me? I was more than enough to be able to take care of her, and protect her from all the other assholes out there. I'd already shed blood for her, and I could be loyal.

I'd been loyal to Cindy and her bitchy ways for years. She'd been the one that carried things too far when it came to Lee. When had she targeted the woman, and what made her think she could go after her without my interference?

Lee arrived in the doorway, a chair wedged under her underarm and beads of sweat dripping down her cheeks. She pushed me out of the way and set it down in the middle of the shower with a little huff. "There," she announced with a grin. She gave me a mock bow. "Your throne, asshole."

The urge to grab her and kiss her cute little mouth took me by surprise. I couldn't do anything like that until I handled things with the others. Still, the fact that I had the urge at all, shocked me. This was more than teasing her, or trying to make her a cute little pet.

Something deeper was going on when I interacted with her, and for once, I wanted to prove myself. She hadn't seen me try to impress her yet, but that was going to change.

CHAPTER 21

SHOWER SERVICE

Lee

Getting Julian into the seat wasn't too difficult, but hovering over him when he was dripping wet and shirtless was a little more than I'd prepared myself for. I grabbed the rag and gently tended to the gaping bite he'd had taken out of his shoulder. He'd been bitten down to the bone, the muscles were barely covering it, and I could feel it quivering beneath my touch.

I moved around him the best I could, but to really get close and inspect it, I was going to have to move closer to him. Could I trust him?

He cocked his head to the side, exposing his shoulder. "Here. You should be able to get to it from the back like this, right?"

What? Why was he being so... cooperative? It was so unlike him. He tensed beneath my touch, but didn't try to interfere. He bit his lip, hissing, as I gently cleaned the spot. His skin was barely starting to knit together. He wasn't going to stop bleeding until it did.

He stuck his head beneath the stream of water and let it flow down his face. If it was painful, he was hiding it. "Do you..." I paused. Asking him anything was awkward.

He turned and shook his head, sending water droplets everywhere. "What is it?"

"Your hair. You can't wash it like this. Did you want me to help you?"

He gave me a grin. "Yeah, thanks, Lee, I'd appreciate that." He frowned, and sat up. "Hey, don't think that just because I'm hurt right now I can't keep you safe. I promise that if anyone tried to come after you, I'd fight. No one is going to hurt you while I'm around."

He'd been the one who had hurt me at first, it was hard to wrap my mind around this idea of him protecting me instead. "I've got it."

"You've gotta use the color-safe shampoo," he grunted. "I don't want to lose my streaks."

I giggled at him. "Don't want to look too much like Elijah?" I challenged.

He blew out a spray of water as it cascaded down his face, and ran his free hand through his hair. "Yeah, I know you don't get it, but that would be the worst, looking like him. I'm not the perfect little son, I'm sure you've noticed that. I'm content just being myself."

What would it be like if he looked like Elijah? Would I have this same incredible urge to get closer to him if he did? Was it just a physical thing? I wanted to deny it, but I couldn't discount the possibility.

Shaking my head and forcing myself to focus, I grabbed his shampoo, and gently lathered his head. He grunted and leaned into my touch. It wasn't a grunt of pain this time, but almost contentment.

It made me shiver.

I hurried, trying to finish as quickly as possible. Reaching up, I grabbed the showerhead and aimed it at his head to get the soap off of him as fast as possible. The water pounded against his bare chest and I swallowed.

I needed to escape.

"You need to get out of here," I blurted.

He brushed his wet bangs from his face and gave me a smile. "What's wrong? I thought you were going to help me shower, Lee."

The way he said my name made me want him to just call me doggie again. There was something in the way he spoke that made me shudder. "Sorry, you're all done, and I want to take my own shower." I pointed to the door. "You look like you've got a bit more color to you. You'll be fine making it back to bed."

He chuckled. "Fine, but can you get me a towel? I"m soaked. I'll go get changed, you stay in here, unless you're wanting that show."

I did not want a show, even if he was built like Elijah. "Here," I snatched a towel hanging off a rack, far too nice for Julian to have picked it up himself. This had to be Alexandra's work. I tossed it at his chest. "Now go."

He took his sweet time wrapping the towel around his waist, and a moment later, his pants dropped to the ground. Despite myself, I yelped and whirled away from him. I hadn't expected that.

Instead of teasing me, like I'd been preparing myself for, Julian chuckled again and left me in the shower alone. "I'm going to throw some dry pants on, I'll try to take care of the bed to make sure you're comfortable."

What did he mean by that? I wanted to question him more, but there was no way I wanted to come face-to-face with him anytime soon. I locked the door and leaned against it.

Damn, I hadn't thought about what I was going to wear if I took a shower. I didn't really want to wear the same clothes, but I wasn't about to just crawl half-naked into Julian's bed either. What was I doing here? This was insanity.

"Lee, we need to talk."

Barb? She'd been so quiet lately I'd almost forgotten about her. I sighed. She was probably going to try to push Carl and Henry on me again. *"What is it?"*

"It's about Carl."

How had I possibly known?

"I'm not sure what is going on, but I'm afraid I have to admit you were right. When we saw him tonight..." She growled, and shook her head. *"It wasn't the same as the first time."*

"Is it because of Lewis?" I guessed. Maybe because we'd already created a bond with another, it would cancel out the tentative one she swore we had.

Barb huffed. *"No, it's not the same, Lee. I'm pissed about it. I feel so used. We have to figure out what was done to us. I won't forgive anyone messing with a mate bond."* Her growls filled my head and I shuddered. Barb had never been this intense before. *"The thing with, Carl... was not the same as what we have with Albedo. I might not approve of it, but I can tell the difference."*

"What should we do, Barb? Albedo marked us, Sterling is Rusty, and I still can't help the way I feel around Elijah," I sighed.

"Not to mention how you act around Julian," Barb added.

A chill crept down my neck. *"No,"* I shook my head violently and fumbled with the shower, turning it on full blast and stripping out of my clothes.

She laughed at me. *"You can deny it all you want, but you're not immune to any of them,"* she sighed. *"And right now, we have to depend on them until we get to the bottom of this. Maybe we can trust them, and maybe we can't, but until we understand more about what's going on, we have no choice."*

"Lee?" Julian's call came from just outside the door. I tensed beneath the spray. Would he try to come in? "I'm putting one of my shirts on the door for you. I'll ask Alexandra to bring you some clothes for tomorrow. She brought some other things for you, but forgot shirts. It's all on the handle when you need it."

"Thanks," I mumbled.

A nice Julian wasn't normal. It left me floundering for a reply.

My fingers brushed against my mark, and I gasped as the sparks danced across my skin. Slowly, I raised my wrist to study the handsome wolf. I wouldn't reject him, but I still found myself torn. There was no way I could betray Sterling either, not after everything we had been through.

So where did that lead me? I didn't want to reject anyone, was I just going to collect all of the Alpha Gods like some sort of collectible pets? What kind of person was I becoming?

"*Why not?*" Barb questioned softly.

I froze. "*What?*"

"*There's something that's been bothering me since we were marked by Lewis. Something I noticed.*"

"*Oh?*" I scrubbed myself raw beneath the hot spray. Anything to try and keep my mind off of her words.

No. She couldn't be suggesting what I thought. There was no way.

"*I felt the mate bond with Albedo,*" she admitted.

Soap dripped down my forehead and into my eyes. I didn't even flinch. "*Excuse me?*"

Albedo was my mate? Not Elijah, or even Rusty, but Albedo?

"*And then again with Sterling, it's the same sensation you get around Elijah as well, and while I haven't felt it around Julian, I'm guessing that if he wasn't an Alpha God, we would feel that as well.*"

"*That doesn't make sense, Barb. The Moon Goddess couldn't have decided to give me four mates. That's crazy.*"

"*It's not up to us to question her. All I can do is tell you what I've noticed. I can't tell you what we should do about this, or even if this is the best thing for us. It's true they are our mates, but I'm not sure we can trust them.*"

"*Didn't you just say we didn't have a choice to?*" I frowned. Why was she contradicting herself?

"*We don't, not until we get to the bottom of this, but it doesn't mean I completely trust them. The only one I do is Lewis.*"

"*And Rusty,*" I added. How could I not trust him after everything we'd been through? It was still hard to believe that my sweet Rusty was really Sterling. But the more I thought about it, the more our stories meshed together, and the cracks he made about his friend's pet started to fall in place. How had I not put it together sooner?

And despite being bonded to Albedo, he still wanted me.

"*Why wouldn't he?*" Barb questioned. "*He's been there for us for a long time. I admit, I didn't think he was our mate so didn't want to give him any credit, but that's changed.*" She fell silent as I rinsed out my hair. "*The real question, Lee, is how will you convince all these men to accept that you're their mate, and they have to share?*"

"*I don't know,*" I admitted. Heck, I couldn't even get Elijah to acknowledge me. If I was smarter I would just accept that he wanted someone else, and no matter what I did, I couldn't change that.

But...

But!

Despite what I knew I should do, I couldn't stop it. It was a sickness that hovered over me. A burning desire for that spark when our skin touched.

Why couldn't Elijah accept me as his mate? What would he have to do to me to make me ultimately give up? He'd scared me so much the last time when I'd pissed him off, and yet I'd forgiven him for it. My dumb ass was here and ready to try again to get him to accept my feelings, despite all the extra baggage I carried now.

"*You keep forgetting Julian,*" Barb added.

"*Why the hell would I add him? Even if he's being nice now, and even if he got hurt like that for us... That's no reason to forgive him for everything else he's done. I'm only tolerating him because he knows about King, and could use him against me!*"

She laughed. "*Oh? You should admit it. You're softening to him. You can't hide it from me.*"

My cheeks burned and I stuck my head under the water, turning it on full ice setting, until her mocking laughter was washed away.

There was no way that I would ever want Julian as a mate. It was impossible, and if I was acting funny around him, it's only because we were in a strange situation.

It had to be because I'd found out about his connection with Elijah.

That was it.

I was *not* falling for Julian.

CHAPTER 22

FIRST REBELLION

ELIJAH

I stared up at the ceiling. Baron was quiet, but I didn't need his input to not be haunted by the day. I'd been trying to sleep for hours, but my father's words rang through my head, needling me.

I understood not everyone liked Julian. Hell, most people couldn't stand him. I had my own share of issues with him, but the way our dad treated him always got under my skin. It wasn't like he'd always been the black sheep of our family.

In fact, it had been the opposite. Growing up, Julian had been the big brother, by several seconds, that I always strived to be more like. He was the one who had inherited everything, and I was the spare.

Julian had always defended me when I'd been the one that could never measure up, but I was never able to truly confront my father and repay the favor.

No, I was always the dutiful son, eager to fill out any orders given to me, no matter what they consisted of. When the shift of power happened, I never fought against it, or even questioned it.

I should have confronted him on the phone, but I let it slide. I'd gone home and went to my room, without even trying to argue.

"*We should have stayed with Julian,*" Baron huffed.

"*I know,*" I agreed. "*But Lee will be okay. Julian won't try anything.*"

"*That's not why,*" Baron complained. He sighed. "*I wanted to spend more time with her.*"

"*No.*" Why was he being like this? "*I know-*"

"*You think,*" Baron corrected me. "*Did you notice how she reacted to us earlier? She pushed us away.*"

If I didn't know better, I'd think my wolf was pouting over it. Throwing the blankets off the bed, I crawled out and ran a hand through my hair. Everything should be perfect. My room was fit for a prince.

Once Julian had rebelled, I was given the best of everything. My brother had been kicked out, and his room locked, only father had the key.

Not that Julian would ever stay under the same roof with us again anyway.

I walked to the balcony and slid the door open. The crisp night air had a slight chill but I welcomed the cold.

I couldn't get her eyes out of my head. Obeying my father hadn't been the only reason I hadn't tried to stay at Julian's place.

Lee was still scared of me. Sure, she was hopeful I'd change my mind and accept her, but there was that moment's hesitation and her desire to create distance between the two of us, and it stung.

No, I wasn't romantically interested in her, I couldn't be. Baron was being ridiculous. I loved Alexandra, and she was the only one I needed. Though, I needed to make things up to Lee somehow. I hated being the cause of the fear in her eyes.

What were they doing? Was Julian harassing her? Or was she sleeping by now? After the events of today, I could understand her needing to rest. We had to find out everything we could about the history of our school, and the Alpha Gods who used to rule it.

"*How are you going to make it up to her?*" Baron questioned.

I raised a brow. "*Make it up to her?*"

He growled at me. "*That wasn't much of an apology, and it didn't work.*"

"*Baron, why are you insisting on this? You can't believe that she's our mate. She's already got Albedo, and I doubt Sterling will hand over the woman of his dreams without a fight. She doesn't need us.*"

Baron huffed. "*Are you fine with her having that shimmer of fear in her eyes when she looks at you? Think about it, Elijah. You're the one that did that to her, you need to be responsible for fixing it.*"

Why in the world was my wolf scolding me like I was a misbehaving kid? What was it about Lee that bothered him so much? "*What do you expect me to do? I already apologized. Why are you so bent out of shape?*"

Baron fell silent, and I almost thought he was ignoring me before he sighed, long and hard. *"It's the mark,"* he admitted.

"Lewis's mark?"

"Yes, it's made me think. Something was different about her tonight. There was a strangeness in the air, I want to see her again, Elijah."

I snorted. It didn't matter what he wanted. I wasn't about to go take a midnight trip to visit Julian's apartment again.

"You left them alone together," Baron added. *"Think about it, do you really trust your brother to do the right thing? What will you do if he crosses a line?"*

I shifted, trying not to think about his words. He was being an asshole tonight. *"There's no way I can fix it now. I'll talk to them tomorrow. If he hurts her, I'll handle it."*

"That wasn't the kind of line I was talking about. He's called her, his, multiple times. What if he marks her too?"

I sat up. No. I couldn't let that happen. He would hurt her, I couldn't allow it. I jumped out of bed. It would be the first time I disobeyed my father. He would expect me to stay here the entire night and likely talk with him over breakfast about the issues that had arisen at school.

But I wasn't going to be here when he came to get me in the morning.

My heart raced.

I was acting like Julian, though in his case, he wouldn't be nervous about slipping out. What was I planning to do?

"Apologize properly," Baron insisted.

I rolled my eyes. He wanted me to apologize? Fine. I had an idea of what would shut him up, and maybe help take the fear from Lee's eyes, even if it was just replaced with laughter.

Baron chuckled. *"That's your idea?"* he grinned. *"Well, it's at least a solid start. I approve."*

It didn't matter if he did or not. I still would be determined to do the same thing. Despite my rush, I still found myself making my bed and tucking it securely.

Would I be disowned after this night was through?

Julian's old room was right next door, but if I was found creeping there through the hallway I'd never be able to explain myself, especially for what I was planning. Instead, I turned my attention to the balcony and let the night air sting my cheeks.

With a mere jump, I was on Julian's balcony and I slid the door to his room open. It didn't surprise me he never locked it. The man had zero thoughts about his own safety. Then again, who would dare to mess with Julian besides me?

The room was empty. None of the things that Julian loved or cared for remained. If he had left them behind, my father would have broken them apart, just to drive his point home. Betrayal was not something he took lightly, and not following the perfect plan he'd written for us since birth, was the perfect betrayal.

It didn't take me long to find what I was looking for. It was hidden underneath the bed. One board sounded a bit different when tapped, to all the others around it. Sliding it open, I pulled out the worn collar and the spotted Dalmatian ears that had been hidden away for years. It took only seconds to find the tail that went with this particular set, and I fashioned it securely around my waist.

The ears were easy, I didn't even think about it as I perched them on the top of my head. But, I froze when I lifted the shiny red collar. It was worn from age, but had been well-loved. Putting it on would be almost taboo. If my father ever found me with any of these things, I'd be cut out of his life without a second thought.

Julian was going to be pissed, I grabbed any of his things.

I hid the rest of his secrets and secured the board back. Now was the hard part, leaving the mansion and returning to the apartment. It wasn't that I feared getting caught, my parents probably wouldn't notice me gone. They had absolutely no reason to believe I would ever question their judgment.

No, the part I struggled with was disobeying. I was supposed to be the 'good' kid, the one that was perfect and caused no problems.

I glanced in a mirror at the sight I made. My lips twitched. This should really do the trick. Maybe after Lee was done laughing I could find a way for us to be friends. I liked her, though not in the same way I loved Alexandra. I owed it to her to work harder so we could still have a friendship when this whole mess was over.

Hopping from the balcony, I landed on the ground and stayed still, listening hard to see if anyone had noticed what I was up to.

We had no guards, my father was too confident that we would never be targeted by anyone. Our blood was one of the oldest lines in the area. We were untouchable.

Until Lee showed up anyway.

I jogged down the path, sticking to the shadows. As I ran, I let my mind wander. I didn't know how Lee would react to this, but hopefully, I could make her smile again.

Just the memory of it made my heart ache, and I almost stumbled.

Wait... No. Baron was rubbing off on me. There was no possible way I was feeling anything like that about Lee.

Baron smirked.

CHAPTER 23

BLOSSOMING FEELINGS

I MADE IT TO the apartment without running into anyone. It made me wonder if I was incredibly entrusted, or incredibly controlled. Even when Julian hadn't been the black sheep, he'd never had this degree of freedom.

Before I knew it I was at the apartment door. The silly ears on my head were heavy, and I twisted a bit of the tail around my finger.

I was nervous.

On the other side of this door was a woman I had wronged, one I wanted to be friends with. Would she accept this apology?

Taking a breath, I knocked on the door.

"Coming," Lee's soft voice called. She paused to argue with Julian, and I imagined she forced him to lie down again. Moments later she cracked the door open and studied me. "Elijah? Is something wrong?"

My brain short-circuited. It was Lee, the same one I had become accustomed to, but my senses were on fire. One of Julian's shirt's hugged her body, ending at her knees and her hair was damp.

She shifted, and a faint apple scent tickled my nose. Baron drooled. It was just shampoo, why was he being so ridiculous?

"Elijah?" she questioned again.

I should never have left them alone together. What had been going on? "I was worried about you."

Her lips twitched and she put a hand over them. "What are you.... Wearing?"

I knelt on the ground before her, my forehead touching the cold floor. "Lee, I know I apologized earlier but what I did was not right. I truly am sorry, and I'll be wearing this tomorrow to prove it. No one will even look twice at you."

She giggled. "But, why would you even do that? It makes no sense."

It made perfect sense to me. "Because I really crossed the line. We're not mates," I was quick to add before that hopeful sparkle appeared in her eyes, "but, I want us to be friends, good friends. You're important to my life and I ruined everything because I couldn't control myself. I should have just talked to you."

She bit her lip and glanced at me and then behind her. "I'm not sure if this is a great idea," she mumbled. Her eyes shimmered.

Fuck. I'd almost made her cry again.

Baron growled at me, and forced me back to my feet and toward her.

With every step, the apple smell grew stronger.

There was another fragrance beneath it. One I hadn't noticed before. I'd expected to find Albedo's, since he was her mate, but there almost surrounding her, was my brother's scent.

I followed her into the apartment, closing the door behind her, but caged her against it. She stared up at me, at least there wasn't fear in her eyes anymore, but there was something raw, and almost desperate, in the way she stared at me.

"Elijah?" she whispered my name, I leaned closer.

Why couldn't I stop? This was supposed to be about apologizing, making things better for her. But here I was ready to... what?

She shifted against the door and her shirt rode up her legs.

Why was she dressed like this with Julian? And why did she smell like him? What had they been doing before I interrupted? Something strange stirred beneath my skin, and it wasn't just Baron. "Lee," my voice was husky, and her eyes widened at the sound of it.

She licked her lips as her eyes darted to the side. I couldn't stop myself from watching the path her tongue took.

Had Julian kissed her?

I shuddered at the thought. Why was my brain betraying me? What was going on? But the closer I got to her, the more my control eroded away. I pressed closer until her scent threatened to drown me. "Elijah," she whispered, reaching out for my cheek.

Lewis's mark caught my eye and I couldn't look away. It was a declaration that she belonged to someone else, I had no business doing this.

The realization struck me, and I only kept upright by leaning against the door and squishing her against my body.

Mate or not, I wanted her.

Her eyes flickered to the side, searching.

Had Julian done something to her in the time I had left her alone and defenseless? Or worse, had they done something together?

"You're going to get sick with your hair that wet, and you should be wearing something warmer," I whispered into her ear.

She trembled against me, but didn't push me away. She tilted her head back to meet my eyes. "My clothes got drenched when I was giving Julian a shower."

My perfectly crafted world cracked around me at her words. Despite myself, I envisioned them in the shower together. Lee's neck arched back as the water ran over her hair, with Julian behind her, his hands wrapped around her waist.

She reached for me again, her fingertips gliding across my cheek. Her scent wrapped around me and reminded me of fresh apple pie. I drooled. Baron strained to rip control away from me, he was desperate to be closer to her.

I pinned her wrist above her head, took my other hand and tilted her chin up before I pushed my lips against hers. She tasted exactly like sweet spiced apples. Her sweet scent completely enveloped me and I inhaled it.

She didn't resist, or shove me away. Instead, she kissed me back.

My hand slipped from holding her chin up, to grabbing her by the nape of her neck as I deepened the kiss. Everything I had ever known crumbled away in an instant. Her arms slid around my neck and she melted against me. Her sweet lips parted and I wasted no time, too eager to know if all of her had the same tantalizing taste.

Something hard thumped against the wall.

Pulling away from Lee's all too willing lips, I turned to meet the crimson eyes of my brother. Rage flickered in him like a flashing neon sign, and through our bond, a typhoon of fury threatened to be unleashed.

Lee's eyes slowly opened and she tilted her head to see what was going on. When she recognized Julian she paled. "Julian," she whispered.

"Elijah," Julian growled softly, stalking toward us. "What the hell are you doing here? And if you don't give me a good enough answer, I'm throwing you out of the fucking window."

Considering what I was doing, I fully expected that kind of reply. "I've come to apologize to Lee."

"By what, gagging her with your tongue?" he snapped. The wound on his arm was still red, but at least he wasn't bleeding any longer. "Weren't you going to be the well-behaved boy that listened to dad? He's going to be pissed when you're not there for him to force-feed his shit to tomorrow."

"I'm staying here," I replied instead. "With Lee."

Julian's nostrils flared and his body trembled. He crossed his arms and his tendons stood out as he clenched them. "Well, I hope you know I'm not giving her up, not even to you."

CHAPTER 24

LINE IN THE SAND

JULIAN

Even wearing a pair of Dalmatian ears, a bright red leather collar, and a long spotted tail, my brother managed to keep his superior air.

Wait, why the hell was he wearing that? I couldn't tear my eyes away from how his hand rested possessively on Lee's hip.

She flinched with every step I took. Was I really such a monster that she had to stare at me like that? Sure, I'd teased her, even bullied her a bit at the start. But that was over now, why couldn't she get over it? Elijah had physically threatened her and she'd already forgiven him, if the whole tongue tennis thing was to be believed.

What was I missing? What was different between our situations?

Elijah stared at me, challenge glistening in his gaze. "I'm staying here."

I growled and Oni snarled, prepared to take over and teach my brother a lesson. "The fuck you are."

Elijah gestured to Lee. "I can't leave her here alone with you. I was a fool to do that in the first place. I'll help her stay safe."

Like I couldn't do that? "Didn't you leave her here so I could take care of her in the first place?" My shoulder throbbed, but I refused to show any weakness. "Come on, Lee. It's time to go to bed. I'll sleep on the floor, you take the bed."

There was no way I was going to try sleeping back-to-back with her as I had before. Even before Elijah had showed up I'd been setting up the bed so she could be comfortable. It had taken me longer than I wanted due to my injury, but I didn't want her worried that I'd try anything.

Lee rolled her eyes at me, but there was something softer in her expression than had been there before. It was similar to how she had been when it was just the two of us. "You dummy, you're the one injured. You need the bed." She gestured to one of the chairs where my robotic kitty was curled up. "I'll just put a few chairs together. They're soft enough."

I snorted. "No, I'll take those. You're sleeping in the bed, Lee." I glanced Elijah's way and he nodded.

Lee frowned at both of us. "You're not supposed to gang up on me like this."

"Julian, you're sleeping in the tub," Elijah announced.

And leave him alone in the same room with Lee? No way.

"This is nonsense," Lee complained. "Julian, we'll sleep in the same bed. There's enough room, and we'll just be back to back. You're injured, I'm not letting you sleep anywhere but the bed."

"Fine," I grunted. It was better than being stuck in the bottom of the tub. "I'll help Elijah get set up. Go to bed, Lee."

She opened her mouth to argue but stopped, and with a shake of her head, she sighed. "You're right. I'm exhausted. Tonight has been... something." She glanced at Elijah beneath her lashes, but he wasn't looking at her, he was too busy petting one of my dogs. "Goodnight," she whispered before she scampered off.

Elijah waited until the bedroom door closed before he glanced my way. "Julian."

"Elijah," I countered. Never had I wanted to punch him more than I did at that moment. "Care to tell me just what the hell happened? I've never seen you kiss Alexandra, who you supposedly love so much. What happened to her being your mate? Why are you kissing mine?"

We both froze.

What had I just said? Oni cocked his head, and nodded.

It was one thing for me to declare her as mine and to want her, but actually calling her my mate opened up a whole new world to me. Maybe it wasn't clear because of what we sacrificed as Alpha Gods, but there was something about Lee that kept attracting me. What else could it be but a mate bond?

One she didn't seem to share.

"Julian, yell at me, I don't care. I can't even tell you what happened. All I wanted to do was apologize for everything. That's why I'm dressed like this," he tugged on his collar. "Something about her scent took me over, but Julian, she can't be my mate. I love Alexandra."

Oni snarled. Despite us wanting her, the callous way he just disregarded what happened crawled beneath my skin. He'd gotten to kiss her. Only Albedo had been that lucky. And now he wanted to protest that Alexandra was still his one and only?

I should be happy. If he was obsessed with her, then that left Lee's heart open. But no, I was pissed. Why the hell did he kiss her if he was just going to crush her again? "That's enough, Elijah."

His head jerked up and he studied me. "What's wrong? What's going on?"

I nodded to the room where Lee was likely pushed against the door listening to us. I hoped not. This conversation would only hurt her. "Elijah, I'm tired of you fucking with her heart. You're either going to choose her, or you pick Alexandra and walk away. No more trying to be her friend, or make things up to her. I won't let you keep both."

What the fuck was I saying? Every word that escaped me I yearned to take back, and stuff deep down. I didn't want him choosing Lee!

Elijah groaned, running his hands through his hair and tugging on the ends. The motion made me chuckle. At least there were some things we still had in common.

Another thing now, since we both wanted the woman that was in my bed.

"Julian, I never said I wanted her."

A sea of red washed over my vision and Oni lunged, desperately trying to break my control and take his revenge. It took everything I had to stop him. "You bastard. You're the one who is denying that she could be your mate. Why would you need to say that if you really believed there was nothing to worry about?"

Elijah took a step away. "You're wrong. It has to be Alexandra."

I scoffed. "You're such an asshole, Elijah. Isn't it obvious to you that Lee's head over heels for you? I promise she wouldn't have just kissed anyone else like that. Why would you take advantage of her feelings if you don't want her?"

Why the hell was I saying all this shit? If I didn't know better, I would think I was encouraging him to be with Lee. Why the fuck was I sabotaging myself? I didn't want to hand her over!

Elijah sighed. "Julian, you're right."

I stared at him. I had to be hallucinating. He had not just agreed with me.

"I haven't been treating her properly, and as for why I kissed her? I really don't know myself. However, there is something more important that we need to discuss; we are the only Alpha Gods left in the school able to protect her. No matter what happens, we have to be there for her."

I huffed. "That's a given. I'm going to get to the bottom of what the Dean and that Inu guy are trying to do. Whatever it is, I'm putting a stop to it. I'm protecting her."

Elijah nodded then glanced back at the bedroom. "You do know I'm not going to let you sleep in there with her alone, right?"

I raised a brow. What the hell was his problem? "Sure, you can join us, but I'm sleeping in the middle. I have to be careful of my shoulder, remember."

Elijah laughed. "In that case, you should be sleeping on your good side against the wall. I'll sleep in the middle."

"After this?" I snorted. "Yeah fucking right. I don't trust you. I'm either in the middle or you're not sleeping in the bed, Elijah."

He shook his head but sighed. "Fine, whatever. But this thing between us isn't over, Julian. Just consider it tabled for now."

He could think whatever he wanted. But I was more determined than ever to win Lee over to my side. There had to be a way to get her to see that Elijah wasn't the right one for her.

I was.

CHAPTER 25

CRAMPED QUARTERS

LEE

The instant I heard the scuff of shoes on the floor heading my way, I dashed away from the door and dived back into the bed.

My heart was thundering and I could barely keep my breath steady.

I'd heard everything.

Julian thought I was his mate? That was insanity. Why would I be mated him?

Barb was cracking up. Her snickering drowned out my panicked breaths. "*Told you,*" she insisted.

My face burned like a million suns, and I buried it in the coolness of the pillow. I was crammed all the way against the wall so that Julian could take the other side, and not irritate his still-healing wound.

For a moment I considered flopping over and staying in the middle, but the idea of being between both of them after that conversation cured that stupid idea.

The door opened and I held my breath, the bed dipped as the two climbed in.

They really were both going to sleep with me.

"Get out of the middle, Elijah," Julian growled softly.

"You need to be on your side to take care of your shoulder. If you sleep in the middle you're going to bump it."

"I don't trust you," he snarled. "Not after what you did."

Elijah groaned. "Come on, Julian. Just lie down."

"No fucking way. I swear, I'll pick up you and throw you out of the window if you don't move now. You've done enough damage for the day."

I winced. As wonderful as the kiss had been, and as amusing as it was seeing Elijah dressed like a dog, the moment was already rotting after listening to their conversation.

Through the strength of Morgan, I persevered in not touching my lips. Had I meant anything to him? I wish I knew what to do. Everything was going topsy-turvy.

Albedo was my mate, Sterling ended up being one of my closest friends, and Julian was trying to be nice, and failing, but at least he was attempting. And Elijah... kept crushing me every time I turned around.

"You're such a baby," Elijah grumbled, but I could tell his voice wasn't next to me. "If you try anything, Julian, I'll be giving you an ice shower."

Something heavy landed on my chest and I gasped, my eyes flying open. The robotic cat meowed at me before turning in a tight circle, and making a nest of my chest.

"Damn it, Julian," Elijah complained.

Seconds later the rest of the apartment's occupants scrambled onto the bed, until it was covered in the pets. They all took turns rubbing against the three of us, and I couldn't hold it in any longer.

I giggled.

Elijah sat up and looked over at me. Our eyes met, and the memory of the kiss burned bright. There was no way he could have kissed me like that if there was nothing between us. And how in the name of Morgan did he look hotter with a leather collar around his neck?

I wanted to grab him by it and drag him to me for another kiss. The only reason I didn't, was the other pair of eyes studying me from the other side, an identical set.

Oh.

Julian had beautiful eyes too. I was lost in the deep blue that reminded me of an encroaching storm. My heart beat faster, and despite my proclamations of hardening my heart against him, I softened.

He'd stood up for me. I couldn't believe it, but he had been the good guy against Elijah's bad. Did anything make sense anymore?

"Get off," Julian ordered a robot monkey that had curled itself up in his hair.

"He's comfy," I chided. "You should let him sleep."

Julian gave me a deadpan look before the cat that was using me as a pillow kneaded me with razor-sharp claws. I gasped as I moved it to the side. "Okay, never mind. Off is good," I agreed.

The dog scratched at Elijah's stomach, as if he was trying to dig a hole, and the man grunted, but didn't move it. Instead, he idly scratched behind its ears. "We're in their spot, it makes sense they want to get us out."

Maybe Elijah just had abs of steel. I glanced back over at him, my eyes dropping down. I wanted to feel them, and compare them to Julian's of all things.

I could have slapped myself. What was happening to me? Instead of focusing on this whole mess I was in, like I should be, I was worrying about these two assholes.

One had tried to crush me mentally, and sure, he was being nice now. But was he really? Would this whole act of his vanish, and he'd have some big 'gotcha!' moment? I wanted to believe that he was changing, but based on his past behavior, it was going to be hard to trust him.

And when it came to Elijah? He was his own set of problems. I couldn't help how I felt about him, even now. However, I wasn't going to let those feelings get in the way of my common sense.

He'd hurt me. More than once now. Not only physically, when he's scared the crap out of me, but emotionally as well. If that kiss meant as little as he stated, he was just toying around with me. Like Julian had accused him of.

"*Another point for Julian,*" Barb pointed out with a chuckle. "*What are you going to do if he comes out ahead?*"

I could have strangled the wolf. Considering I was already Albedo's mate, I shouldn't even be worrying about these two. "*I'm not going to do anything. We've got enough problems to worry about without more mates, and in case you don't remember, Julian was a total ass to us when we met him.*"

"*And yet, he's the one defending you, not only from his brother, but he took a nasty attack from Carl just to protect you. He didn't have to do that.*"

I sighed. Why couldn't she stop making sense? I didn't want to think of Julian like that. "Julian?" I blurted. He sat up on his elbow and stared my way. I shivered at the darkness in his eyes. "I thought your eyes were red."

He laughed. "Nah, I wear contacts, and dye my hair too, in case you thought those were natural." He smirked at me, but it didn't have the same barb in it that I had noticed from before.

He was teasing me?

"Why do you do that? You've got gorgeous eyes."

Oh, Goddess. What did I just say? What being had possessed me to even think such a thing?

Julian stared at me. A red flush crept up his neck and into his cheeks. He didn't answer, but quickly looked away. "Thank you," he mumbled. His monkey screeched at his head moving, and pulled his hair hard, forcing him to look at me again. His entire face was beet red.

"Lee?" Elijah called, pulling my attention away from his brother. "You do know that Julian and I are twins, right?"

Twins?

I stared at the two of them. Granted, their hair was different, and Julian had piercings, but when I saw their eyes, there was no denying it.

It explained so much. No wonder I was attracted to Julian! He had Elijah's great looks. That's why his eyes were suddenly something I could get lost in. A weight rolled off my chest.

"*You really think that's why?*" Barb laughed. "*Oh, Lee. You can try to fool yourself all you want, but what you're feeling isn't because he looks pretty. Give yourself more credit than that. It's the same thing we've been experiencing with the others, even if the direct sparks aren't there. I've felt it enough times now, he's our mate too.*"

No way. Impossible. Inconceivable. A miracle would have had to happen for that to be the truth, or more like an epic disaster. Julian could not be our mate.

"*He is,*" she insisted with a shrug. "*We should make him grovel more before we forgive him.*" She wagged her tail and chuckled. "*Hey, do you think we could get him to dress up like a kitty and roll on his back for us?*"

I imagined it. The outfit he'd worn during the truth or dare, but this time, he was just wearing the cat ears and a collar alone.

With a yelp, I buried my burning face deep into my cold pillow and ignored the two men beside me.

This was all Barb's fault.

CHAPTER 26

BREAKFAST WOES

I DIDN'T REMEMBER FALLING asleep. But when I woke up, an arm was wrapped protectively around my stomach, and someone snored in my ear.

Was Julian really holding me?

Slowly, I turned to check out the situation. My hair brushed against his nose, but besides him wrinkling it, he didn't show any signs of waking. Elijah was on my other side, sprawled in the small space, and all the pets had decided to sleep on top of him, even the monkey.

I was still tired, what had woken me up?

"Julian?" A woman's soft voice called into the apartment.

Wait, that wasn't Cindy. Was he cheating on her? I scowled. What the hell was his problem? Why would he say I was his mate if he had someone else?

The snoring stopped. Julian pulled me closer against his chest. "Shit," he whispered.

I opened my mouth to ask him what the problem was when the bedroom door creaked open, and a stunning young woman stared at the group of us. Her eyes glazed over Elijah and the army of pets, and settled on me and Julian.

She smiled.

"It appears the rumors are true. That Cindy child was trying to betray you again, darling." She nodded to me. "Once you find a way to wriggle out of my son's tight grip, I think we should get some breakfast. What would you like, dear? I'm not the best at cooking, but I'll do my best."

Why wasn't she upset and yelling at me? There was no hostility from her at all. Her eyes were like theirs, but the dark blue was friendly, and her mouth was crinkled from smiling all the time. She adjusted a long blue feather sticking out from behind her ear.

"Eggs?" I blurted.

"Ah, I can actually manage those." She brightened. "Though sometimes they do come out crunchy. Hopefully, this won't be one of those times." She scuttled away and back to the kitchen before I could answer.

"That's your mom?" I hissed to Julian. Elijah was still dead to the world.

He slowly nodded, his eyes still on the kitchen entryway. "Yeah, uh, Lee, you don't have to answer anything you don't want to when it comes to her. In fact, you can feel free to ignore her. It's fine."

I raised a brow. "Why would I do that? She's your mother. What could she possibly ask?"

Slipping out of bed I stretched, and Julian's shirt rose to my thighs. With a yelp, I put my hands down. I'd completely forgotten I had used his clothes to sleep in. I peeked at Elijah, but the man only snored in response.

"Go ahead and change in the restroom. I'll find you something to wear," Julian offered. "It's bad enough mom saw you in the bed, but if she saw that... it would get worse."

I didn't have to ask what that was, I understood what he was referencing. Slinking into the bathroom, I escaped being seen, and breathed a sigh of relief. She hadn't spotted me at least.

"Mom, are you really making eggs?" Julian's voice carried through the thin walls.

"Of course, dear, I'm making you bacon instead. I bet you thought I forgot about your condition. I'm not your father. You know I won't force you to eat them. Now about that girl."

I found myself leaning closer. Were they talking about me? Or was it about Cindy again?

"You've had this apartment for a long time now, and I'm well aware of the fact you've never let anyone else enter it. What is she to you that you not only invite her, but the brother you've had so many issues with?"

"Mom, it's not like that. Listen, she needs a safe place to stay. Something weird is going on in the university." He took a deep breath. "And I want to protect her, more than anything. I know the promise I made to you, but this is important to me."

Based on what he was saying, I expected to hear her yelling and screaming at him for breaking rules. Maybe it would be best if I gathered my things and got out of here. I did my best to ignore the warm feeling flooding my heart at his words. There was no way I could let myself be swayed.

"You know, Julian, considering your behavior right now, and that look in your eye, I would say that you've finally found your mate."

"She is... But she's not just mine. She belongs to all the Alpha Gods."

I couldn't say I liked how he was wording that. It wasn't like I was an object they could just stick on a shelf. Still, it was shocking to hear Julian say this, of all things. He'd been so possessive and obsessive. Now he was willing to share?

Barb grinned. Her tail was going a mile a minute, but she didn't add anything else. There was a smug sense of rightness about her and I didn't want to get involved in it.

A soft knock at the door made me freeze. Julian and his mom were still conversing, so that meant the only one it could be was Elijah.

"Lee?" he mumbled with a long yawn.

He was so adorable it made my teeth ache. I wanted to fling the door open and observe him, but I was still wearing the long shirt. I couldn't believe I'd actually worn that in front of him the night before.

"You in there?"

"Just a minute," I muttered. "I can't come out like this."

Elijah yawned again, loudly. "Alexandra was here yesterday. She's really organized, check under the sink on the right-hand side. She probably put emergency supplies in there for you."

Confused, I crouched down and inspected the spot. Tucked inside the cabinet, pushed to the back, there was a small box and it not only contained feminine products, but a change of clothes, including said shirts that Julian had been convinced she had forgotten.

Granted, they were far too fancy for someone like me. But beggars couldn't be choosers. With a sigh, I pulled them out. I found myself taking one last breath of the shirt that clung to me currently. Julian's scent was strong, and I'd never ever admit it to him, even if my teeth were being plucked out, but it was reassuring. It calmed me in a way that didn't feel right.

I was safe. Despite my past with the man, there was no doubt he was a solid protector, and though I still didn't understand how the relationship we had turned from enemies, into whatever this was, I knew he could keep me safe.

"But you'd never think of him like that, right?" Barb teased. *"Just admit it, Lee. I don't know how it happened, but they're all our mates, even Julian."*

I would never admit it. With a final hug to the shirt, I peeled it off and set it aside as I slipped into the things that Alexandra had left. Despite the quality of the fabric being the softest thing I'd ever touched, it fit me perfectly.

Taking a deep breath and preparing for battle, I opened the door and nearly bumped into Elijah nose first. I'd forgotten about him waiting for me.

"Hey, careful," he cautioned. He grabbed me by the shoulders so I didn't fall back, and before he let me go, he gave me a gentle squeeze before tensing and pushing his way into the bathroom.

He could keep fighting it, but eventually, Elijah was going to have to accept that we were mates.

And though I'd never ever say it out loud. Maybe... just maybe, Barb was right about Julian.

CHAPTER 27

A NEW MISSION

I SHIFTED IN MY seat and stared at the innocent eggs on my plate. Almost innocent, I spied multiple eggshells in our breakfast.

The brothers' mother gazed expectantly at me from across the table. A hopeful smile tugged at her lips. "Well?"

Now that I got a close-up look at her, I was even more intimidated. She was gorgeous, flawless even. She looked like she had waltzed off the pages of the most fashionable magazine. Her skin was clear, and from this close, she didn't look like she was old enough to have kids.

Her soft black hair was pulled back into a trendy bun with tendrils of hair framing her face, and her makeup was a work of art. She studied me with the same dark blue eyes of her children, though the lingering smile on her lips was softer than anything they'd ever given me.

My eyes shifted back to the eggs. I took my fork and stabbed a few of them, that hopefully didn't contain crunchy surprises.

"You don't have to eat that, Lee," Julian objected. "Mom knows she can't cook."

"Julian!" his mom protested. Her eyes shimmered with about to be shed tears, and my mind was made up.

I took a bite. On the third chew, there was a glorious crunch as I bit into a piece of the shell I'd failed to find.

"Well?" she questioned, still smiling hopefully at me.

Telling her how awful it was would only serve to hurt this precious being. "Delicious," I gasped out. With a little wince, I stabbed some more eggs and felt the fork scrape against more egg shells. How much had she managed to drop into breakfast?

She clapped her hands and grinned. "Wonderful!" She glanced over at Julian and smirked. "See? Not everyone hates my cooking, Julie."

"Mom!" Julian glared at her and glanced my way. The bridge of his nose was beet red. "Don't call me that!"

Her eyes widened, and she put a hand to her lips. "Oh my, I'm sorry. I forgot." She glanced my way again and smiled. "But aren't you going to introduce us properly?"

"I've got it," Elijah interrupted. He was fully dressed in some of Julian's clothes, but they hung differently on his frame. His aura of being polished didn't vanish just because he was in a t-shirt. "Mother, this is Lee Suga, she's a scholarship student at Silverton, and due to what's happening there, she's currently staying here with us so we can keep her safe. Lee, this is my mother Mika."

Julian shot him a death glare, and his eye twitched. If I didn't know better I'd think he was upset that Elijah took the job away from him. Elijah for his part, ignored it.

"It's a pleasure to meet you, Lee. I can't say I've gotten a chance to hear all about you yet, but knowing my Julie, I'm sure that will come in time." She reached over and took my hands in hers and gave them a squeeze. "Considering you're going to be part of our family, I can't wait to hear everything."

My face burned. "I've got a mate," I blurted. I flipped my wrist around to show her Albedo's mark. "So you see, I can't be part."

Julian came up behind me and wrapped an arm around my shoulders. I tensed at his touch, but his smile was warm, dare I even say sweet? "Lee, you're going to be the mate of all the Alpha Gods. I can't explain it, but you've got connections to each of us."

I stared at him. Sure, I'd heard him say as much when I was hiding in the bathroom, but I hadn't expected him to just blurt it out like this. "I haven't even accepted you."

He shrugged. Instead of looking hurt, he flashed a wicked smile that made my toes curl. "I'm not worried about that, you will."

His mom grabbed a clean plastic spatula and smacked him on the top of his head. We both whirled to face her, but she frowned at Julian. "Julie, that is no way to talk to your future wife. You will respect her feelings and if she needs time or space, you're going to give it to her. I will not let you bully her."

I couldn't help it. I giggled. She was a little late on that front, but it was interesting to see how different she was from her son.

"You know I love you, but you need to know how to take care of someone you love. It's obvious to me from what you've told me that you'd do anything for this young lady, so waiting shouldn't be hard. If you are truly mated, you'll end up together."

Julian stared down at the table and grabbed his plate. Instead of the crunchy eggs I got to enjoy, he had singed bacon for breakfast, extra crispy. He crunched into it and didn't say a word as he ate the whole thing without a wince.

"Now, I'm afraid we need to get down to business. As much as I'd love to just sit here and get to know you, Lee. From what I've been told, and the state my Julie is in, I'm afraid that something horrible is happening in that school, and I intend to get to the bottom of it. Please, tell me everything."

Elijah snickered as he grabbed his own plate. "Yes, Julie, we need to tell her everything."

"Eli," Mika threatened with a cool glare his way. My normally suave Elijah froze in place. His eyes widened and he paled.

"Sorry, mother," he apologized.

She nodded.

Considering the brothers were occupied, I decided it was best for me to break the news. I took my time and explained everything I could. Starting with scholarship students and their eventual fate, and ending with the missing former Alpha Gods. The entire time Mika merely sat there and listened to me. Her face was passive, but her eyes were sharp.

When I was finished she nodded. "Is that everything? This Inu is someone that no one has ever met. The fact he targeted you all worries me. I feel you were hiding something else, and that it concerns one of the boys."

I glanced at Julian and Elijah. Was it really my position to talk about Albedo and what was going on with him? But it wasn't like his father was something that couldn't hurt others if he chose.

"There's one more thing. The Dean of the school is abusive. I can't tell you which student he's done anything to, but he's thrown them into a cage, beat them, and made them suffer. He's not fit to remain in power."

Her eyes narrowed at every word, and they focused on Julian. "Julie, why didn't you tell me about any of this earlier? Or you either, Eli?"

Both men shifted in their seats. Instead of answering, they crammed more of their breakfast into their mouths.

Cowards.

"It's likely they didn't know. We didn't find out a lot about this until the last twenty-four hours. I'm not sure what happens to the Alpha Gods, but I'm sure it's nothing good." I inhaled deeply. "And no matter what it is, I'm determined to help protect them."

Julian spat out bits of black bacon. "We're protecting you. You're not putting yourself in danger for us."

The more I thought about it, the more sense it made. Albedo and Sterling were banned from the school already, and Julian and Elijah were on thin ice. "I'll get proof of what's going on with the Dean. He's the type to brag about it. I don't want you to have to rely on hearsay since what we're talking about is so serious."

Mika stood up and gave me a smile. "Lee, I wouldn't dream of putting you or the boys in danger. I see how you are all responding to this, and more importantly than that, you're here in this apartment. Julie has kept this place to himself for years. He wouldn't willingly bring you here if this wasn't a serious matter."

"Your husband then, he won't believe me unless he has proof, right?" I pressed.

She pursed her lips and sighed. "That is true," she agreed. "However, he might not even listen to your proof in the first place. My husband is a bit of a..." she trailed off.

"Asshole," Julian helpfully offered.

"Julie!" she scolded. He smirked in response. "He's not pleasant," she added instead. "I will do my best to get you a meeting, but I worry about you putting yourself at increased risk. Are you sure this is what you want to do, Lee?"

Maybe with proof, I could find some way to even things out, and not just for my sake, but for King's as well.

Two could play this blackmail game of theirs. Surely the other families would not so willingly sacrifice their children if they discovered that the whole Alpha God schtick was a scam, right?

CHAPTER 28

GROWING CLOSER

MIKA SMILED AT ME as she gathered the plates from our breakfast. "Since you are determined to do this, I think it's only right you cement your current bonds. In case anything happens, it will help protect you, and also ensure there are no regrets."

My current bonds? I glanced at the dark wolf on my skin. Did she mean Albedo?

She nodded, as if she could see into my head. "That's right. I'll be taking the boys, and you will be inviting him here. You need to, at the very least, mark him."

"No fucking way," Julian growled.

Without missing a beat, Mika grabbed her trusty spatula and smacked him on top of the head again. "Language, Julie!"

He growled, but slunk down. "But, you know what will happen if we leave them alone."

She shrugged. "Don't you understand that's exactly my intention?"

Elijah pressed his lips together hard enough to make them white. With a grunt, he excused himself and retreated to the bathroom.

I slipped out of my chair, and followed. No matter what he'd done to me before, there was a magnetic pull I could not fight that always dragged me to him.

I got to the door before he did, and he glanced down before looking away. "Sorry, I'll go to the one in the building."

Shaking my head, I put my hand on his arm. The familiar sparks danced beneath my fingertips, and Barb nodded. "*There is no doubt, this is the same as it is with our mate. You have to accept them all, Lee. They all belong to us.*"

That still didn't make sense to me, but what was more important right now was not letting Elijah out of my sight. Maybe it was a predator's instinct, but I saw him softening to the prospect of us.

He was jealous of Albedo, he had to be.

"Elijah, I want to talk with you."

The collar from before was still wrapped around his neck, even if the cute Dalmatian ears were lost to the bed somewhere. It was a wonder his mom hadn't noticed them. "You heard mother, I need to get ready to leave."

"Elijah, you can't tell me that kiss meant nothing to you." I was positive about this. Besides the spark of touching a mate, there was the added heat. If Julian hadn't been there, who knew how far things would have progressed?

He turned and looked down at me. Slowly, he reached down and tilted my chin up. "You're right, I can't say that anymore. But that doesn't change that I have my heart set on Alexandra. Even if we are mates, Lee..." He winced. "I-"

"We are mates, Elijah," I corrected. I took a breath, steeling my resolve. "I think I am with all of you, even Julian, and as strange as that sounds, I'm willing to accept it. If you truly can't let go of Alexandra, and you can ever get her to change her mind, go to her. But, I'm going to fight for you."

He opened his mouth to ask me what I meant, but I pushed myself up on my tip toes and kissed him hard. His back hit the wall and I buried my hands in his soft dark hair. He groaned beneath me, but gave in and held me against his body.

Everything around us faded away. His scent wafted around me, and the taste of him danced through my senses as I deepened the kiss. My tongue tangled with his, and I gently bent down with just enough pressure to get his attention. I broke away from the kiss with a sharp tug of his hair.

His eyes flew open and he peered at me, and I stared back.

"Elijah, I'm telling you right now, you're mine, and you'll always belong to me. I'm going to win your heart, no matter what it takes, and once I do, you're going to apologize for everything you've put me through when you denied us. That little Dalmatian stunt was only the beginning." I smirked. "I hope you're ready to be my bitch."

With a kiss to his cheek, I wiggled my fingers and ducked into the bathroom, locking the door behind me. Oh Goddess, I can't believe I said that! Or did that!

My heart was racing a mile a minute. I'd never been that bold before, not even when facing former bullies down. What if I'd made a mistake and that made him back off? What if by pushing him I ruined everything?

"*No,*" Barb protested when I went to open the door. "*You did the right thing. Baron was impressed.*" She smirked. "*We've won his wolf over completely.*"

I hoped she was right. Despite the boldness, I couldn't help but doubt my actions. I wanted all of my mates.

It took me a while to get my heart back under control, and to adjust my appearance. I didn't want to come out looking like I'd been kissed senseless, though I'd been the one doing the kissing.

Silence greeted me. There was no Elijah nor Julian, or even Mika. Walking into the kitchen, I scanned the table and saw a handwritten note. It was too stylish to be Julian, and the characters were too curvy to be Elijah's.

It had to have come from her. It was a simple note with only two words written in calligraphy style.

Have Fun

A soft knock on the door stole my attention and I looked away from it. It felt strange being in the apartment alone. The robot pets were still asleep curled up in a ball on Julian's bed, right where Elijah had slept. Those two might have problems, but it was cute to see Julian's pets loved his brother.

The person at the door knocked again, and I peeked through the hole. The man standing on the other side made my chest ache.

Albedo lounged against the door frame with his hand on his head. I could hear him muttering, but not loud enough to understand the words.

Slowly, I turned the locks, opened the door, and froze. Something was different about my mate. His dark hair had streaks of blonde racing throughout, in a not-too-different style from Julian's.

He rushed into the room, grabbed me tightly, and gave me a huge squeeze. The fire spiraled through me wherever we touched, and I gasped. While with Elijah it was sparks of lightning, when I was with my mate, the sensation was even stronger as if I'd been plunged into a waterfall of lava. It burned, but in a good way.

"Albedo, what's with your hair?" I questioned, grabbing one of his styled spikes and twisting my finger around it. They weren't as stiff as they had been before, it was soft and silky to the touch.

He chuckled, kissing the top of my head. "Thank the Goddess you're okay, Kitten. I was worried sick. As for my hair?" He shrugged, glancing away. "Do you like it?"

Puzzled, I wriggled out of his tight grip and locked the door. "Do you really need to fish for compliments from me when you have a whole fan club of women ready to throw their panties at you?" I scoffed.

He gave me a wink. "I only want your panties."

I rolled my eyes and snorted. "Anyway, why wouldn't I be okay? Why are you so worried?"

"Mika contacted me saying it was an emergency. I needed to come to Julian's apartment and take care of you. She also said I couldn't leave until it was done. I thought he hurt you, or that Inu found you."

I shook my head. "No, I just stayed the night here with those two. No one hurt me," I paused. Should I reveal to him that he'd been sent here to be claimed by me? It wasn't exactly something you blurted out, even to your mate.

But no matter which way I thought about it, I couldn't come up with any other answer but the truth.

"Mika sent you here so I would claim you."

His eyes widened, and a grin spread across his lips. "I knew I liked that woman." He paused, his brows furrowing. "But wait, I would think she'd want you for a daughter-in-law for at least one of her sons. Is she trying to keep you away from them by throwing me at you?"

"Not... exactly."

How should I explain the rest? It was one thing for me to accept what I was about to say, but it would be quite another for him to do so.

"Is something wrong? You're worried..." He looked me over, inspecting me for injuries. "Did they hurt you somehow?" he growled softly.

"Albedo, before I claim you, there's something we need to talk about. It concerns the Alpha Gods as a whole. The originals I mean, not those others."

"Lee, as long as you're the one claiming me I don't care what your next words are. Since the moment I locked eyes with you, something inside of me just knew you were the one I should be with."

He gingerly grabbed my arm, and his fingers glided over the mark that bound me to him. Flames danced beneath his fingers, and all the tension in my body faded. I could trust him, but how could I possibly explain this? "You're going to hate me," I whispered. Barb whimpered at the thought, but didn't intervene.

"Hate you? I could never do that." Albedo frowned. His sea-green eyes sparkled in the light and reminded me of the calm of an ocean. Would they darken when he learned I wanted to take others as mates?

"I don't want to just claim you."

He blinked. "You mean Elijah finally warmed up to you, Kitten? That's great. I know how much you've been pining for him."

How could he talk like that? Go on as if he didn't mind at all about me thinking about another man? I wasn't sure how the mate bond worked for him, but if Ms. Pink decided to try any of her nonsense around me I was going to replace her shampoo with glue. "You're not mad?"

"You should be the one mad at me, Lee. I was the one who took the choice away from you. I meant what I said, if you want to reject me, I'll take it."

"Never," I hissed. I put both of my hands on his cheeks, and stared into his eyes. "Albedo, we are mates, and even before you claimed me, that was a fact. But, I've come to realize I'm also mates with the other Alpha Gods."

He blinked again. "All but Julian?"

I winced. "Even Julian," I mumbled.

He laughed, and pulled me close to his chest. His warmth threatened to engulf me and he kissed my forehead. "You know, Jules is pretty rough around the edges, and he is an asshole, but deep down inside he does have a heart. It's just it has been covered in so many layers of rock lately that no one wants to try to break through. Not that I blame them, he *is* an asshole."

I giggled. "Did you have to say that twice?"

He nodded, and taking one of my palms, he gently kissed it. "Yeah, I do. But I also know him and Elijah are the only ones who can keep you safe in that school until we get to the bottom of all this. But I can at least protect you while you're here."

He wasn't going to be happy when I revealed I was about to dangle myself in front of his father like delicious bait. I considered hiding it from him, but if he did find out there was no doubt in my mind he'd come barreling into the school, spells or no, and end up getting himself killed.

No, best to be upfront.

"I'm going to see your father in the morning. I'll make sure I catch his words on tape to prove to others what's going on with the Alpha Gods."

CHAPTER 29

ALBEDO'S TRUTH

ALBEDO TENSED AND A deep growl rumbled from his chest. He turned from the heart-breaker I knew, into a true Alpha. "There's no fucking way I'll let you," Albedo snapped. "Do you know what he's capable of?" His fists tightened at his sides, and he took a step away from me.

"It doesn't matter. I need proof of what he's doing to the Alpha Gods. If I can get support, maybe we can put a stop to all of it and save everyone."

Albedo sighed, giving me a hard look. "Lee, I'm going to show you everything that bastard is capable of, and if you can't look at me the same way after, I accept it." Slowly, he peeled his shirt off, throwing it onto the kitchen counter.

I yelped and covered my eyes, turning my back on him. "Albedo!" I hissed in protest.

"You can't run away from this, Kitten. I need you to look."

Slowly, I turned on my heel and peeked through my fingers. My hands dropped to my sides and I stared at his body. Everywhere a t-shirt covered was riddled with layers of scars. Long, short, deep, shallow, one even looked like a star because of how many rested beneath it.

A vicious snarl erupted from Barb. "I'll kill the fuckers!" She promised. "Let me at them! I'll rip their arms off, eat their livers, pull out their teeth!"

"Albedo," I whispered. My lips trembled, and hot tears clouded my vision. "How did this happen?" I stepped closer, inspecting a spot around his belly button that had various cigarette burns. "I don't understand. We're wolves. How is none of this healed?"

With a shake of his head, he chuckled softly, though I could find no reason to be amused. "This? It's because my dear sweet father forbade me from healing any of it. He nearly broke Lewis to teach me such a neat trick. Each of these are supposed to build character, and make me remember every mistake I've ever made."

Barb was wild. She bounced back and forth in my head, desperate to seize control and send us into battle. The man who had done this was someone I was about to confront, but instead of being scared, I was more determined than ever to put an end to him. One way or another.

"I can't tell you how long it took before I could stop healing everything that was beneath the shirt. He kept me in a half-dead state until I learned it. No food, minimum water, and beatings constantly. Lee, this is the kind of man he is, this is what he does. I won't let him destroy you too."

Reaching out, I brushed a finger against a long skinny scar on his stomach. He winced at the touch. This was no true playboy, the rumors about him had to all be wrong. How would he ever reveal this to anyone? "Heal it," I ordered.

"What?" He blinked, staring at me as if I'd asked him to reach up and pluck the sun out of the sky as a gift. "That's not possible."

"Have you ever tried?" I pressed.

He winced. "No..."

"Then, heal it. I promise you'll never be in a position he can hurt you like this again. Albedo, I want you to heal every last one."

He shuddered. "Lee, what you're asking..."

"Demanding," I corrected. "I know this is scary, but I don't want that monster to have even a tiny bit of power over you. You're free, Albedo."

Glancing down at his chest, he bit his lip before turning his piercing gaze back on me. "Promise me you won't go tomorrow, that you'll stay far away from him. Better yet, let's just both get out of Silverton completely. I've got friends in some of the other academies. We can hole up somewhere, get on our feet, and escape all of this. Do that, and I'll try it." He took both of my hands in his, and knelt at my feet. "Kitten, let me protect you."

I hated doing this to him, but I couldn't let him put a stop to the plans I had constructed. It was too important. "Lewis," I called. Through the bond, his wolf surged at my voice, and Albedo's eyes flashed gold as his wolf nearly took control. "Please, would you heal him for me?"

Albedo scowled, but Lewis was all too happy to answer my plea. He fought his way to the surface, and his eyes glowed pure gold. The scars on Albedo's body slowly shrunk and faded before my eyes. His wolf healed them one after the other.

"Damn it, Lewis," Albedo snarled, but he was hopeless to wrest control back.

I pulled Albedo to his feet and ran my fingers over his now smooth flesh. It was as if he had gone back in time, and the horribly mangled canvas that had been his skin was healed. "Lewis, thank you," I whispered to the wolf.

Lewis smirked. "If you're so thankful, prove it, mate. You already told us your intention, but if you want my help keeping this one under control, I only desire one thing. Mark us so I can feel my mate. Do that and you'll have all the power you'll need to go against his asshole of a father. Albedo might have always been scared of him, but I know how weak he truly can be. You can take every last ounce of power out of my body if it saves you from him." He frowned. "I swear on the Goddess Morgan, I will never let anything happen to you."

I shivered from his intensity. "Lewis, you barely knew me, and yet you claimed me as yours the second you had the chance. What made you so sure? The Alpha Gods were blocked from all of that. Wasn't that the sacrifice they endured to become so powerful?"

He cocked his head. "Isn't that obvious? I knew you were the one fated for my soul from the start. Albedo might not have figured it out as quickly, but nothing could keep me away from you. You and Barb are my destiny."

My insides turned to warm jelly. Should I really be surprised that even his wolf was good with words? "You're sure you're okay with all of this? I know Albedo said it doesn't bother him, but you're a wolf..."

Lewis chuckled. "I can't keep control from him too much longer. The healing has taken a lot out of me. But if you're worried because you also feel the pull of the bond with the others, I'm not going to get in your way," he chuckled. "Besides, no matter what, I'll always be your first. The first to claim you, and the first to be claimed."

I buried my head in his chest. I'd almost forgotten that agreement. Despite the surety of his words, his heart raced beneath my cheek.

Barb nodded, pleased with my decision. "He's right, Lewis will always be special to us. I have no doubts he can protect us."

"Lee," Albedo whispered. His eyes had returned to the sea green I loved so much. "I'm ready." He tilted his head to the side, exposing his neck.

Barb pushed forward, eager to take this next step. My fangs grew larger so I could carry out this important task. More than anything else, I wanted Albedo. The flames of desire could not be denied a moment longer. I wanted to give in to them and let this man do what he willed, even if I ended up with a broken heart.

Leaning close, I brushed my lips against his chest, right over his heart. "This is going to hurt," I warned.

He chuckled at me, ruffling my hair gently before petting me. His head rolled back and he stilled as he took deep steady breaths. "I want this, no matter how bad it gets, I won't regret it."

Nodding, I opened my mouth wide and bit down into his chest. The bond was like a raging river breaking through a dam. It smashed into us tying us together in a way that no one would ever be able to pull apart.

Albedo was mine forever and always, and I wouldn't want it any other way.

CHAPTER 30

TIME TO HEAL

ALBEDO

Lewis purred.

Wolves shouldn't purr.

In any other situation, I'd be pissed he was acting so strange and lecture his ass. However, this time I agreed with him. If there was ever a moment to purr, it would be the instant we were tied together to our mate forever.

The bond settled over us and the floodgates of her mind were opened to me. Barb was overjoyed, the wolf bounded around Lewis, they were like two overgrown puppies.

Lee's soft touch left fireworks across my skin. Each fingertip lit up sparks and I groaned under their assault. "Lee," I moaned.

She had placed her mark over my heart. A pretty little wolf booped noses with that damned Clevania mascot creature. I growled at seeing it, and she peered up at me. Her cheeks were dark red.

Her eyes danced and her lips twitched, despite her embarrassment. "You can't be too mad. I didn't pick that."

I snorted. "Why am I not surprised you're that crazy for the game, Kitty? I bet Sterling has one matching it."

A haunted look flitted across her face. "Sterling," she echoed, biting her lip. "This is really going to hurt him. Everything I'm about to do. Yes, he said he didn't really care and he'd love me no matter what, but..." I gestured to his mark. "I claimed you, Albedo. How could he still?"

I resisted the urge to snort. How could she not see it? "Do you seriously doubt the devotion that man has for you? He's been saving himself all this time for his precious, and the first time he felt anything for anyone else he was devastated. He's been so fucking relieved that you are his Kitty. You are his queen, and he's just a helplessly devoted servant willing to do whatever it takes to make you happy. You could claim all of us, and he'd still throw himself at your feet to do your bidding. I promise, Lee, nothing will ever take his love away from you."

She shook her head, brows scrunched. "I chose you first, it's going to hurt him more than anything else."

This woman. What was I going to do with her? Gently, I took her wrist and rubbed a finger over the dark wolf before I pressed a soft kiss to it. "Lee, Lewis forced this on you. You had no obligation to return it, or even keep our bond. No matter what you want to do, I'll never stop you."

Her cheeks turned to pale pink roses. "Albedo," she whispered. I felt like purring at the sound. It hit differently now that we were bound as tight as mates could be. Almost as tight as mates could be.

I kissed her wrist again and her eyes fluttered as her breath caught.

Oh? Did that make her heart skip a beat like it did me? The tingles of the bond sparked an inferno inside. I smirked.

Time for an experiment.

Keeping my eyes locked on hers, my tongue darted out and traced over her mark. She moaned, leaning against me for support.

Oh, this was all too perfect. I grazed it across my teeth and she clenched her thighs together, releasing a soft little whimper.

"Albedo, if you keep that up..." She bit her adorable lip as I did just that.

"Yes?" I asked innocently. It was time for me to push this experiment a little bit farther. Besides, every sound that came from her was addictive, and I never wanted it to end.

I grazed the length of the mark with the tips of my teeth, not enough to hurt, but she shuddered beneath the assault.

"Albedo," she growled.

I chuckled, and pulled away. "Yes, kitten?"

She turned her head toward my chest and pressed her sweet lips against the mark there.

I was the one to lose control and moan. It was like a wall of fire slammed into me. My naughty little kitten wasn't done torturing me. She licked at the same spot, sucking harder before nipping.

My entire body was dipped in a pool of lava. The heat wave rushed over me and I growled as my control crumbled. Pulling Lee into my arms, I buried my head in the curve of her neck and scattered kisses across it. "Are you sure?" I whispered. "I won't be able to hold back."

I needed her too much for that. Her soft teases had done more than drive me crazy. And if I couldn't find my own release, I would at least give her hers.

"Positive," she whispered, angling her head back more and giving me better access. "We should go to the bedroom," she suggested.

I shivered at the implications. I'd never have imagined any of this could really happen. I was the one that flirted, I never was the one falling hard. So hard I'd never recover if she decided to break me. Not that I'd tell her that, I wouldn't dare try to control her decisions.

"You're thinking too much," she scolded before grabbing me by a handful of my hair, and wrenching my head to the side. She copied my teasing kisses, but added soft little licks that made my whole body tense.

"I'll fix it," I promised. I put my hand over hers and guided it to my hair until she took a handful of it. She tugged softly and I hissed as I groaned.

Something was wrong with me. I was broken forever because of my past, and this was a side of myself I never shared. Wincing, I spared her a glance to see if disgust or anger had crossed her face.

She untangled her hand from my hair and gently stroked my cheek with a palm. "No matter what you need, Albedo, I'm your mate. We'll form our own way of doing things, and right now, we need to get to that bed before I strip right here."

My eyes rolled to the back of my head as I imagined that. My pants grew unbearably tight, and with a groan, I nodded before following after her like an obedient puppy.

The bed barely fit in the room, and it was covered with an assortment of robotic pets. They looked up at us when we entered.

"Out," Lee ordered with a snap of her fingers. "I don't know if you guys have any recording capabilities, but this is private and I'm not about to share it."

The cat meowed at her and fled the room with its tail held high, followed by a dozen dogs, and a monkey.

Since when had Julian gotten a robotic monkey?

Lee smirked and locked the door behind him. Keeping eye contact, she grabbed the hem of her shirt and pulled it up and off of her body, tossing it in the corner as she went. Next, she wriggled out of the skirt she wore.

There was a confidence in her movements I hadn't witnessed before and I couldn't tear my eyes away.

"Keep your eyes on me," she ordered before reaching behind her back and undoing the hooks on her bra. Her breasts bounced as they were freed and I licked my lips. More than anything else, I wanted to bury my face between them and breathe in her scent.

"Always," I promised. It took all of my willpower not to reach into my pants and torture myself as she gave me this slow tease.

Her thumbs hooked on the band of her panties and she slowly pushed them down, taking way more time than she could have possibly needed. Inch by delectable inch, she revealed herself to me until she was bare, and oh-so beautiful.

"Lee," I breathed out. I didn't trust myself to be able to say anything else.

She climbed onto the bed and leaned back until she supported herself by the elbows, and she crooked her finger at me. "Your turn."

I hesitated. True, most of the scars had been healed earlier, but there were still many she hadn't been exposed to yet. Doubt stirred inside.

"Bedo?" My nickname slipped from her lips far too easily and a wave of warmth flowed through me. How could I love someone this much?

"I'm okay," I assured her, as I kicked off my pants and let them slide down my legs. Her eyes traveled from my chest, down, and narrowed.

Shit. I forgot how bad some of these were.

"Albedo, why didn't you heal it all?" she whispered. She crawled off the bed towards me, letting her fingers graze across my skin. Licks of fire followed her path. She paused at the jagged knife wound that stretched across my hip and traveled down my groin.

"He's a monster," she whispered.

I didn't disagree, but it gave me all the more reason to want to keep her safe. He was the monster that my little mate was about to face head-on, and I couldn't even stand by her side. "It's over though, this is the past, Lee."

She pulled her hand away as if I burned her, and slipped off the bed. My heart sank. Was this the end of my fairytale? She turned away from me and her shoulders shook. I reached out for her and she whirled on me like a wildcat. Tears shone as they trailed down her cheeks. "Lewis!" she screamed my wolf's name, and he responded with a deep grunt.

What was she up to?

"Every spot I kiss, I want you to heal," she ordered.

She put her hand on my chest and shoved me backward until I tumbled onto the bed. She stood over me, with a smirk, before she crawled after me.

Before I could stop her, she grabbed my ankle and pressed her lips against the holes left when my father had transformed, but forced me to remain in this form. He had pushed his claws into me, seeing how far they would go before he hit bone.

Of course, I hadn't been allowed to heal it.

The skin stitched together beneath her touch. Lewis was quick to obey. In seconds, what had been with me for years was just a bad memory.

She didn't stop. She crawled farther on the bed and found a slash across my knee. I'd gotten that trophy from when I took Fireball into the house without his permission. He'd hated my cat, but I'd protected her until she passed away from normal old age. It didn't matter how many battle wounds I acquired in the process.

"Damn it, Lee," I groaned. How was I supposed to be able to do the right thing by her if she kept this up? I'd forced all of this on her, and she deserved nothing but the best.

And that wasn't me.

With every touch, she tied me to her in a way even more intimate than our bond was. I'd never be able to let her go.

"What's wrong?" she whispered before kissing my inner thigh. That had been the time that father had pierced me with a fire poker. He'd liked the mark it left, as if I was branded cattle. That had been the punishment for my first failing student.

After that, I'd taken to sweet-talking the women in my classes, and sending them to help anyone else who was likely to fail. They were willing to do anything to spend time with me, and I was determined to not suffer under my father's wrath again.

I swallowed hard, as even the burn vanished.

I was whole again, pure.

"Lee," I whispered, she raised her head to meet my eyes. Hers were still full of tears, but her rage wasn't focused on me.

Hopefully, she wouldn't hate me for this.

"I love you. I know it's too soon to say that, and all of this is just too emotional, but I can't fight it anymore."

She didn't answer, instead, she crawled higher and kissed my lower stomach. One of the cigarette burns had been low on my hips, hiding under my pants.

Her closeness and her warm breath was more than I could take. My dick bobbed against her chin. "Shit! Sorry," I whispered, reaching down to adjust myself.

"Bedo," she whispered, kissing my side where he had plunged a knife into one of my kidneys. Lewis was all too willing to heal every single spot, not caring how much energy it took from us as we turned back years worth of time.

"I want you to want this too," I whispered.

She backed up, sitting on her heels, and raised a brow. Tucking a strand of hair behind her ear, she gave me a heated look that made my toes curl. She leaned over and her tongue flicked out; brushing from the start of my balls, working her way up my shaft with the most intricate swirls and twists that I thought I was going to explode in her face.

Her lust tugged at me, ready to devour me in its own inferno.

She wanted me.

I could hardly believe it, but her emotions were all too easy to feel through the bond.

She got to the tip, and her tongue tickled it before she glanced up at me. "What do you think?" she quipped.

I lost the battle, and my head fell back onto the sheets as the vixen continued to kiss away every other injury that had ever been left.

There was no doubt in my mind that I was about to take another of the firsts away from the others, and I prayed they'd forgive me. It might be the last chance we got before all hell broke loose, because no matter what, I would keep her safe from my father, even if it killed me.

CHAPTER 31

SWEET SURRENDER

LEE

By the time I was finished with him, he was a shivering reddened mess, but at least his scars from the abuse were gone. I only wished I could take all those memories away as well. How could anyone treat their own child like that?

"You still okay?" I questioned, smiling down at him.

"Yes," he grunted. His voice was gruff, deeper than I'd heard him use before. It was strange though. The way he responded to me was almost fragile. Wasn't he the heartbreak king? Shouldn't he be more confident?

I ran my fingers over his chest, eyes still locked on him and he trembled like a fawn beneath my touch. He took a sharp intake of breath, panting as I pulled away.

Crawling on top of him, I hugged him tight, listening to the rapid beat of his heart. He didn't try to progress things, and after a few moments, I chanced a peek, to see what was going on.

He stared at the top of my head with a beet-red face. The bottoms of his ears were fire engine red. "What's wrong? Am I moving too fast?" Oh Goddess, had I just read things wrong and shoved myself on him?

The raging inferno he had set aflame with that accident of his would be hard to tamper down, but I didn't want him compelled to be with me because of this bond of ours.

"That's not it." His voice was soft, almost fragile as if he was worried about how I was going to take his words. "I want to, Lee, more than anything. But..." He trailed off and looked away.

That single word held so much weight I could scarcely breathe. I reached out, palming his cheek and he turned into my touch, surrendering himself to me. "Bedo, whatever is stopping you, I'm here for you. We don't have to do anything if you're not ready, we can easily go to sleep."

A tear trailed down his cheek, but he made no move to brush it away. Instead, he gazed at me. "Are you sure? You're not... disappointed in me?" His voice caught at the end as if he was barely holding himself together.

How could he possibly think like this? I trailed my fingertips down to his chest and over the mark I'd given him. "I want you, I won't lie, but I'd rather us both be on the same page when that happens. If it's not good for you or something you don't want to do, we won't do it." I shifted my weight, and curled against his side. "This is just as good."

He chuckled wryly. "Oh, it's not nearly good enough," he growled softly. "In fact, while I'm not too comfortable with you taking care of me, I'm more than competent of being able to take care of you." He smirked. "Let me take you to heaven, mate."

This man. I shook my head and gently kissed his cheek. "I'm not having fun without you, mate."

He trapped me against him by wrapping an arm around my back and I submitted against his warmth. I flopped over to use his arm as a pillow and turned to peer at him.

"We can cuddle if you want," I suggested.

As I wriggled into position, something hard poked me in the center of my back and his breathing became ragged. "Sorry," he whispered huskily. "That can't be comfortable digging in your back."

"You know, you could just turn over and I could hold you," I offered. "It'll probably be more comfortable for both of us."

Slowly his brow raised, and his chin tilted down. "You? Hold me? You do remember I am an Alpha, right, kitten?"

I answered him with a flick to his forehead. Twisting a strand of his new hair color around my finger, I brought it into his view. "My very insecure Alpha, or are you going to tell me you didn't do this because you were jealous of Julian?"

Red splotches popped up on his face and he turned away from me, burying his head in the pillow. "Shut up," he pleaded.

I giggled. "You didn't have to do it. I think you're amazing no matter what, and," I paused to take his hand in mine, and intertwine our fingers, "you're my mate, no matter what. My first mate, no one can ever take that away."

"Are you going to hold me, or not?" he mumbled his voice muffled. The bottoms of his ears were still incredibly dark red, and his new highlights made them stand out even more.

Another burst of warmth filled me. It hadn't really dawned on me before, but this was a side of him that he didn't share with anyone else. We truly were special to each other.

I crawled closer, wrapping one arm around his chest while with the other I hooked it around his shoulder so he could use it as a pillow. I pressed my body against his and gently kissed the back of his neck.

Sparks threatened to consume me from the smallest of touches. However, I was determined to keep my word. "Bedo?" I spoke softly into his ear.

He shivered at his name. "Yeah?"

"Does this mean... all the rumors are fake? You really haven't done anything with anyone else before, have you?"

His body tensed, and I could hear his teeth grinding together before he let out a shuddering little sigh. "Kitten, you saw my scars. There's no one alive in this world that would want to be with a freak like me."

"What about Zelda?" I blurted, and instantly regretted it.

He chuckled. "Do you think I'd expose my vulnerabilities to someone like her? She's seen a few marks after they were given, but she had no idea that I hid them like this. She's been exposed to my father's rage, but not really the results of it." He shrugged. "No, kitten, only you have gotten to see this ugly side of me."

I scowled and bit into the back of his neck. He gasped and moaned against the assault. I pulled away and licked the tiny wound I'd left. Maybe I'd been too rough. He backed his body against mine and I buried my nose in his hair. "You're not ugly, and I'll protect you from that asshole. You'll never be hurt again."

Barb huffed and rolled her eyes at me, and Albedo chuckled.

"Lee, I'm the one that will protect you. I swear."

I sighed, men and their insistence on being some tough asshole that could handle everything. "Bedo, you don't have to be tough with me. We're mates, you don't need those walls, and I will never judge you for what lies beyond them. I'm on your side, always."

The back of his neck turned red, and my lips twitched. Tormenting him was quickly becoming a favorite pastime.

"Thanks," he grunted.

"I do have a question though. If you really haven't been with anyone else, why is every female student in that university chasing you so hard? You could have your pick of so many beautiful women, and yet you're settling for me."

"Settling?" he snorted, grabbed my hand curled around his stomach, and pulled it to his lips. He kissed my wrist, his tongue swirling over the skin in a delicate dance. I shivered as a moan slipped from me, and my body throbbed in desire.

Damn, I'd been trying to control myself.

I bit into his shoulder again to stop the unending moans, as he continued to tease me. Albedo moaned against the assault, and he let my wrist go so he could reach back and bury his hand into my hair and press me against the spot I bit. "Lee," he groaned, his voice shaky. "More."

Who was I to deny him? I bit harder almost to the point of breaking flesh again, and he panted hard. Instead of pain twisting through our bond, it was replaced with excitement and lust.

"Fuck," he moaned, his entire body trembled.

I licked the spot and nuzzled him. "Albedo?"

He took deep shaky breaths, as his heart galloped.

Shame washed over him and tainted our bond. His body clenched and he slowly let go of me. "Damn, I'm sorry. I didn't realize I was such a twisted little fuck. Goddess, Lee, you're perfect and I'm just a worthless piece of corrupted shit. I'm sick."

"Why? Because you like a little pain?" I blew against the top of his ear until the tension drained away. "That's not anything that's wrong with you. There are lots of people with that kink out there, even those that don't have your history."

Slowly, he propped himself up on an elbow and turned around. His eyes searched mine. "You're seriously telling me you don't have a problem with that? You're not the least bit disgusted with me?"

I scoffed. "You can feel our bond as well as I can. Did you feel any disgust?"

He shook his head and stared. "Lee, you're stuck with me forever. I'm never leaving you. I'm sorry."

"Why are you sorry?" I tugged on one of his blonde spikes. "You keep apologizing and acting like you're the worst. You were the victim in all that. Don't you understand you deserve love?"

I crawled on top of him and grabbed his wrists in my hands, pinning them above his head so I could stare into his sea glass like eyes. "I love you, Albedo."

He swallowed hard. "Even though I'm a shitty friend?" he whispered. "I found out who you were when I remodeled your room. I kept it from Sterling because I didn't want to share you. Despite knowing how you two felt about each other."

I wrinkled my nose. "You did?" He nodded. My eyes widened and my lips twitched. Maybe I was a horrible person too. "Does that mean you did the VR date just to taunt him?"

He chuckled. "Yeah, and you can see how that turned out." He shook his head. "You'd have been better off not accepting a fucked up mate like me."

"Idiot," I scolded before leaning down and capturing his lips in a kiss. He moaned, melting beneath me. "It's too late, you're mine and I'm never giving you up. You're worth so much more than you treat yourself, and I'm going to make you realize it."

Albedo pulled his hands free of my loose grip and looped his arms around me, deepening the kiss. His tongue plunged inside and tangled with mine. Holding me close, he rolled us over until he was the one on top.

He pulled back and smiled down at me. "I'm taking care of you right now, little mate, I can't wait to watch you lose it as I make you come."

CHAPTER 32

INTERRUPTED PLAYTIME

ALBEDO

The Goddess Morgan truly had felt pity for me. She'd let me have such a sweet and perfect mate. One that tasted of juicy sweet apples and the delectable spice of cinnamon, that stung my senses. Her scent wrapped around me, becoming a part of me and overriding my own.

I wanted to smell like her forever.

Pulling away from the kiss, I gazed down into her eyes, never had I found the pink sheen of them more appealing. Her cheeks had turned into rosy red apples that I wanted to nibble.

I kissed her chin and peppered her with soft feathery kisses as I made my way down. "I-love-you," I whispered between kisses. The words came easily, and just saying them made a wellspring of warmth rush through me.

All of this felt so right, like we were always meant to be.

I pressed my lips against her throat.

A long moan escaped her, and she bit her lip to try to keep them locked inside. I didn't give a damn if the whole apartment complex heard us. "It's okay, kitten," I assured her. "You can sing for me as loud and long as you want."

I was determined to give her a blissful moment of pure release. If she'd let me. Kissing my way down her neck, I made my way to the little v between her breasts and I lapped at the skin there.

"Bedo," she whimpered. Her body trembled beneath me like a little defenseless bird.

My tongue circled around one of her erect nipples and I rolled it into my mouth, capturing it as I teased her sucking tightly on its peak. She rose off the bed toward me, lost in her emotions. A fresh wave of arousal wafted over the sheets. I doubted any of the others would complain about that.

Lee grabbed handfuls of the sheet as she twisted beneath me. She was so worked up; she was more beautiful than any other woman I'd ever seen. No matter what it took, I'd make sure she got everything she deserved.

I let her nipple go, and brushed a soft kiss over the other. She gasped beneath me, waiting for me to tease that one as well, but instead, I moved my kisses lower. I worked my way down until I knelt between her legs.

Her breath came in little pants and she stared down at me. She sucked her bottom lip into her mouth, and bit down hard on it.

She still hadn't learned her lesson about the sweet song I wanted to hear.

Slowly, I pressed her thighs down until they were completely flat against the bed. My little mate was fighting her arousal so hard, but her body was betraying her. It was so thick I could almost taste it. My eyes drank in her every curve and the pinkness of her skin.

My control was way better than I had assumed it would be. How had I held myself back from feasting on her? I was dying to find out what she tasted like. However, there was a certain bliss in this moment of forcing us both to wait until our insides burned with need.

Leaning down, I grazed her inner thigh with eager lips, and nipped her skin.

She wound her fingers into my hair and tugged at my short locks, trying to guide me to where she wanted.

Chancing a glance up at her, I watched as she stared down at me. Her whole face was red and she was tormenting her poor bottom lip. "Bedo," she whined.

"Impatient," I scolded nipping a little harder. "Don't worry, kitten. Lay back and relax, I'll take you straight to heaven's gate. All you have to do is let me," I purred.

Her head thrashed back and forth on the pillow. She let her poor lip free, as keening moans tore from her. Each kiss and suck against her skin brought me closer to what she so desperately wanted.

"Bedo!" She howled. "Please, please, please," she begged.

I chuckled. My poor baby was about to fall apart. It was too cute, but it also woke the beast inside, and it was all I could do to hold myself back from completely devouring her. But no, it was more important that she reach bliss, she needed it more than anyone else.

Slowly, I brushed my tongue against her sweet pussy. I took slow leisurely licks, like she was the finest ice cream I wanted to savor. I followed her soft curves and circled my tongue around the hood of her clit before I gently sucked on it.

I pushed her over the edge and she came undone. Her grip on my hair tightened and she shoved me into position. My name echoing through the small room did wonders for my ego. She was so much sweeter than I'd anticipated. The apple taste was still strong, though the spices had dialed down. My tongue twisted and twirled over her until all that was left was an unending series of moans and grunts.

It had been mere seconds since I started, but my little mate was already so close to exploding, and thanks to our bond, she was forcing me to that point as well. The last thing I wanted was to finish on the bed, without the excuse of her touching me.

She lost the ability to form words as I tormented her. Her taste got stronger, and her scent completely engulfed me until all I could smell was her. For the first time in my life, I wanted to have sex. No, more than that, I wanted to become one with my mate.

But there was no way I could give her everything she deserved with just that. No, instead I was going to make her come harder than she ever had in her life. She'd never be able to erase me from her mind.

I slipped a finger inside of her wetness and her moans gave me new life. Twisting my finger around, I searched for that perfect spot. Her eyes rolled in the back of her head, and an endless streams of oh my goddess escaped her.

Any moment now she would lose the battle with herself, and I would get my sweet reward.

Off to the side and from the direction of my pants, something vibrated. I pulled away to glance in that direction.

Lee scrambled up from her position to glare down at me with her precious scarlet cheeks. "Don't you dare," she seethed.

This woman was too adorable. "Just give me a minute, love," I requested. "I have to make sure nothing else happened." Leaning over the bed, I grabbed my phone with one hand and continued to torment her by sliding a finger in and out of her slickness.

The phone continued to vibrate nonstop.

What had happened now? I steeled myself for the worst.

"Bedo," Lee whimpered. Her hips rose and fell as she worked herself against me. She was chasing her orgasm without me.

Her body was flushed, as was much of her face, which had turned into a mask of open lust. Had I ever witnessed her eyes that dark? They were as almost as red as Julian's. Lewis was pissed at me, he didn't want to stop. We were so close to pushing her over the edge and making her break for us.

We had plenty of time for that, what was important was keeping her safe. I pulled my finger free and sucked on it before I casually answered the phone. "Hey."

"Hey? That's how you answer the damned phone? I heard that you're alone with my Kitty, Albedo! I might have been kidnapped by Mika, but that doesn't mean I'm going to let you get away with whatever you want."

I chanced a glance at the woman in question and she stared at the phone with her fingers to her lips. Damn it. She didn't need to feel guilty for this. "I'm here with her, she's safe. That's all that matters."

"Sterling-"

"Excuse me," Lee mumbled. She pointed at the phone and snapped her fingers. "Let me see that."

"Kitty?" Sterling gasped. His excitement clearly bled through the line.

She cradled the phone between her cheek and shoulder. "Rusty, I want to be upfront with you always. You mean the world to me, but you already know that. I marked Albedo, and I will be marking all of the Alpha Gods in time. I hope you were serious about what you said earlier."

He swallowed. "Whatever makes you happy, Kitty. That's all I care about."

"Thank you, when I'm finished with my important business with him, I'll call you and you can come back to the apartment. Just wait for me, okay? I want all of you here with me tonight."

"I'll be there," Sterling promised. "Albedo, make sure you take care of her. Put those skills of yours to use, It's our job to make her blissfully happy, and if you fail, I will punish you."

Lee chuckled at the phone before hanging it up and tossing it in the corner. She reached down and grabbed me by the back of my neck before she guided me back to her quivering wet pussy. "You, on the other hand, are going to get to work right now, Bedo. You can't get me that close and abandon me like that," she growled. "Take care of what you started."

I loved this woman so much. Laughing, I licked my lips and slowly went back down on her. I had no intention of failing Sterling's challenge. I'd been given orders, and I wasn't about to fail.

CHAPTER 33

FULL HOUSE

LEE

Albedo was lucky he'd tossed that damned phone. I was ready to open the window and throw it out of the apartment. How could he stop when I'd been that close? It was a special kind of torment I didn't deserve.

Thankfully, he didn't make me suffer for too much longer. He crawled back on the bed, pushing my knees back to the surface, and his hot breath warmed my thighs. He stared up at me, his eyes so dark they reminded me of a typhoon. His intensity made me glance away.

"You're so beautiful," he whispered, gently kissing my groin. He took his time with tiny little kisses crawling closer to that oh-so-perfect spot. With a whimper, I collapsed back to my pillow.

My senses were going haywire. Every moment that had existed before this one paled in comparison. How could having a mate change things so drastically? No wonder fated mates were so treasured, and I was lucky enough to have this connection with three others?

Albedo growled, and his sweet kisses were replaced with bites to my chunky thighs. "You're not focused on me, kitten," he scolded.

My heart thumped harder, and the always present sparks with him exploded like fireworks, threatening to consume me in their blaze.

He brushed his nose along the line of my inner thigh, and a string of unintelligent gurgles erupted from me. "Lee," he teased, and with effort I focused on him. He slowly pulled my pussy lips apart. "You're even blushing here."

I trembled, melting into my pillow. Nothing else existed in the world except the two of us.

His breath got hotter and his tongue slowly swirled across my exposed bits. He pushed the same finger from earlier back inside, and gently pumped it in and out as his tongue got more aggressive.

Oh Goddess, I couldn't hang on any longer. My thoughts dissolved like drops of dew as all I could focus on was the delicious tension building up inside. My body spasmed, and the heat of his breath only intensified his every motion.

Grabbing tightly to his hair, I held him in place, pushing against him as I hit my limit. My world exploded and I fell back onto the bed in a satisfied little puddle. Instead of letting me go, he held me tighter, but slowed down to lick me clean in a new sweet assault.

Reaching back, I grabbed handfuls of the pillow and pulled it out from behind my head so I could scream into it. My mate didn't know the meaning of the word mercy. The soft gentle licks had turned back to twists and twirls of torment, he plunged his tongue inside me and there was no stopping.

He didn't even stop to tease me about the pillow, instead, he sped up, and his tongue took complete control of twisting inside me while his fingers went to my clit and he rubbed it in a quick hard circle.

The fireworks popped before my eyes. How could I stand this? I wanted to pull away and run into the bathroom, but I also wanted to hold my thighs apart and let him have full access. The razor edge between pleasure and overstimulation was too much for me to endure.

Why didn't I stop him the first time? I didn't have any strength left in me now, and the urge to stop him quickly faded. I'd never felt like this before, no other sensation that existed could rival this.

Pride and satisfaction seeped through the bond, and I could imagine the man smirking against me. Instead of being upset at him for being so smug about making me lose my mind, I decided to spread my legs to let him torment me in more of this blissful sweet way.

Maybe I loved being tortured too.

Why wouldn't he let me return the favor? I wanted to watch his eyes roll into the back of his head. Just a crumb of all the pleasure he was forcing me to endure. Then again, I could understand his hesitation, but now that his physical injuries were healed, I wanted to help him erase the scars left on his soul.

It wasn't fair that I was the only one lost in this sea of bliss.

His tongue delved deeper than ever before and I gasped as he sucked on my clit at the same time. How could he even reach both at once? In seconds he had driven me right to the brink again. "Bedo," I gasped. I tried to slam my thighs shut. It was too much, I couldn't take anymore.

He chuckled, and pulled his tongue out to flick it over my sensitive little clit in a rapid assault. I screamed into my pillow again as all my control dissolved away.

He chuckled, but he didn't stop. Instead, his tongue circled around my clit and he pushed two fingers inside, scissoring them to drive me right off the point of no return, again. How many more of these would I be forced to endure? My pulse sped up and my eyes rolled once more, until my vision was nothing but a patchwork of white and sparkles.

My mate was a master at this.

All too soon I screamed as I couldn't take anymore. I gasped, and the delicious tingles consumed me. He licked me again and I shrieked, and bodily pulled him off by a handful of his pretty new hair. I glared at him as I panted and squeezed his cheeks with my thighs. "No more," I snarled.

"Okay, I give," he conceded, kissing each of my thighs gently and backing away. "Did you find heaven?" His question was accompanied by a lazy mocking smile, and I wished I could throw something at his head. He licked my juices off his lips, and then sucked what was left off his fingers. He moaned the entire time, letting his tongue slide between his fingers as he gathered every last drop.

When he was done he gave me a wink.

"I wish you'd let me take care of you," I complained.

"Later, kitten," he promised as he crawled back up the bed and pulled me into his arms, snugly against his chest. "In time, just not tonight. I ... can't." He took a shaky breath, and his lips trembled as his smile threatened to vanish.

Not on my watch. I wrapped my arms around him and hugged him tightly. "We're going to be okay, Bedo. No matter how much time it takes, I'm here for you, and even if you never get to that point, I won't ever force you. We've got all the time in the world."

It wasn't like I hadn't just given myself a serious case of blue clit, but I would keep true to my word.

"That's just me though, I know that later Lewis is going to want to have some special time with Barb. He's been giddy ever since you marked us. If I didn't know any better I'd say he was the kitten that ingested catnip."

I snorted. Was my wolf really going to get lucky with my mate before me? That would be my luck.

A knock on the apartment door stole our attention. I tensed. "I should get that. It might be Mika. We're supposed to go over our plan for tomorrow."

Albedo grabbed the sheets on the bed and pulled them up and over me so I wasn't exposed. He grabbed his pants and thrust his feet back in. "No, I'll get it. You stay here. You're the one that needs to be protected. If it's her I'll let her in, but if its anyone else, I'll handle it." He smirked. "I am an Alpha, even if you choose to keep forgetting that."

Show off. I nodded and adjusted myself to be more comfortable in the bed. I relaxed against the pillow. The whole room smelled like me. My face burned at the implications.

Instead of Mika's voice, I heard the rest of the Gods. Dread hit my stomach, twisting it into a series of knots. Of course I was going to tell them, but I hadn't expected to deal with them so soon. They were already aware of what happened, there was no doubt about that, and I figured that's exactly why they were here.

"No, you can't come in yet," Albedo argued. "I don't care if this is your place, Julian. She needs her privacy right now."

"Damn it, Albedo. I already know what you two did."

"Oh? I'm sure you don't have any fucking idea what we just did, Julian."

"Will you two stop it?" Elijah requested. "You're going to upset her."

"What, do I have to deal with you too?" Albedo groaned. "Whatever, fine. You can come in, but she's not ready to receive visitors."

These guys. I climbed out of bed and grabbed Albedo's shirt. It didn't travel quite as far down my thighs as Julian's shirt had, but at least I was well covered. I ran a hand through my hair and fluffed it up before I steeled myself and cracked the door open.

The arguing fell silent as I slipped out to join the group. Albedo broke away from the others first, taking a position between me and the rest. "Happy now?" he huffed.

"It's fine," I promised. I put a hand on his shoulder and he relaxed beneath my touch before nodding.

Julian's eyes glittered like hard sapphires. The highlights were gone from his hair, the red streaks were just completely gone, and his eyes were back to dark blue. Had something happened to his contacts?

"You guys knew we were cementing our mating bond," Albedo scolded. "Did you really have to interrupt us?" He shrugged. "Besides, you already know of her little plan to go toe to toe with my dad, but did you know she was planning to do it solo?" He turned a hard look on me, and I winced.

Maybe I had been wrong about him accepting my plan after all.

CHAPTER 34

PREPARING FOR WAR

STERLING

"Kitty, that's too dangerous," I growled. If Elijah was at her side I'd be far more reassured, or I'd even settle for Julian. But her facing that asshole by herself? "We saw what he did to Albedo, there's no way we can approve of that. He can't be trusted."

She opened and closed her mouth, desperate to argue, but unable to from the circle of glares.

"I didn't say that I did trust him," she grumbled.

She shifted closer, and that sweet scent of hers filled the room. Her scent mingled with that of Albedo's, but not in the sexual way I'd have imagined. Rust grumbled, but I didn't let him have control.

"I'll do whatever it takes to stop him, and Inu," she explained. "He'll trust me, and I'll make sure that the trap springs on him. That demon will never hurt anyone else. And with this proof, we can get multiple people involved, instead of just a bunch of college kids."

"You really think those pompous assholes are going to help?" Elijah questioned. He rested his hip against the counter and his eyes were dark, almost black, with his simmering rage. I didn't have to be connected to him to feel it. It was radiating off of him like a beacon.

Lee tensed. Not that I was surprised. She probably had only been exposed to pissed-off Elijah a couple of times before, and the last time the fucker had pushed things too far. I still owed him for that.

"What other choice do I have? We have to put an end to it, not just for me and you all, but for the future. I refuse to believe everyone will turn a blind eye to this. There's no way everyone is so callous and power obsessed."

Oh, if only she knew the depths of our world. Or rather the shallowness of it. The only decent adult I knew, was Mika. Many of the rest were too busy being obsessed with power and control to care about the fates that went to Silverton.

But I wasn't about to tell her and break her heart.

"Damn it, Lee," Julian growled. He stalked toward her, and I joined Albedo's side in forming a barrier between them. He leaned to the side to make eye contact. "Even if all of that is true, which I know those shitty people, they won't give a flying fuck, that still doesn't explain why you have to be alone!"

"Calm down!" I snapped back. Lee was shaking, but she didn't cower. She stared steadily at the twins like they hadn't just both jumped down her throat. "Yelling at her isn't going to change anything. I'm not happy about her plan either, but we can do better than scream at each other."

Lee crossed her arms over her chest and raised her chin to stare at them. "I'm not backing down on this. Even if they don't listen, I'll know that I've done all I could to change this, and if it doesn't work, I'm not going to stop looking for an answer. There are other universities out there under the same umbrella that Silverton is. You can't tell me that all of them have just as twisted assholes operating them."

"What are you going to do about Inu?" Elijah pressed. "He's not like the Dean. He's not someone that can be easily taken out of power, and in case you weren't paying attention, he was able to freely use magic."

"Talk to him," Lee replied. "We know that the Dean is a lost cause. He's a cruel bastard that gets pleasure from others' pain. Inu at least was willing to talk with us. If I can have a one-on-one with him, maybe we can find a solution that works for everyone. He's got his own plans, but until we know what those are, and his intentions, we're working in the dark."

Elijah and Julian both mirrored her body position as they loomed over her. "There's no fucking way," Julian protested.

"We are not letting you be alone with that man," Elijah added. "You should stay here in this apartment until we figure things out and stay out of danger. Julian and I can handle Marcus."

"Who?" Lee's brows scrunched.

"My father," Albedo mumbled, glancing away. He shook his head. "He doesn't play fair, even if you two fought against him, he'd find a way to get an upper hand. He's dabbled in a lot of messed up things over the years, and has access to products that make you go weak with one sniff."

Lee hugged herself. "What do you mean sniff?"

"They're potions?" Albedo guessed. "I don't know where he gets them from, and it's not like he uses them a lot. Just on me, as far as I know. But he's got a collection." He shuddered.

"What makes you think you can just waltz into his office and him not know what you're up to?" Julian stressed. "What possible reason could you have to join his side and go against us?"

"My family," she answered simply. "He knows exactly why I'm in this school, and what I'd sacrifice to save them. He's counting on me being in that situation so he can retain control over me. I can make him believe me."

"I still don't like this," Albedo objected.

Julian nodded. "In any case, we're taking you to school and staying at your side before and after this little meeting of yours. You can't stop us, Lee."

Fuck. Why did I have to think of things like they were video game missions all the time? Still, whatever I could to do improve her chances of success, and keep her safe, I would do. This was just an annoying as hell stealth mission, that's all. "I... have an idea. I really fucking hate it, but it'll lower his guard."

Albedo tipped his head back, scanning me. It was hard to take him seriously with the new bright streaks of his. He had no shame for what he'd pulled. No, that wasn't important right now. We'd deal with that topic later, when we got some time to hang out on our own.

I pointed at Julian. "His little pet play kink."

"Hey!" Julian protested.

"You know how he likes her to wear that collar, and treat her like a dog kind of shit? She can go to the Dean and report it again. He, of course, ignored her the first time because of our status, but now that there are cracks in that, it gives her an excuse."

Lee scowled. "I just managed to get away from all that. Why do you think I'd ever put it back on?"

"Why, to hide your marks, Kitty," I replied smoothly.

"What marks?" Julian grumbled, he eyed her closer, and she took a step back from him. "I don't see anything."

I waved my hand. "Oh, I don't know about the rest of you. But I'm not letting her leave this room tonight without claiming her. I've waited way too long."

She held up a hand to cover her neck, and glanced away from me. All that mattered was she didn't say no. Julian and Elijah turned twin death glares on me. I expected Julian, but Elijah's took me by surprise. What had gotten into him, and when did he start copying his brother? Those two could barely stand each other for years.

Lee shook her head. "No. I'm not being marked by anyone else tonight. Albedo is my mate, and we've claimed each other, but I'll be the one who decides when I make that kind of bond with the rest of you." She paused. "But, I have decided that as long as you'll have me, I do want it," she mumbled the words fast, so we could barely catch them.

"Even Julian?" I found myself asking.

"Maybe," she agreed with a soft chuckle. "But in any case, it's been a long day already. I know the sun hasn't even set yet, but I'm going to bed early. You can wake me up for dinner, or don't. Tomorrow I'm going to need all the strength I've got, but I promise the Dean will believe every word I say."

"Fine," Julian agreed. "But we're all staying here to keep you safe. This is my apartment after all."

She raised a brow. "You're not kicking everyone out and trying to throw a tantrum to get your way?"

He scoffed. "Woman, you've already agreed to belong to us. And if I have to share with anyone, at least it is these guys. It'll be a tight fit, but we can all share the bed. That way no one gets farther ahead than the rest."

Julian was willing to share, and even more so, Julian was letting us all stay?

Maybe that asshole friend of mine had finally found someone to move his cold heart. I couldn't be too surprised though, my Kitty was truly that special.

"You're not all sleeping with me," Lee protested.

"We're just sleeping by you, like Elijah and I did, promise," Julian interrupted. "Tomorrow we do this secret mission. Albedo and Sterling will stay here and treat it like a command center. For now, it's off the Dean's radar."

Well, it looked like I'd be having that little talk with Albedo sooner than I'd imagined.

Lee rolled her eyes. "Fine. I'm tired of arguing with you. Do whatever, but I'm getting rest." She stretched and her shirt rose teasingly high, revealing her creamy thighs that were covered in kiss marks.

I just might have to strangle Albedo.

True, I knew that they were not part of my happily ever after, but I was going to get my revenge before I let that happen. After that, I'd make her the happiest woman in the world, no matter what.

First, we needed to get through the nightmare that was going to be tomorrow, and I hated the fact I had to rely on others to keep her safe. But with being expelled and a magical spell preventing me from entering, I had no choice. At least it was men I knew, and I respected their strength, but would they really have the resolve to protect her, no matter what?

"How can I trust you two?" Albedo pressed, as he eyed the twins. "Elijah, we all know how you feel about Alexandra, and Julian, you've never been serious about anything in your life. If anything happens to her, I'll kill you both."

I put my hands up. "Enough of that." Lee gave them a cold look before she retreated back to the room. Maybe she'd been too tired to even break up arguments. For some reason, it made me even angrier at Albedo.

"I've got this," Julian promised. "She's my future." He frowned, and shook his head. "No, she's all of our future, and even if we all have to die, she's going to survive this."

For once, I actually agreed with him, but I couldn't help but hope it didn't come to that. I wanted to spend the rest of my life with my Kitty, and dying wasn't on the list.

CHAPTER 35

BATTLE PLANS

LEE

The others stayed up late into the night. I could hear their chatter, but I didn't have it in me to go check on them. I was still drained from all of Albedo's earlier attention. How in the world was I going to survive if any of the others were like that?

Julian's pets crept into the room and made themselves comfy, finding spots as near me as they could get. The monkey took the pillow next to mine, and made a nest out of it while hugging a fluffy robot kitten.

I had acted bravely in front of the others, but they hadn't seen what Albedo's father was truly capable of. Though my worry wasn't for myself, but for my family. I didn't care what happened to me, but I'd lived for my family for so long, I didn't know how else to operate.

I would make this work, he would believe me, and I'd put a stop to him. The Alpha Gods would be saved, and my family would be protected. That's all that mattered.

I'm not sure when I fell asleep with my thoughts, but I did notice when the others crawled into bed. They argued over placements and through a vigorous rock, paper, scissors tournament, it was determined that Sterling got to sleep behind me, that Julian got to sleep on my other side, and that Elijah and Albedo had to sleep at the bottom.

I almost cracked an eye open to laugh at them, but kept it together.

The room was full of snores in little to no time. Julian's lips were at my ear as he nuzzled his nose in my hair. "Doggie, I promise, no matter what I'll keep you safe. I know you're asleep, or I wouldn't have the confidence to say all this. I want you to be able to count on me. Even if you end up rejecting me, I've decided to take care of you for the rest of my life." He groaned. "Damn it, if the others hear this shit they'll never let me live it down. Sleep well, Lee, and I hope you forgive me for having to be such an asshole tomorrow."

He huffed before he flopped onto his side and curled into a ball. One of the robot cats left my side to curl up against my other side so it was between the two of us. How advanced were those things?

Soon even he was asleep, and I found myself submitting to slumber at long last.

When I woke up, I found myself in a more tangled position than I had before I fell asleep. Julian had ended up on Elijah's back, mouth wide open as he snored, and his pets were all over his stomach. The robot monkey had found Elijah's hair again, and used it for his new nest.

Albedo was curled up into a sad little ball at the end of the bed, almost doubled over, like some guard dog. I could barely move without kicking or elbowing someone in the face.

"Good morning," Sterling greeted with a faint smile. He brushed the hair from my eyes. "I've always wanted to watch you wake up, Kitty."

It was strange, but I somewhat missed being tagged as scholarship all the time by him. "What are you doing up so early? Everyone stayed up late last night."

"I wanted to spend what time I could with you before all of this comes to a head. Maybe even convince you to change your mind? We could get out of here right now, just vanish and leave everyone else to sort out this mess. You don't have to be in any danger."

I had no doubt Rusty would sacrifice the entire world for me. "It's okay, Rust. I've made up my mind about this. Besides, if I just ran away this whole event would just play out again in the future. No, I have a chance to put a stop to this."

He sighed. "It's not fair, I can't resist you. You're making me put my trust in those two to protect you, and it's killing me."

I bit my lip. "Then have faith in me. You know what kind of person I am, and the sort of decisions I'll make. No matter who I have to face, I've got this. I know how to use my charisma stat," I promised with a wink.

His smile didn't reach his eyes. "Give them hell, Kitty."

Julian's deep snores came to a halt, and he groaned. He put a hand on his cat's body as he sat up and cradled it. "What time is it anyway?" He glanced my way. "Did you change your mind?"

"Not a chance," I said as I held my hand out to him. "Give me the collar and ears. I'll wear them. I'll give my best performance ever, the Dean won't doubt my story."

Julian scratched his chest and yawned before falling back to sleep. Elijah groaned beneath the weight, but continued to snore. Albedo whined and curled into a tighter ball, hugging my feet and snuggling against them. He smiled and relaxed.

And to think. Not even a week ago I'd been terrified, and prepared to fight these four. Now I was willing to help fight for them.

"That's what being mates means," Barb added. *"The Goddess blessed us with four fated mates, I still can't believe it myself. We'll keep them safe, Lee, I promise."*

I had no doubts she was capable of it, but it was hard to believe that I'd gone from not really believing in fated mates, to having four of my own.

"I've got to get ready, Sterling." I braved a smile for him. I couldn't risk showing even a crack of doubt. "Do you know where Julian put his collar? I'm sure he's got one I can use around here somewhere."

"I'll help you," Sterling offered. He slipped off his side of the bed, and helped extract me from the tangled mess of limbs. With his hand around my waist, we left the room and headed for the kitchen. He helped me perch on a stool, and wandered off.

It wouldn't be a problem convincing the Dean that I still had an issue with Julian, even after the incident with Inu. But, I didn't want to leave any doubt. In order for him to believe me completely, I had one more plan in mind.

"Here," Sterling handed over the items. "Are you sure you're going to be okay?"

"Rust, don't underestimate me. I've got this." I secured the collar around my throat and pulled out the clothes that Alexandra had left. How had she known to leave a school uniform, and why hadn't she checked in with us at all the night before? Did she have her own plan in motion?

"You're right. I'm sorry, scholarship." He ruffled my hair. "I do know better than to do that."

"You should get Julian up," I suggested. "I need him to get into a fight with me in front of the school."

"What the hell? Why would I do that?" Julian staggered into the room. His uniform was half disheveled, and he looked like he hadn't slept for a week. "I'm taking you straight to the Dean, just like last time."

"Last time we didn't give him any reason to believe we were on the same side, because we weren't. Now, we have to play our cards wisely. We're going to have a fight, you're going to call me the worst things you can think of, and then I'll report you to the Dean. Something about you not being fit as an Alpha God."

"None of that makes sense," Julian complained. "Just do it my way, doggie."

"Julian, you need to use that thing that sits on your shoulders. If I'm going to the Dean to talk about you bullying me, why would my bully accompany me straight to the door? Besides, if we pull a good enough show, he won't even suspect us."

Julian crossed his arms over his chest. "And tell me, why would I fight with you? What possible reason would make me treat you any differently than he saw me before?"

"Cindy," I replied without missing a beat. "Her and Zelda had me in that strange room with Carl, and that weird-smelling stuff. I know they took pictures." Beside me, Sterling growled. "But we can use those. You can say you saw them, and then be pissed off at me."

"Fine... But that doesn't provide a way for you to be dropped off at the university today. I was going to take you. If we're fighting as much as you claim, why would I let you in my precious car?"

"I believe that's where I come in," Elijah offered, as he too stumbled into view. The monkey was still curled up in his hair, and he'd somehow made it out of bed without disturbing it. "I'll take her, you know I won't let anything happen."

The warmth that filled his voice made me want to grab him by the collar and kiss him senseless. But no, not yet. Elijah had a ways to go before I could forgive him for everything he pulled, and I had to bring him to heel before he got any rewards.

"Here, let me help with those." Julian pushed past the others and adjusted the wolf ears on my head. "If that fucker does anything shady, get out of there. Don't let him trap you. If we have to, we'll tear the entire place down to get to you."

"Elijah, once you're done with breakfast, we'll go." I couldn't bring myself to eat. My stomach was nothing but a ball of nerves. "Albedo, Sterling, I'm counting on you two to stay here and keep this place safe. You're our backup plan in case everything falls apart."

"Wait." Julian grabbed my wrist, but his touch gentled as he tugged me to turn me around. "Hey, what I'm about to do, don't take it to heart, okay? I know you told me to do this, but damn it, I don't want to be this kind of guy to you." He ran a hand through his hair. "Please," he grunted.

When had this man been able to be so gentle? It should have been a concept foreign to him. "Julian, do whatever you have to in order to sell this. Whatever you have to throw at me, I can take it." I forced a smile. "And I won't judge you for it."

Julian sighed, and his chin hit his chest. The glitter in his eyes died. For a moment he looked tormented, and I wanted to hug him close and let him know everything was going to be okay.

No, I didn't have the time for that. What awaited me next was a grand battle, and nothing would stop me.

CHAPTER 36

POKING THE BEAR

As much as I wanted to talk to him, Elijah drove me in silence until we got to the university. My mind was racing with everything that could go wrong with my plan, far too much. But what other chance would I have, besides this, to try to get to the bottom of everything?

Elijah leaned over and paused with his arm outstretched to open my door. "Lee, are you sure about this? We can find another way." His soft voice sent tingles throughout my body. It took all my willpower not to just jump onto his lap and try to win him over.

"Positive. I know this is dangerous, Elijah. I'm not running in there blind, but it's not just my life that I'm worried about." I stared into his eyes. "I'm going to save everyone."

He sighed. "Why do that to yourself? You don't need to have the weight of everything completely on your shoulders."

"Goodbye Elijah," I answered instead. I leaned past him and opened my door, slipping from the car and heading for the dining room. It was time to head to war.

"Goodbye, Lee," he whispered behind me.

I strode through the campus for only a few minutes before Elijah caught up to me. I raised a brow. "We just said goodbye, you're going to ruin everything if you're here."

"I can't do it. There's no way I can let you do this alone."

The stone statues that were scattered throughout held a new meaning to me now. Instead of being a legacy left behind by the former Alpha Gods, they were more like tombstones.

It gave poor Max's fate a new spin. It was childish to believe that the former Alpha Gods could be saved, but somehow, deep inside, I couldn't squash the hope.

I reached out to touch the nearest statue.

"Filthy fucking mutt," sneered a nearby all-too-familiar voice.

Of course it would be those two. Then again, for once I could make use of them and their endless hatred. I turned to eye the two. "How can I help you girls?" I questioned.

Cindy scowled and Zelda cocked her head to the side, sniffing the air. "Wait," she ordered her friend. She took a step closer and kept sniffing the air. Her eyes darkened. "Slut," she sneered. "You really cheated on your fated mate with my man?"

Her eyes glowed, as her wolf threatened to take control and fight me. Elijah stayed to the side at least, a fact I was grateful for. He kept his focus on the women, prepared to intercede if need be. Not that I needed him to stop my fight. I'd put these women in their place once, I was more than capable of doing it again if needed.

Slowly, I twisted my wrist around to show her the mark left on it. Zelda trembled like I'd struck her. "I spent time with my mate," I corrected. "Not that Albedo is any of your business anymore, Zelda."

Her face turned brick red, and her breathing got heavy. The cute little pink leather clutch she held in her hands was shredded as her claws slipped out. "You tricked him," she snarled. With a wild cry, she chucked her purse at my head.

The purse flew through the air for two feet before thumping on the ground, several feet away from me. She seriously was pathetic. I'd worked my ass off to get into this hell hole, and had the skills to prove it. "Lewis marked me, and last night I marked him. He's mine, you missed out."

"No!" Zelda howled. Her eyes turned pure gold, and she snarled. "I'll never accept it! I'll make him reject you, bitch! Albedo is mine! He's been promised to me since I was a child!"

Elijah shifted his weight back and forth, keeping his eye on both women. They didn't even register him being there, they were far too invested in watching me.

"You're coming with me," Zelda growled. "It's time you have a talk with the Dean. He's going to set you straight about who does, or doesn't, belong to you."

She was going to waltz me right into the office? Maybe I wouldn't need Julian and that other plan after all. I smirked, and gave her a mock bow. "Lead the way, dear classmate." She reached for me, claws still exposed.

I stepped out of reach, and she bared her teeth. "The Dean isn't going to let you get away with this, bitch. But first, I'll tear you apart myself and give him the remnants."

"Get moving you filthy mutt," Cindy sniffed. "Be sure you don't touch her, Zelda, who knows what kind of diseases you'll pick up."

"Are you saying Albedo has diseases?" I asked innocently. "That's really mean to say, isn't it?"

Streaks of red blossomed on Zelda's face. Her cheeks puffed as she struggled to contain her rage.

Cindy scowled at me and put a hand on Zelda's back, gently rubbing it. "Don't get cocky, mutt. You haven't won this, and you're still going to waltz your slutty ass to the Dean."

I yawned. "Is that the only insult you can come up with? I thought Julian had that one covered?"

"Don't you even say his name, you bitch. You pretended to hate the Alpha Gods, and yet you've gone after each one like a desperate little whore. I can't say I'm that shocked you grabbed the lowest-hanging fruit. That guy was desperate, so pathetic. The rest won't fall for your little bullshit games, Lee. They're smarter than that."

Zelda whirled on Cindy, and the other woman was forced to jump back as Zelda clawed at the spot where the other had stood. Every breath in made her shake. "How dare you," she snarled. "My Albedo isn't low-hanging fruit!"

Cindy rolled her eyes. "Seriously, Zel? Everyone knows he's the king of desperation. Think about all the problems you had with him before. Are you really trying to fight me over that scum bag? He doesn't deserve to be an Alpha God, period."

Raw fury licked at my insides. However, I held back. It looked like Zelda was doing more than enough to protect her former fiance's honor. "I'm tired of you thinking you're better than everyone else, Cindy. Don't forget, your precious little Julian is on this bitch's side as well."

I hated how these two slandered my mates, but for now, I would endure it. I needed this friction to sell this entire scheme. "If you were expecting me to snap and attack you, I fear you're going to be disappointed. I'm not getting thrown out of this school for the likes of either of you."

Cindy snorted and tossed her hair. "What? You think I'm that pathetic, and I would need to stoop to a pathetic ploy to be able to take care of a peon like you? What a desperate little mutt. All you've done is find the one man in this school who was horny enough to settle for whoever landed in his lap. Zelda is far too classy to mess around before marriage. You were merely a cock warmer. There's no doubt that he'll return to who he's supposed to be with. You're like the flavor of the week, Lee."

"Weren't you going to march me to the Dean's office?" I asked the two, trying to get them back on track. I turned away. "If that's it, I'm going to head to classes."

I froze, and Barb growled.

Standing in front of me, Rue and Carl stood side by side. Carl smirked as soon as he saw me while Rue put a hand on his arm, and prevented him from coming closer.

"Mate faker," Barb snarled. She desperately wanted to take control and make the man pay.

Elijah joined my side, now that the little issue with the women was over. "Don't worry," he whispered. "I'm here."

"Elijah, I've got this," I told him instead. But instead of listening to me, he took my hand in his, and any resistance I had against him dissolved away.

"You've always been too nice," Cindy scolded. "You shouldn't touch something like that, you'll get a disease."

"Lee," Carl snarled, striding toward me. "You are the mate of an Alpha God, why are you causing a scene in front of the school? My mate needs to be better behaved and come to heel."

Elijah's eyes flashed gold, and I gave him a warning glare. I could handle this. "I'm not your mate, Carl. I thought Alpha Gods were supposed to be smart, as one of the conditions for the position. Haven't you been able to tell there's nothing between us?"

Elijah, thankfully, stayed put. If Carl believed me, maybe I could finally take one enemy off my list. Then I'd just have to handle the two bitch slimes, and the boss monster.

CHAPTER 37

ABOUT TO BREAK

JULIAN

While getting prepared for the day in the bathroom, I stared at myself in the mirror. For so long I'd tried to avoid looking like my twin. He was the perfect one, and I was just the fuck up. Now because of Lee I had put all of that behind me.

I wanted to be the perfect one for her.

Right now, she needed my help. I had to pull this off to help her succeed. Normally, I wouldn't have given a damn if my actions helped someone, or not. If it failed oh well, it didn't effect me.

But this?

Even if this didn't work and everything fell apart, I was going to protect her.

I grabbed a brush and studied my raven hair. I missed my old look. In some strange way it had been like battle armor. I grabbed a tub of the temporary dye I kept at my place, and worked it through my hair until the wild red streaks had returned.

If something happened to her before I got there, and Elijah let me down, I was going to kidnap his precious Alexandra and ship her off to another country. She was too good of a friend for me to hurt, but I could still make sure that Elijah never got to see her again, if he forced me to it.

Damn it. Why was it so hard to focus? I slapped my cheeks hard enough to leave red hand prints. Right now, all that mattered was I focus. It was time for me to be the big bad wolf and sell this fake little scene.

It was almost enough to make me laugh. I'd been the type of person that delighted in torturing others, breaking them had given me a little high. And now? I wanted to be Lee's champion, and I regretted my past. How could she change me like this?

Oni chuckled, but didn't engage. Whatever he found amusing he wasn't willing to share. The bastard was probably sitting back and judging me again.

Giving my hair a final ruffle, I left the bathroom and made my way to the front door. I needed to hurry if I was going to go play my part.

"Julian, we're counting on you," Sterling calmly informed me the moment I entered the kitchen.

"Don't fuck it up," Albedo added. "If anything happens to my mate..."

He didn't have to continue for me to understand what he was trying to say. "Albedo, if that bastard tries anything, I'm gonna rip his heart out."

Albedo smirked and nodded. "Thanks."

"Good luck," Sterling added.

It's not that I needed it, but I accepted it with a nod and strode toward the door. Enough putting it off, it was show time.

The car ride to campus was well beyond the speed limit, but any cops that saw me fly by, were already familiar with the make and model of my car and they knew better than to snag me.

My car screeched, as I swung into my parking spot before scrambling out and I strode across the campus. It didn't take me long to find her; she was in the middle of an argument with Cindy and Zelda, and that asshole Carl.

Oni snarled. My wolf was ready to rip everyone between us, and our mate, apart. My fist clenched, as Zelda and Cindy took turns berating her. This was far harder than I thought it would be.

"Seriously, Lee?" Carl said with a huff. "I'm not sure what you're trying to pull, but I know you're my mate and I refuse to let you act like this in public anymore. I guess that Julian guy was right in collaring you and forcing you to behave."

The bastard reached for her, and useless Elijah stood to the side, watching and clenching his fist but not interfering. What the fuck was up with him?

"Don't you dare touch me!" Lee stepped back and out of his reach. "I don't know why you're so dense you can't figure it out. We're not mates, we never were mates, and I'd die before I let you so much as touch me."

"You bitch. How dare you try to humiliate me at my school. I'm going to have to teach you a serious lesson. The collar won't be enough, I'll tie you up and beat you with a belt if I have to. I know what I felt."

"You stubborn asshole!" Lee growled, then grabbed his wrist, staring at him deadpan. "No sparks, nothing."

Carl frowned. "What are you trying to do?"

"Prove that you mean nothing to me," Lee replied with a shrug. "It's not like when I touch Albedo and I feel like there are firecrackers going off under my skin. You're more like a cold fish. I could never be with you."

Cindy spotted me and her face lit up. "Julian!" she called, with a little hop, waving her hand in the air.

Never had I wanted to toss her in a vat filled with piranhas, more than I did at that moment.

Oni wanted nothing more than to take control and rip Carl apart. The wound he gave us was all but healed, but the spot burned with an intense inner heat, reminding me that I owed this fucker.

Lee spotted me and her features hardened. "Oh great, the king of the assholes has shown up. Leave me alone, Alpha God," she mocked. "In fact, it would be great if all of you could. I'm so tired of your shit. You want me to go to the Dean so much? Sure, let's go, I'll report all of you."

"Watch it filthy slut," Zelda snarled. "You're not going to get the warm welcome you're expecting."

Lee pushed past them and headed toward the Dean's office.

I knew the plan, and understood what she wanted from me, however, I didn't want to carry it out anymore. Watching her march down the hall, in that angry stride of hers, made my heart ache.

Cindy wrapped her hands around my shoulder and rubbed her cheek against it, like she was some damned cat. "What a bitch," she sneered. "I'm glad to see you've come to your senses, Julian. You had me worried."

My smile felt like that of a serial killer. I wrapped an arm around Cindy's shoulder, and hated myself for it, as we strode after Lee. "You better keep walking, bitch," I called after her.

Lee whirled around and gave me a double middle-fingered salute. "Fuck off," she called. "The Dean is going to listen to me this time."

"Come on, Julian. Just ignore her. She can talk to him until she's blue in the face, but there's no way that he'll ever betray Zel. He knows what's best for his future."

"Yeah, you're right," I grunted.

Cindy grinned and brushed a kiss against my chest. My skin crawled. "I'm so glad to see you've returned to your senses. I'm sorry that bitch ever fooled you for a second. I don't blame you, I blame her. She got her claws into Albedo, I feel so bad for Zelda. Can you imagine what it feels like to see her future mate's mark on another woman? That slut stole her happily ever after right from under Zel's feet!"

I held my tongue. Until I could calm down, if I dared to speak, I'd put all of these people back in their places when it concerned Lee. Besides, in order for this plan of hers to be truly believed, I still had some more scenes to endure.

"Hey," I greeted Carl with a nod.

He glared. His anger seeped through our Alpha God bond, pathetically attempting to engulf me. This disgrace of a wolf couldn't even build a mental wall to try to damper some of his emotions? Both he and Rue were easy to read, far too easy.

"What do you want, Julian?"

"Calm down, Carl," Rue requested. His eyes weren't on his companion though, but rather on Lee's fleeing back. The man was pale, but if he truly cared about her, he should have been in a fight with Carl, not trying to calm the man down. He really was a pathetic white knight.

"Wow, Carl, you're a total saint to have to deal with that shitty mate. I'm sorry you got saddled with a mutt. If you need help putting her in her place, let me know. I can help break her down."

A couple sentences was all it took for his suspicion to melt away, and be replaced with awe. "Thanks, man! I really appreciate that. Sorry about the whole shoulder thing last time around. I snapped and didn't try talking to you. But don't worry, I've got a plan to break her. I've just got to get hold of her while she's asleep, and all these little spats will be a thing of the past. I've got it all planned out."

My unspeakable rage ratcheted up another notch. Throwing this asshole in a volcano wouldn't be enough to appease the monster in me. Because I was a master at hiding my emotions, neither had a clue of my true thoughts. "Oh?" I asked, with a casual glance his way. "Going to hypnotize her?"

"Nah, nothing like that. But," he dropped his voice and leaned close. "The Dean is incredible. He gave me these sticks of incense and told me that as long as these are burning around Lee, she'll remember she's my mate. Apparently, Cindy and Zelda used these last time, but they used like a quarter of a stick. This time, I'm going to make sure there are multiple burning so she falls back into her place. It's a little risky, but worth it considering how she's embarrassing me now that I'm an Alpha God."

A generic Alpha God, he was beyond pathetic. Bile built in my throat. Even though it was part of the plan to ferret all this information, I couldn't help the wave of nausea rushing me. This fucker could never be a real Alpha God. "Just remember once you've got her, humiliation will work wonders on her. You can get a lot if you push her the right way."

Carl laughed as if I had told a damned joke. It reminded me of a weasel, with a ball stuck down its throat. He slapped me on the back. "That's what I love about being an Alpha God. You always have the best ideas. Rest assured, I'm not going to let your legacy down. The incense is only the first step, after I remind her where she belongs, I'm going to punish her in front of the entire school. I've got a great collar to slip around her neck, one that has a little bite to it. I showed it to you before. I can't wait to hear her cries, and watch her dance when I push that little button."

Fuck.

How was I supposed to just let that slide? I needed to teach his ass a lesson, and I needed to do it now. Being tied to the peak of the school wouldn't even start to be close enough. No, I was going to strap him to the wall outside my apartment building, where one wrong move would be a messy death.

He deserved no less.

"You're going to have to rethink your plans," seethed a familiar voice from behind.

"Oh yeah? You going to stop me?" Carl mocked.

My normally mild-mannered brother punched Carl with a cross punch, and stood over his body as he went down. "I've had enough of your shit, all of you," he included me in his glare. If I didn't know better, I'd think he really was that pissed.

"You hit him!" Cindy shrieked. She hugged my arm tightly, like she was going to dislocate the damned thing.

"No matter if you fucks are Alpha Gods or not, I'm letting all of you know, Lee is under my protection and none of you are going to lay a finger on her." He strode over to me, and poked me in the chest, driving me several steps back. I was only half-faking by this point. "And Julian, that goes double for you. Enough of your shit, or I'll show you why I'm the stronger brother."

CHAPTER 38

INTOXICATING NIGHTMARE

LEE

I marched into the Dean's office, slamming the door behind me. I was shaking, and it wasn't from acting. I'd put up with a lot worse by this point, but the mean comments today were digging into my soul.

Julian being hateful was nothing new. But seeing Cindy rub all over him like a desperate dog in heat was driving me crazy. It lit an irrational fire inside. I stuffed my hands in my pockets and stared up at the ceiling, as I struggled to control my racing heart.

My hand brushed my phone, I fished it out, and flipped the recording software on. I would get the bastard's words on tape, and nothing would stop me.

The secretary stared at me cooly from her chair. "Dear, can I help you?" she questioned with a raised brow and a wrinkled nose.

"I'm here to see the Dean," I calmly replied.

The fake smile melted from her lips. "He's not seeing any students today. There have been some family troubles, and he's taken the time off."

"Don't worry, he'll agree to see me," I pushed. He would probably think that I had come to admit defeat. Without his supposed help I was powerless against the Alpha Gods, and after seeing what he was able to do to half of their numbers it made sense I was trying to reach him.

He had no idea that I knew of his sins, and that I'd make him pay.

The secretary's cheeks puffed out and she leaned forward. Her curly hairdo bobbed with the movement. "He most certainly will not. I don't know why you think you're so special, but you're going to have to come back another day young lady."

I took a seat across from her. "Push the button, tell him Lee is here. I promise he'll let me in. It's likely he's waiting for me anyway. He knows who I am."

The older woman sighed and took off her half-moon glasses, setting them to the side and rubbing her forehead. "Listen you little shit. I'm tired of dealing with the likes of you. Students come parading in here thinking they're too important to listen and follow the rules. You could be an Alpha God today and the Dean would still refuse to see you."

"Then it should be easy to prove. Just tell him I'm here," I pressured.

Her eyes flashed gold as her wolf peered out. "Listen bitch, get up off my chair, take your scrawny ass out of this office, and get out of my sight before I eat you for dinner. Come back another day when he's willing to see you. If you continue to challenge me like this, I'll be sure the Dean labels you as a troublemaker and will personally see to you getting expelled from this university. Obviously, you don't belong."

"That's an awful lot of words for you to say, you just don't want to do your job." I got to my feet and wandered near the door. "I'll be back," I promised.

She huffed and turned to reach for her glasses. I slipped outside, but used the toe of my foot to prevent it from shutting completely. I sat there in the hallway, and waited, listening intently to what was going on in the room.

"Seriously, what an outrageous student. Such riff-raff! In my day something like that would never be allowed in these sacred halls. We had standards. Only purebloods were allowed in Silverton, and that's when the school was at its best. I swear if I was Dean I would solve so many of our problems."

Why did it not surprise me? I let her rant and rave, and waited. In time she returned to her work and the clicks from the keyboard filled the room, speeding up as she lost herself in her task.

I took a deep breath and pushed the door open before racing for the back office.

She screeched like a faulty smoke alarm and lunged across her desk trying to grab me, instead of doing the smart thing and going around the obstacle. "You can't!" she shrieked.

I shoved the door open and almost fell over, as I threw myself into the Dean's office. I nearly tripped over a student just outside his door, with his head in his hands. I couldn't make out who it was, and I didn't have time. "Sorry," I mumbled before slamming his door shut behind me. The faint fragrance of orange lilies drifted through the room.

The Dean looked, up and his eyes narrowed. "Why Ms. Suga, you've decided to grace me with your presence again. Tell me, what is it this time?"

I huffed, throwing my shoulders back. "I'm here to demand you do your job, Dean. I've been threatened more times than I can count, and the Alpha Gods will not stop harassing me. I saw what you were capable of when you expelled two of them, you can't sit there and tell me you don't have the power to put a stop to this."

His shoulders shook as he laughed dryly at me. "Pathetic, Ms. Suga. Do you recall what happened in our previous encounter? Those so-called bullies of yours were falling all over themselves to protect you. What kind of fool would believe that in this short amount of time that they had turned on you again?"

"Protecting me? They were kidnapping me! Do you really think I want anything to do with those assholes? You remember what they did to me in the cafeteria, in front of everyone!" I pulled at the collar around my throat. "Do you think I'm wearing this because I want to? It's all part of their sick little fantasy. Just expel the last two like you did before. None of the former Alpha Gods deserved their position."

"Ms. Suga, to think you would just throw yourself into my office like this, and on today of all days. I don't know what little scheme you think you're passing here, but I did want to see you today. Though, I am more assured now, than ever, that you were never right for this school. No one with actual intelligence would have put themselves at risk by meeting with me personally."

There was something sinister in the way he spoke. It wasn't as if he was trying to just lord his power over me, rather it was like a snake that had cornered a rat, and was taunting it before it went for the kill. There was something this man had planned that I hadn't accounted for.

"If you refuse to do anything about this bullying situation, I'm going to go to Inu. I'm sure when he founded this school he didn't plan for it to be a hellhole like it is."

"Ms. Suga, please sit down. It's time that you and I had a little talk. You've forgotten some important pieces of leverage I have."

I hadn't forgotten, but two of us could play this blackmail game. Though I was doing an awful job of actually harvesting any information from this asshole that I could use.

"I insist you sit down," the Dean added, waving a hand at the chair.

Something about his voice forced me to obey. My head felt heavy, and my limbs were unresponsive. I plopped down in the seat, my head hanging. "Keep them away from me," I wheezed. Every word was a challenge to produce. "Since I'm sitting, will you stop them?"

He grinned at me and rubbed his hands together. "Good girl," he praised. It made a wave of disgust wash over me. He leaned over his desk and pushed the intercom button. "May dear, please be a doll and send in my guest. I've kept Ms. Suga waiting long enough for my little surprise."

Damn it. What was he planning now? I steeled myself, prepared to fight whatever I had to. Even if I had to go one-on-one with him, I wouldn't let him win. He needed to start blabbing, so I had proof of his rottenness.

"Are you just going to act like our last encounter never happened?" I sneered. "All your rotten plans."

He smirked, and the door creaked open. An occupant hobbled into the room, and it took only a second for me to recognize him.

"No," I whimpered. My worst nightmare had come to life.

The Dean continued to grin. He got up from his seat and helped my brother take a spot beside me. "No? Is that any way to greet our newest student, Ms. Suga? I've managed to pull some strings and talk to the Founder of the school. This year we'll have not just one scholarship student, but two. He's already passed all the intellect-type tests, and as for physical, we're bypassing those due to his medical conditions. We're even setting him up in your previous room. It's almost like he's taking your place." He clapped King on the shoulder and laughed as if he'd told some great joke.

The Dean met my eyes and his intent was clear. I'd never had the upper hand on this man, and even if I could have gotten him to spill even one word, none of it would matter. The only way I was going to escape the hell that waited for me was if I was willing to thrust King into it.

My hand slipped into my pocket and I turned off my phone. The Dean had outplayed me this time, but it would be the last. No matter if it cost me my life, I would make sure I was the last sacrifice in this school. My mates would hate it, but I'd be relying on them at the end to save King from the Dean's maniacal plans.

CHAPTER 39

SECRET DEAL

"KING," I GREETED. My voice was thick and I blinked away the forming tears. I couldn't break down in front of him.

He grinned in response, not even noticing my distress. His usual happy smile was at full strength and I'd never seen him look so healthy before. I suppose that made sense, they would need a healthy sacrifice, not one on its deathbed.

"Sis!" He greeted as he stood up, and flung his arms out to the sides. "I've got a uniform and everything! I'm a Silverton!"

I glanced above him and into the smirking expression of the Dean. No wonder he'd been so confident from the moment I'd barged in. He'd already laid his trap. One day this evil monster would be torn apart limb by limb, and if not by me, by the mates I left behind. I'd never rest until he came to justice for putting my baby brother in danger.

"Wow, King. I'm shocked you managed to enroll here already. I thought you were a few years off from being able to get into college."

"Nonsense," the Dean remarked with a little shake of his head. He turned and adjusted a little warmer on a shelf behind his desk. The emerald elephant's eyes turned gold, and the scent in the room intensified. "Poor King here has missed a lot of school, but after extensive testing, we are more certain than ever that this is exactly where he belongs. You'll have to watch out, he might take your spot."

King grinned, pride shining through his features. He was eating up all this attention the Dean was lavishing him with. The boy had no idea how much of my life he'd just ruined. Even I wasn't sure of the extent of the damage just yet. "King, are you sure you want to go to college so early? You've just gotten better. Maybe you should stay at home with mom and dad. You can play Clevania all day."

"Oh, I think you misunderstand my plans for King here, Ms. Suga. He's not only the answer to my problems, but the answer to yours. He's a scholarship student now, but I truly believe that he is going to excel and take over the position of an Alpha God from that pesky troublemaker, Julian. You did point out he was a huge thorn in your side. I'm sure we can both appreciate King's calm nature in comparison. This fine young man will be an amazing Alpha God, I'm positive."

The Dean had won. He had to know I would do everything I could to keep King out of Silverton, and especially out of anything involving the Alpha Gods or the special scholarship position. I wanted to scream, throw that heavy warmer at his face, and burn his office down, but I couldn't do any of it. He was in too solid of a position. Instead, I gave him a strained smile.

My shoulders slumped forward, and deep inside I felt Albedo's concern through our bond. I tried to reassure him, but it was hard to focus. The Dean's face swam in front of me. "I've got another question," I mumbled.

His smile flickered. Did he know that I was aware of his sick history? His brows furrowed and his eyes flicked towards King, then back to me. "Oh? And what would that be, Ms. Suga? I'm here for all of my students."

Albedo's name burned on the tip of my tongue. If King wasn't here I would have confronted him on each and every injury he'd ever made my mate suffer through. What kind of monster could do those things to their own child?

But with King here, my priorities had to change. All I could do was protect him, and try to keep him from getting involved with this toxic mess. "Is there a way you can get me into contact with Mr. Inu? He's given me an extra credit assignment, and I'd like to let him know I've chosen to accept it. I'm well aware it will be difficult, but I'm prepared to put it all on the line for the sake of the team."

He chuckled. "Well, I'm very happy to hear that. Yes, it won't be a problem to arrange a meeting for you. I just have one request before we get to that." He glanced at King and gave him a broad smile. "Son, I have to have your sister sign some confidentiality papers. Would you mind finishing up your paperwork with Ms. May?"

"I can't stay? Aww," King complained. "Okay, see you later sis," he said as he left the room, and I was once more alone in the room with a monster.

"What is it you want?" I growled. As he raised a brow at me and gave the door a look, I sighed and repeated the sentence calmly. I hated the smirk that crawled across his lips.

"Much better. As for what I want, I need you to bind yourself in a promise. It'll make me feel less worried about your conduct, and what goes on around you, and you'll know exactly what you need to do to have a successful life at Silverton."

I scowled. This asshole. I wiped it from my face and settled for staring at him. I needed to be careful, the smallest mistake could ruin King's life. There had to be something I could still use against this monster, some crack I could use to free my brother from this mess.

But if the Dean turned up being a dead end, I would use Inu. He had more power than the Dean and if I had to side with him to keep my family safe, I'd do it. "What kind of promise?" I asked.

The Dean chuckled and turned, grabbing the glowing elephant. He placed it between us on the desk and turned it up. I whimpered, and collapsed onto my seat. "First of all, I think it's important that you show me the respect I deserve, Ms. Suga. If you continue to defy me, or if you decide to run off before the end of the Alpha Gods of this generation, I'm going to be forced to have your brother replace you."

Show him respect? My lips lifted as I tried to force a smile, but it wasn't working this time. Not after the threat to my little brother. "Keep your paws off King, you fucking monster. I know what you did to your son."

"I disciplined him," he shrugged. "Look at me in the eyes, Lee. We're on the same team, the one that will hone the Alpha Gods into the champions they're destined to be." He reached into his drawer and pulled out a golden linked bracelet with a pure pearl in the center. "Put this on, girl."

Despite my fear, I reached for it and slowly set about securing it to my wrist. The air was heavy, and it was too hard to think. "What did you do?" I whispered.

"I'm making sure you can't rebel anymore. You are under my control now, and you're going to bring that worthless brat back into my care. I've got so many punishments in mind for him, daring to stand against me." He grinned. "And if you don't, well I know how mate bonds work. I'll punish you and let him experience every second."

His silky words made my hair stand on end. Barb's voice was muffled, I couldn't make her out at all. The bracelet burned against my skin. What had he done? The white stone glowed against my skin, and a ghostly image of King was reflected inside as he strolled down the hallway.

"What is this?" I whispered. I reached out, desperate to take it off.

"Oh, I wouldn't suggest you try to take it off. You'll hurt your brother severely if you do. Now that little trinket is on you and has touched your flesh, you've become connected to him. Inside that crystal is a strand of his hair. Anytime you break a promise to me, the crystal will darken and it'll release all that negative energy straight into him. Push it too far, and you'll kill him."

I wanted to throw up. This bastard needed to be burned alive. "The Alpha Gods won't let you get away with this, Marcus," I taunted.

"It doesn't matter what they try to do. With this, your fate is sealed. Not once have I lost a scholarship student in my years working here at the university, and that's not going to start with some twisted creature like you. You'll get to visit Inu now, you should be grateful. He's in a passageway behind my office. Before you go, I'll need you to promise that you'll never breathe a word about what's beyond here to anyone else in this world, besides me. You now belong to me Ms. Suga, you are my servant, and if you fight this, I'll make sure your brother suffers."

Tears stung the corners of my eyes, and my fists clenched like useless meat lumps at my sides. Even if I shifted and threw myself at him, until I managed to get this bracelet off and free my brother, it was pointless.

Across from me, Marcus laughed, clearly enjoying my suffering. "That's what I like to see," he snarled, his eyes turning pure gold. "That defeat is the best feeling in the world. Enjoy your little chat, I'll be sure to summon you soon for some stress relief. You'll be my new stress toy since you took my last one away."

CHAPTER 40

WILLING SACRIFICE

THE DEAN PUSHED ANOTHER button hidden underneath his desk, and the office behind him rumbled as the wall slid open. The light didn't stretch far down the path, but it looked like an endless rocky hallway.

As I stared down its expanse, one by one, lights flickered on down the pathway, urging me down into the yawning darkness that awaited.

"Do be careful you don't trip. I would hate for you to get hurt before I'm able to brand you. And don't forget your promise. If you breathe a word about Inu to anyone in this school, your dear sweet little brother will be screaming in agony, and I've wired the bracelet so you'll get to hear every decibel. Have fun."

"Why are you doing this? You've already won, why make this worse?" I hissed.

The Dean made himself comfortable as he leaned back on his desk, and stretched out. "Because thanks to Albedo, I've become well accustomed to screams of pain, and how powerful they make me. Since you decided to make me expel him, you'll be my new source of power. The bracelet on your wrist is bound by you to your brother. If you try to take it off it will shock both of you, and it will drain his life by a year. The more you struggle, the more you kill him at your own hand."

"You truly are a monster... But I promise, you're not getting away with this."

"There's no one left that's strong enough to stop me, Lee," he sneered. "And after your little chat with Inu, I want you to return to my office. You'll be rejecting my son, and ridding yourself of that nasty mark. Hopefully, it kills him off."

"No," I snarled. I held my wrist close to my heart. "I won't let you take that away."

"Lee? Did you forget who has the power in this little circle of ours? Say no again, and I'll let you listen to King's screams. Is the life of one worthless ex-Alpha God really worth that?"

The tears trickled down my cheeks, and I made no move to wipe them away. I envisioned ripping him apart in several different ways, and Barb provided a dozen more. This man deserved a painful demise. "Marcus, my mate bonds are non-negotiable. You need me to be your punching bag? Fine. You want me to willingly sacrifice my life when the time comes? You've got it. I'll even be the most ideal student. But I refuse to reject my mates."

"Mates?" He frowned, measuring my words. "Why Lee, I believe you've let slip more than you meant to. Who else is your mate besides that worthless reject of a son? You'll have to tell me, and soon, or I'm afraid I'm activating the bracelet. Don't keep me waiting."

I lifted my chin and stared at the asshole in the eyes. "The original Alpha Gods are all my mates. Not that cheap knockoff group you're trying to form. All four are my mates, but in return for my loyalty and obedience, you're not allowed to touch them."

What was I doing? This was insanity, I had no business trying to negotiate when I had nothing to offer.

"Even the Julian that's supposedly been bullying you so much, you can't endure anymore? I'll admit, this possibility amuses me. Right now, you only carry the mark of one wolf, and in return, I'll spare that one. You have two days to create bonds with the others, and prove it to me, or I will consider them open game. There are many in this school who would delight in getting revenge on their former tormentors."

His words set me on edge. Why was he encouraging this? I dropped my head, unable to look him in the eye. "Done," I promised. "I'll prove what they are, and you'll keep them off your little hit list."

The Dean chuckled. "I'm looking forward to you trying. But enough chit-chat, run on down the hall. Inu is waiting for you, and he doesn't usually take visitors. You should be honored that he's agreed to meet with you."

"Thank you," I ground out before I strode down the hall. The instant I was in the hallway, the wall behind me rumbled again as the bricks rolled back into place and my only companions were the flickering shadows on the walls.

It was a straight path, with no entrances on either side. I had no choice but to go forward.

"*I don't like this,*" Barb complained. "*That man thinks he can control us? No way! Lewis is going to rip his nuts open so that man can never procreate again. Lee, we can't listen to him!*"

"*I don't have a choice, Barb. He's got control over King. As long as he has that, I'm hopeless.*"

"*He says he has control over King. What if that bracelet is all just a bluff? Are you really going to just believe him?*"

"*I can't risk it,*" I replied softly. "*I'm sorry, Barb. But until I find a way out of this, I don't have a choice. As long as our mates, and King, stay safe, it is worth it.*"

"*Lee, I will tell Lewis right now what you're planning. You cannot let that man do whatever he wants. He's a twisted monster. I will not let you throw yourself in the way of a rampaging bull. This deal is asking for trouble.*"

I sighed. It's not like I didn't understand her concerns, but it didn't matter when everything was on the line. There was not a way to save everyone, and if the Dean needed a sacrifice, I would be it.

Besides, maybe there would be some sort of solution from Inu.

"*Barb, you have to understand. No matter what, I'm going to keep everyone else safe.*"

"*I just wish you cared about yourself half as much, Lee. I'm going to pray to the Goddess that we find some way out of this, because I don't want to lose you. If it comes down to it, I want you to give me full control. I'll take all the pain for you.*"

My heart throbbed. Didn't she understand that I didn't want her hurt either? Somehow, I was going to find a way to get my revenge on this school and its monsters, even if I had to do it from beyond my own life.

CHAPTER 41

NOT ALONE

Barb lapsed into silence, and the lights down the hall from where I had come, went off one by one. It chased me down the long hallway, and not wanting to be left in the dark, I rushed further down the hall.

With each step I took, the lights down the hall behind me turned off faster. I ran, and the lights sped up, until the light in front of me turned off before I could reach it, and the lights ahead all followed suit, one after the other, until they were all snuffed out.

The darkness surrounded me, and the pitch black made it impossible for me to tell one way from another. The winds fluttered around me and I shuddered. How was there a breeze in this hallway? I hadn't seen any vents, or anything, but the endless rock walls. Was this another sort of punishment the Dean had cooked up just for me?

Was he trying to push me to the brink of insanity?

No, if the Dean was trying to kill me, he would have done it back in his office. I was still more valuable to him alive, than dead at this point. I took a breath and forced my racing heart to calm. Reaching out, I let my hand connect with the left-hand wall and I walked forward. I would eventually find my way out by this method.

"Oh? That's very sensible of you," purred a husky male voice in my ear. "I knew you were interesting."

I shuddered and whirled, prepared to fight. I fell into a combat stance and stared into the endless darkness as if I could see through it. "Who's there? I'm not some easy prey. I've been trained in various forms of combat."

A pair of crimson-red eyes opened in front of me. "Me? Why, I'm just an interested observer. It's not often I see those willing to sacrifice themselves to protect everyone else, but those that do, always intrigue me."

"Oh? Good for you," I snapped. Just because whatever this was decided to talk to me, didn't mean that I trusted it. "Going to tell me what you're trying to get from me?"

"Ah, I see you're uneasy around me. There is no need to fear. This situation you're in, with the turned-off lights, is because I wanted to have a private chat with you." He chuckled. "You are not the one I am seeking, but there's an echo of her personality in you. It was enough to get my attention."

Did this mystery creature insult me? "Whatever, just tell me who you are. I don't have time for this."

"Ah yes, names are important to many. I've had more than a few names at this point, but the one I enjoy hearing the most, currently, is Luci."

"Luci?" The instant I said his name, the air around me heated. It was like someone had cranked a thermostat up, or had locked me into a furnace. "Are you ready to tell me what you want with me? I've got an important meeting to attend, and you're in my way."

The figure took a step closer and its hand pierced through the dark to wrap around my wrist. "It's admirable that you are so aware of your surroundings, and prepared to fight, but maybe you should open your mind just a bit more. Maybe it's not what I want from you, but what I can do for you. You do seem to be in a rather dangerous situation right now."

At least it was a human-shaped hand. I stared down at it before snatching my hand back, and rubbing my wrist. "Listen, I don't care who you are, or what you are. It's obvious you're no wolf, and there's no way I'll trust you. Now, out of my way. I have an appointment to keep. Turn the lights back on."

His laughter filled the air, but it wasn't jeering, just amused. "This is the first time I've been turned down. You really are intriguing. She was right about you. Lee, this is your last opportunity. Will you accept my help, or will you continue to waltz down this path of destruction?"

A chill spread through me. I hadn't told this thing my name. I took another cautious step back. Without my eyesight, it would be a hard fight, but I was willing to do whatever it took. "How do you know my name?"

"How long has it been since I've made such a silly mistake? You truly intrigue me."

"Yeah, that's great," I grumbled. I took a step backward. I couldn't see, and running would be dangerous, but what choice did I have? This creature was dangerous.

"I really wouldn't suggest you run, Lee. You'll get hurt and I would hate for that to happen." He took a step closer and a light flickered to life above us, but it wasn't one of the lamps on the walls. Instead, it was a floating globe of light.

Now I had a better look at this dangerous monster.

Or maybe an angel? My brow furrowed. He filled the expanse of the hallway, tall, muscular, but still lean. Long silky black hair streamed down to the floor like a waterfall. They matched his feathery black wings well.

Still, all of that isn't what froze me in place. Not even those blood-red eyes that glittered like rubies made a difference. But this strange creature was the definition of perfect. Every feature reminded me of an idealized sculpture I'd seen in my art history classes, but in this man's case, they were real.

How is it I had stumbled upon someone that was even more beautiful than my precious Elijah?

His full lips parted as he smirked. "It's a pleasure to meet you, Lee," he purred. His eyes flickered as he said my name, and a strange sense of warmth raced through my limbs.

What the hell had I stumbled on down here? Couldn't this university stop trying to surprise me all the time? Just a few moments with this Luci, and I was more than confident that this little meeting had not been planned by the Dean.

"Tell me, do you know what will happen if you continue on this little adventure of yours? Because I do. I know the things that you have been through, and what your future will be if you don't stop this madness. You will be sacrificed in a war that you never signed up for, and it will be a death full of suffering."

"Yeah, I know," I answered softly. "Not the war thing, but that I'm going to be a sacrifice. Listen, Luci, it's nice you're trying to help me and all, but there's no way I can trust you. My life is already fucked up enough, I don't need whatever you are, added to the mix."

"A God," he provided with a chuckle. "The one that created this world."

"Yeah... That's even more reason for me to get out of here. You asked if I wanted your help, and I told you, not a chance." I turned and ran the other way, I wasn't sure if it was the right way or not, but I couldn't risk staying with this man another moment.

There was something strange about him that made my heart race, and I already had my hands full with the Alpha Gods.

"Lee," he called to me. "I promise you're making a mistake…"

He could talk all he wanted. This God, or whatever demon he was, had just appeared in the middle of the hallway and had tried to manipulate me to take his side. Who in their right might would just listen to that?

The lights all came back to life at once, and I was blinded by the brightness. I ended up in front of a black door with a ruby-red handle. I grabbed the door and turned it, flinging it open. I glanced back to see if Luci had followed, but the hallway was completely empty.

Had I hallucinated it all?

"Ah, Ms. Suga. I've been waiting for your visit." Inu wasn't seated at his desk when I entered, but was standing, staring at a stone figure that greeted all that entered.

Large black-painted wings spread across the expanse of the wall. But that wasn't what caught my eye. No, I found myself lost in the glow of the two priceless rubies that were the figure's eyes. Blood-red eyes, and the perfectly perfect face of the God Luci I had just run into.

I shivered as a full-body chill struck. What in the world was going on here? I collapsed in a seat in front of Inu's desk and stared at the man. If I didn't get answers soon, my brain was going to melt.

CHAPTER 42

THE SECRET OF THE STATUES

I WASTED NO TIME and pointed at the mocking eyes of the future. "Tell me, Inu, who is that?"

Inu turned from staring at it and studied me. With his mask on I couldn't get a good look into his eyes. "Before I answer you, Ms. Suga, I have a question of my own. Tell me, do you know the story of our world?"

What did that have to do with anything? "What?" I asked, unable to do anything but stare blankly.

He patted the cheek of the stone god. "Allow me to introduce you then. This creature is the one that created our world, and his name is Lucifer."

The God of our world, and he'd tried to talk to me? What could he have possibly wanted? I shivered. I had turned down a literal god. Would there be some sort of punishment for that?

"Does that make him the God of our world?" I whispered.

Inu's lip curled. "God?" he scoffed. "This creature isn't nearly so benevolent as that. The reason we have the Alpha Gods program, is in order to stand a chance against him when he inevitably turns, and tries to destroy everything he created."

"But they're only Gods in name. They don't have any powers. What could they possibly do against a real," I paused. He didn't seem to like the word God. "Creature with that kind of power?" I questioned instead.

Inu slipped his mask off, and placed it gently to the side. He looked up at me with electric blue eyes. They reminded me of lightning streaking through the sky, and it jolted me to my core. "That's because the Alpha Gods, as you know them, are not complete, yet."

Was I finally getting answers? He'd mentioned this before, them not being true Alpha Gods, but maybe this time he would go into specifics. I'd worry about Luci, and the wrinkles he brought to my world later. "If that's the case, what happened to the ones that didn't get completed? I haven't seen or heard anything about them. It's like they vanished."

Inu scowled. "Their fate is no concern of yours, Lee. You are the one that will help me mold this generation to be ones that can take on the mantle of true Alpha Gods. I'm confident at least one of them will be the answer I seek."

My head swam. I was getting answers, but none of them made any sense. Without knowing the fate of the former Alpha Gods or the scholarship students, I was lost. "Be honest with me, and I'll see what I can do to help your plan." I slipped a hand into my pocket nonchalantly and turned on the recording. If he spilled, I'd have my proof.

His lips twitched. "Ms. Suga, I think you might have misunderstood me. I'm not looking for your help, I don't need you to be willing to get what I need from you. Though, it would be easier if you agree to cooperate because it is the right thing to do."

Damn it. This wasn't going the way I wanted. "How am I supposed to help you if I don't know the consequences of failure?"

He chuckled. "You truly want to know that badly? Well, we'll get the obvious out of the way first. They were all failures, and as such, they needed to be punished."

Something about the cold way he said that gave me the chills. "And then?"

Inu strolled over to a corner of his office where a pair of stone wolves stood guard. Both were in fierce poses. "Here," he patted the top of the stone. "Every single failure has gotten to stay at Silverton in this lovely stone form."

The statues truly were tombstones.

All I wanted to do was run from the office and be violently sick, but I needed to find out more. It was finally a start to everything I needed. I fought the bile that surged in my throat, hot and heavy, and ready to spew. I shook my head and forced a smile. "What way did they fail? I have to keep these current ones from repeating the same mistakes."

"*Careful, Lee,*" Barb cautioned. She was tense, but instead of fight, she was ready to run. "There's something dangerous about this man. I don't think I can take him."

Her entire being trembled. She was focused entirely on Inu.

"Your wolf still wants to run and not submit? That's intriguing. Usually by the time I'm called in, the wolves of the scholarship students are broken down and prepared to do whatever I say in order to escape the torment of their lives."

"You're a murderer," I blurted, and hated myself for it. I hadn't planned to argue, I had wanted to get more on the recording, but I couldn't stop thinking of all the wolves I'd seen in the university. "You killed all of them!"

Inu raised a brow, and drummed his fingers on the stone statue's head. "Why, Lee, I think you misunderstand something very important here. The statues here are not just stone, they are the actual failed Alpha Gods. They're not dead, they're just trapped in this form. They are my special little battery packs, scattered across the campus. It's the only way these failures can be of use, but they'll never die."

Every statue was a real Alpha God? My mind went back to Max, and how Rue hung all over him. Did they have feelings? Were they aware of what was going on around them? Maybe they even tried to warn the students that attended here.

"I'm sorry, Inu, I'm afraid I'm still struggling to understand. These true Alpha Gods of yours, what can they possibly do?"

"Stop Lucifer," he replied. "Nothing is more important than that."

Would this be enough proof? "What is that creature doing that you're so hell-bent on fighting it?"

"Lucifer only has one objective in this world, and that is to find his queen. It's the soul of a woman he lost long ago. There is no telling what kind of person she is, but if she is someone who wishes for the death and destruction of this world, he will carry it out. It's why not only the Silverton Academy, but all the other universities which have been created as well even exist."

The academies are under the same umbrella. I remembered that being mentioned. "How many more are out there?" I questioned, barely above a whisper.

"Eleven besides us. Together, we will do whatever it takes to create the perfect Gods and prepare for battle. No matter what it costs, we will put a stop to Lucifer before he ever meets his queen."

CHAPTER 43

CHANGING SIDES

THE GRAVITY OF THE situation hit me like a bomb. The recorder was still on. "How can these Alpha Gods succeed where the others failed?" I questioned.

Inu frowned. "Your questions aren't about the creature destined to destroy the world, but only about the failures?"

"Because the ones you're judging this time are important to me. I want them to win this challenge, and become true Alpha Gods. Rather that, than being your latest pigeon shit catchers, scattered around your campus."

"Such a narrow-minded view. It doesn't matter how many students must be sacrificed as long as we ultimately defeat that creature. Thankfully, there hasn't been any word of him rising from his prison yet. We have time."

I couldn't stop the smirk that popped on my lips. I knew something this man did not. I'd just been handed leverage, and with it, I could get more proof.

His eyes narrowed. "What is it? It's obvious there's something you want to add to this conversation."

I tapped the bracelet on my wrist. First, I needed to dismantle the Dean's control over me. "You are the founder of this school, surely you're stronger than that, so-called Dean, correct?"

Inu puffed his chest out and scoffed. "Are you trying to tell a joke? The Dean is a mere pawn on the chessboard. The Academy and the Zodiacs are on an entirely different level than the likes of him. He doesn't even know what a true Alpha God is. What's that little trinket on your wrist?"

"I can't tell you too much, it'll end up hurting me." Technically it would be hurting King, but I was forbidden to reveal that.

"Child's play," Inu scoffed. "Here." He grabbed my hand and put a finger over the white pearl. "I'm the one that gave him such trinkets in the first place. I can easily fix this." Black mist seeped from his hand and over the entire bracelet. "That is if I wanted to."

I gasped, as the breath was driven out of my body. An ache filled me, and my body screamed, but the bond with Albedo didn't activate.

"Do you think you're the one in control here?" Inu questioned. "I can turn you into one of my lovely statues, and your precious little Gods would be none the wiser until I take the spell away."

I bit my lip and resisted the urge to shudder. A cold smile played on my lips. "What if I told you that I have a valuable piece of information that's vital to your mission?" I questioned.

"You dare to lie to me?" he hissed. However, when I didn't elaborate his back stiffened and he took a cautious step closer. "If you're playing with me, I will turn the pain of that little bracelet to the max. It's not tied to anyone but you and your precious mate now. But if you're lying, I will turn it black and let them die."

That meant this golden chain really could have made my brother suffer. "It's not a lie, but I'll be honest with you. Luci is already revived."

He was silent, studying me. "Luci," he whispered. His eyes narrowed to slits, and the electric blue of them sizzled.

"Lucifer," I corrected, as I mentally slapped myself. Hopefully, I hadn't just ruined this little plan. "Or it was at least a creature pretending to be him. He was in the hallway when I tried to get here."

Inu absorbed my confession. His eyes flickered to the door, but beyond that, he made no moves. After a few moments, he turned his back and paced from one side of the room to the other. Every now and then he'd sneak a peek at the statue. "That one?" he questioned, pointing at it.

"Yes," I answered honestly.

He blew out a puff of air. "This changes everything. I thought we still had time. Tell me, Ms. Suga, did he mention anything about his queen?"

I shook my head and then froze. "He said that I wasn't the one he was searching for," I mumbled.

Inu cocked his head, weighing my words. "If he has an interest in you, that intrigues me. Your worth has risen, somewhat. I'll keep the curse of that bracelet from coming to pass, but you will help me."

"I turned him down, so he might not care about me anymore."

He shrugged. "Even if you turned him down, you still attracted his interest. I will not be waiting until the end of graduation to test the current group of Alpha Gods. If he's already free, it's only a matter of time before that woman of his is found."

"Please, protect my brother," I pleaded. I dropped to my knees and stared up at him. "You're the only one that can keep the Dean from using him as a chess piece against me, please, protect him."

"I will keep your brother safe, for a price," he agreed. He smirked at me. "Swear here and now that you will not tell anyone about the challenges the Alpha Gods are about to face."

My fingers twitched. Should I stop recording or would this not be considered telling someone else? But I couldn't risk it. I didn't want anyone else to suffer for my decisions. Slipping my hand into my pocket, I turned the phone completely off.

Inu bent down and took my braceleted hand in his. The black mist turned the stone a sparkling red. "This isn't tied to your brother anymore, but I promise you, if you break the rules, the spell will rebound and your brother will suffer greatly before he dies."

What choice did I have? King's life was far more precious to me than anything else, even if it was proof to get the other parents to intervene. "What do I have to do?"

"Put your hand over the stone," he instructed.

I did as bid and I winced at the waves of heat rising from it. "Now?"

"Repeat after me. I promise on the life of my brother that not a soul will know about the tests."

I repeated his oath and the bracelet glowed bright, turning hot on my wrist.

"Good job," Inu praised, letting me go. "If that's the case, then there will be no problems with letting you leave here."

Hopefully, the recording had gone well, and the others would never find out about this deal of mine. Whatever it was going to take to make them true Alpha Gods, I would help them achieve it.

CHAPTER 44

MY DECISION

JULIAN

Cindy never left my side, no matter what I tried. She was like a relentless leech. How long was I going to be required to keep this hateful act up? I wanted to go to Lee's side and check on her, I had the worst feeling.

"Seriously, I can't get over how pathetic he is now. And to think, everyone thought your brother was the better twin. Now he's the freak, he snapped over that worthless mutt." She squeezed me tight, and my eye twitched. "He even looked like he was going to hurt me!" She brought my arm to her chest as she hugged it tightly and batted her eyes at me. "But you would have protected me, right?" she wheedled.

If I had my way, I would have flung her into the nearest trash can. But there had been nothing from Lee yet. This role was still needed, for now.

Carl slapped my back. "Don't worry about that one," he assured Cindy. He was following us like some star-struck puppy. "We'll easily get him out of the picture. They'll replace his sorry ass too. No one is untouchable." He paused, and eyed me up and down. "You're not going to stand in our way or anything because you're brothers, right?"

Thankfully, I was saved from having to answer his ass. A familiar head ducked down the hallways and towards the nurse's office. "You guys go ahead and get to lunch. I'll catch up as soon as I can. We need to sit down and orchestrate our plans of revenge. Elijah will never know what hit him."

"That sounds fantastic," Carl agreed, giving me a high five. Cindy pouted as the other man peeled her away from me, and dragged her away. I breathed a sigh of relief before I hurried down the hallway.

My eyes had to be playing tricks on me. There was no way in hell that I'd just seen King. What possible reason could he have for being here?

I caught up quickly, and King noticed me from the reflection in a mirror. He whirled and grinned. "Julian!" He greeted. "What'cha doing here?"

No one else was around, for a few minutes at least, we had privacy. "I was about to ask you the same thing. I never expected you to show up here. Aren't you still a high school student? Don't you need all those machines of yours?"

King rolled his eyes. "Oh come on, Julian. You and mom sound the same. Listen, I know sis has been having it rough here, and I want to help be there for her. Besides, they gave me a big shot of something, and ever since I've felt way better." He glanced over his shoulder and winced. "At least I did until I was in the Dean's office."

My smile vanished. That's where Lee was. "What are you talking about, man? You're already getting sent to the Dean's office?" I wanted to ask him about Lee, but if I did I was afraid I'd make him worried. It was the last thing that she would want. But I couldn't help but wonder if she needed a rescue from the cavalry. What if that monster had tried to do something to her?

Why had I listened to that shitty plan?

King shrugged. "It was kind of weird. I'm still not sure why I was called in there. He let Lee know I was joining the school, and told her that I was special enough to be a second scholarship student, and that I could even become an Alpha God one day with my potential."

Thank Goddess Lee had been there. But if that was the case, why hadn't she escaped from him? "Oh, Lee was there?" I asked casually. "Did she get in trouble?"

"No idea why she was there. She was really white when she saw me." He laughed to himself. "I thought I was supposed to be the one at death's door. Maybe seeing me up and about was that shocking to her."

"She stayed back in the office?" That bastard better not have put a finger on her, or I'd break all of his, one by one. Where was that woman at?

King shrugged. "I think so. She and the Dean were talking about things I didn't understand. He told me to finish my paperwork, and then his secretary suggest that I go explore the school, and that's when I ran into you. I got myself checked at the nurse's office to make sure everything was okay, but so far everything has been great."

I wanted nothing more than to march into that office and break his door down. If it hadn't been for Lee's request to handle this on her own, I already would have torn the man to shreds. For now, I would protect my future brother-in-law. "You doing okay now?" I asked.

King nodded. "Sure am! I haven't felt this well in years. And to think, all it took was one tiny shot. I wonder how long it'll last." He shrugged. "I'm just going to enjoy what I can, but I'm already exhausting myself. I think I'm going to have to stop for a nap before I hit the cafeteria. The nurse told me I needed to slow down."

"Enjoy," I offered with a forced smile. Hopefully, for his sake, nothing else would happen, and there wasn't anything sinister lurking in that shot of his. I couldn't shake the sinking suspicion that he had become nothing but another guinea pig. I had to find Lee, and soon. To hell with the plan. I needed her to be safe and sound, and away from that demon.

I held myself back until King was out of sight. The instant he turned a corner I sprinted down the hall. Students threw themselves at the walls and out of my way, staring as I ran toward the Dean's office.

I hit his door in record time and burst through it, taking it off the hinges as I went. I ignored it, and stared at the secretary. She tensed, as she stared at me. "Can I help you?" she gulped.

"Here for the Dean," I spat. I ignored her, and headed for his office.

"You can't go in there!" she yelled at my back. I ignored her, shoving his door open.

The Dean's head snapped up, and he gave me a cold sinister smile. "Ah, Julian. We were just having a most interesting conversation about you." He folded his arms over his chest and grinned at a solemn Lee sitting in a chair and staring blankly at the wall. "Here's your chance to prove your words, Lee," he encouraged.

Prove her words? He made me want to snap his neck.

Lee slowly pulled her hair to one side and exposed her throat to me. "Julian," she whispered.

My heart thumped. "Lee?" I whispered back. A part of me melted at the closeness of her, while the other was focused on the violent asshole.

"Julian, claim me," she answered steadily. There was no passion or pleading in her voice, just soft determination.

Maybe I should have turned her down. There were others that deserved to claim her far more than I did, but I couldn't stop the surge of pure happiness that spiraled through me.

Finally, she was going to be mine.

I stood behind her and resisted the urge to gently kiss her. For some reason, this didn't seem the place for that. It was almost like a transaction. "Are you sure about this?" I whispered to her, eyeing the Dean as I did so. Was he forcing her into this or something? My fangs grew.

She nodded, and that was all I needed.

Gently, I bit into her skin and my cocky wolf, with a hoop ring in his ear, wrapped his paws around an exasperated wolf as he licked her cheek. Her cat ears were askew and my heart thumped hard as a wave of warmth hit me.

I had claimed her as mine, once and for all, and nothing would take her away.

To Be Continued

ABOUT MARIA WARREN

Maria Warren is an ambitious author working on a universe that spans 43 books, all connecting with each other in one large story involving Gods, Goddesses, Demons, Angels, and every paranormal creature you can shake a stick at. She's deeply in love with urban fantasy and paranormal romance and loves losing herself while writing it. Inspired by a healthy love of games, anime, and otome, her works focus on reverse harems so the heroine never has to choose, with lots of plot and then hot.

You can visit her online at https://mariawarrenwrites.com/

Want to stay up to date with all of her latest? Join her newsletter on https://linktr.ee/mariawarrenwrites

Join Ream and get the updates as she writes them as well as other benefits https://ream-stories.com/page/lf78xkbeqa

Printed in Great Britain
by Amazon